# MR. ETERNITY

BY THE SAME AUTHOR

*The Ghost Apple*

# MR. ETERNITY

A NOVEL

## AARON THIER

BLOOMSBURY

NEW YORK · LONDON · OXFORD · NEW DELHI · SYDNEY

Bloomsbury USA
An imprint of Bloomsbury Publishing Plc

1385 Broadway     50 Bedford Square
New York     London
NY 10018     WC1B 3DP
USA     UK

www.bloomsbury.com

BLOOMSBURY and the Diana logo are trademarks of Bloomsbury
Publishing Plc

First published 2016

ISBN:  HB:    978-1-63286-093-4
ePub:  978-1-63286-094-1

LIBRARY OF CONGRESS CATALOGING-IN-PUBLICATION DATA IS AVAILABLE.

2 4 6 8 10 9 7 5 3

Typeset by RefineCatch Limited, Bungay, Suffolk
Printed and bound in the U.S.A. by Berryville Graphics, Berryville, Virginia

To find out more about our authors and books visit
www.bloomsbury.com. Here you will find extracts, author interviews,
details of forthcoming events and the option to
sign up for our newsletters.

Bloomsbury books may be purchased for business or
promotional use. For information on bulk purchases please contact
Macmillan Corporate and Premium Sales Department at specialmarkets@
macmillan.com.

*For Sarah*

# MR. ETERNITY

# 2016

---

The ancient mariner got up at dawn in order to drink the dew from the hibiscus flowers that grew in what he called the lee of his house. The sky was a dusty pink and the yard was still dark. I saw him through the gauzy walls of my tent. I heard him singing.

"We have to film you doing this one morning," I said. "Drinking your nectar or whatever it is. It's a significant detail."

He was wearing wide sailcloth trousers, no shirt, no shoes. He had a white beard and long white hair and he was bald on the crown of his head. He was still sinewy and strong but he had shrunk so much that in certain positions his rib cage brushed against his pelvis.

"This morning I want to explain to you about pig toilets," he said. "They were an important feature of life in Goa. The latrine was built over a pigsty. Actually that's all there is to say about pig toilets."

"Pig toilets."

"And the answer is yes. They did eat the pigs."

He called it the lee of his house not because it was the habit of an old seafaring man to refer to everything in nautical terms, but because his house was a boat. He'd been anchored out in the lagoon, he said, just inside the reef, and then an enormous end-of-the-world storm blew up and carried the boat half a mile inland. So providential was his deliverance that he'd felt it was only proper to carry on living in the wreck. Over the years he'd replaced all the original wood, he'd opened windows in the hull, he'd burned the masts for firewood, but he hadn't altered its shape. It looked like what it was. It was a Bermuda sloop run aground.

"Another thing about Goa," he said. "There was a plant that bore as its fruit a tiny lamb, perfect in every detail except that it had no teeth or hooves or eyes. The animal grew inside a seedpod on a long stem that attached just below its shoulders. It would graze and keep the area clear of weeds. The meat was edible, it tasted like crab, and the blood was sweet like honey. You wonder why this plant was never exploited commercially, this meat- and wool-bearing plant, but I think maybe it was condemned by the Inquisition."

Azar and I had come to Key West to film a documentary about him, but neither of us had any experience with filmmaking or, more significantly, any special interest in filmmaking. I'd written the ancient mariner a letter to suggest the project after I saw an article about him in the Travel section of the *New York Times*, but from the beginning I was only looking for some pretext to leave New York. I hadn't expected an answer, and I hadn't expected Azar, a friend since college days, a listless and detached young person like myself, to insist on coming. I certainly hadn't expected to be here, sleeping in the yard and fumbling with an expensive little video camera.

And there was something more: The ancient mariner had agreed to participate in the documentary on the condition that we help him with some digging. He would not say more than "some digging."

"We used to drink feni," he said, "which was made from fermented cashew fruit, and we'd wander around the old city, and the moon was huge and red, and the air smelled like pepper, and we'd pet the little eyeless hoofless toothless lambs and feel ourselves very far from home."

He told us that he was something like five hundred and sixty years old. He told us that his name was Daniel Defoe. He told us that for most of his life he had been searching for a woman named Anna Gloria, whom he had seen in Spain as a young man and had vowed to marry. I could not understand whether he believed these things himself or whether he was making fun of us. He had cautioned us several times against revealing our true names so freely. A name was something to conjure with.

And now he had to scramble up the rope ladder to the deck and speak his prayers. I sat down at the little wooden table in the yard and put my head in my hands. Key West, the middle of May, seven o'clock in the morning, seventy-five degrees. I was not hungover. I was not unhappy. I'd been a graduate student for a little while, but it didn't take, and then I'd worked for an environmental advocacy group in New York, but that didn't take either, and now I'd given up my apartment and left my job and I was nothing. I was staying with Azar and telling people I was on sabbatical. I was trying not to be so gloomy all the time. I was twenty-seven.

## 1560

---

First I was only an Indian. I was a Pirahao girl from the city of Anaquitos, which the Christians call El Dorado. My mother was dead and no one said anything about her, and then my father was dead also and I was sold to the traders on the river. I was loaded into a canoe with the dyewood, the Brazil nuts, the bundles of dried monkey meat, the flying dog wool, the rubber toys. I was sent down the river to the city of Omagua, and then to another city, and then to another. Then I arrived here, in the small Christian city of Santa Inés, in the New Kingdom of Granada, where the Pirahao River plows into the Caribbean Sea. The ocean does not exist in Pirahao, and I could not see it until I learned to say the word in Spanish. I was a slave and then, because I am so beautiful that men become drunk when they look at me, I was sold to the Señora at the brothel and I became a whore.

Now I am both an Indian and a Christian. When I'm asleep my name is Xiako and I speak Pirahao and nothing exists that can't be seen. When I'm asleep I want to return to Anaquitos and live as I did, among people and not among Christians. But when I'm awake I speak Spanish and God watches us from his heaven and my name is Maria. When I'm awake I know about vengeance and I want the Christians to destroy Anaquitos as they are said to have destroyed Tenochtitlan and the cities of Tahuantinsuyu. I want the Pirahao to die and I want them to know they are dying because of me, because they sold me like a rubber toy, because they took my life from me when I was small and alone.

At the brothel I meet soldiers and clerks and notaries and I tell them stories about Anaquitos so they will hate that place as much as I do. I say that the king and queen have regal titles so long that one lifetime isn't long enough to speak them in their entirety. I say that they only eat human flesh. I say that they make drums from human skin, and they make necklaces from human teeth, and from the skulls they make the ceremonial cups from which they drink manioc beer. I say that they pray to the mountains, which are their gods. Sometimes I laugh when I tell these stories. The soldiers are horrified by this. My stories are true in Spanish, in which everything is true, but they are not true in Pirahao. There are no gods in Pirahao. There are no kings and queens.

I can say whatever I like because the Christians believe in everything, even things they don't believe in, even things that don't exist. They tell me that everything they do is done in the service of God. There is no other god but God, and God is three gods, all of whom are the same, and there are many other gods also. Some gods exist and some do not. There is Maria, the mother god, who gave me her name. There are the saints and virgins and angels and there is the devil, Satan, who lives in the world beneath the world. There are so many gods that they are like the insects that scatter when a rotting log is disturbed, although none are as important as God himself, whom the Christians thank for every bee sting and fear more than anything else, more than Satan, more than death, more than the worst pain. In Spanish, it is because of God that the world exists. In Pirahao there are only things that exist, and the world, like things, exists for no reason.

For the Christians it is a sin to eat pineapple before taking Communion. It is a sin to change the bed linens on Friday. It is a sin to say that fornication with an Indian is no sin. However, it is not a sin to fornicate with an Indian. This is an enigma and a mystery of the Faith and the result is that many Christian officials have Indian concubines, although they do not say so. One afternoon two soldiers bring me to the alcalde mayor's official residence and I become a concubine myself. This is very fortunate. It is easier to be the alcalde's concubine than it is to be a whore, not only because the alcalde is a kind man, always trying to be better and do honor to God, always affirming that Indians are true human beings and not simply beasts, always fretting and worrying in his anguish for salvation, but also because his appetites are depraved and he never touches me. His intention is to disguise his real desires, which have to do with animals, with young pigs, not piglets but young adult pigs. He does not touch the pigs either. He does not even touch himself. He stands in the pigpen and prays to God, poor man, and he mourns the fact of his desire.

I live very well in the alcalde's house. I drink cashew wine until I am so stupid I forget my Christian name. I eat guava paste and porpoise pepper steak and seabird eggs. No one bothers me. When I need something I steal it from the alcalde or lie down with one of the guards at the residence. But my life is not my own. No one listens to me and I have no power to make things happen. I think of the Pirahao in their white city and my anger is a thing I can hold in my hand.

And then one day I see an opportunity. One day a wrinkled conquistador in a red Toledo cap comes walking out of the forest. His name is Daniel de Fo and he is one hundred years old and he is the only survivor of the Lopez y Barra expedition to the land of cinnamon, which is what the Christians call the inland forest through which the Pirahao river flows. The Señora gives him a room at the brothel and he sleeps for three days, and I am there visiting friends when he wakes up and begins to speak of a city in the forest.

Daniel de Fo can't tell his story without speaking heresies. He says, "There are things in the forest that not even God knows about. An ant bit my foot off, or he bit me and then my friend had to cut the foot off, but it was fine because the Indians had a medicine to make it grow back."

The soldiers put their hands over his mouth. They say this is witchcraft and they won't let him damn himself by talking about it. They won't let themselves hear the story. But he doesn't care. He laughs and laughs, a sound like haha. I don't care either because I know that in Anaquitos this medicine exists. I know that he has been there. I know that he wants to go back. I can see the web of God's design shining in the sea light.

In Pirahao, the truth is only what happens and time is an animal that sleeps all day. In Spanish, the truth is whatever a woman tells her gods, a different story every day, and time is a river in which she struggles to stay afloat. When I speak Pirahao, I want to return to the city and eat inaga fruit in the central plaza, but when I speak Spanish I want to see the city burn, and it is only in Spanish that it's proper to act. It is this difference that dooms the Pirahao.

# 2200

---

I went out to get my breakfast just a sweet potato and coffee but it were ten years before I come home. I were down on the harbor walk under the Spanish moss groaning holding my head chewing my potato so sad for I were up all night drinking corn whiskey in Madame Caitlin's a whorehouse. It were just another morning nothing unusual same headache same sadness same poverty but suddenly I were so tired of it all suddenly I couldn't stand it. I had never been out of Boston I had never thought of leaving but when I seen the boats yachts ships headed God knows where to New York to Baltimore suddenly I were asking each captain was he hiring. One captain told me yes he were hiring yes and this were how it happened. Strange thought you could say I were gone ten years because one night I were drinking corn whiskey and in the morning I walked down to the water and not up the hill as I did on other days. These are what is called vicissitudes. I remember it were a cool day light breezes long shadows I wore my sweat shirt even it were so cool. It were January the year 2200 it had just begun a new century. My name it were Jam it still is it were never Jim as some think.

I were ignorant of yachts sails waves winds the sea and for many days my only concern were learning the ropes. It were truly learning the ropes not just an expression for there was ropes to pull on I were learning which ones. It had an old sailor who taught me they called him Old Dan. Good gravy said Old Dan you don't know nothing. I admit it were the truth. In Boston I had got my money selling salvage plastic fruits whatever I could find but I had never learned no true skills. I had never learned to sail.

We was heading down the coast all the way to Florida and the seas beyond. We was sailing down into the heat and light close to the sun where pearls grew and gold and jewels and polyester. They needed the light to grow said the captain. He were very interested in pearls he talked of pearls nonstop. Pearls they grew in the stomachs of jellyfish so he said. He thought we could be rich men if we crossed into distant waters like in old days and brought home these products and novelties. Old Dan however he cared nothing for riches he were after another kind of riches he were after a woman. She was called Anna Gloria she was his long lost love.

I thought of pearls too and rhinestones and gold jewels plastics. I were carried away by this dream of riches. I used to lie in my berth thinking of the rich men in Boston which had motored boats and drank clear water out of plastic bottles a fresh bottle every day. It had semi-trailers that delivered them boxes of fruits vegetables bread butter milk oil cream the truck were cold so this food didn't spoil. The rich people could have whatever foods they liked any time any day they was like kings. Their houses was cold also it were called air condition it were a old very expensive technology. You run it off sun panels or you run it off electricity if you can pay the carbon tax. It were a terrible thing electricity air condition trucks and the rest it were the cause of all our ills. It were the electricity plus motor vehicles plus factories plus cows caused climate warming they said. However I did not care I wanted very much to be rich to lie in bed shivering drinking water from a plastic bottle it would taste so sweet. What did I care about climate warming I would have air condition I would have sun panels everywhere on my cars on my gazebo on my dog I would have a plastic bathtub I would pay the carbon tax without a care I would be so rich.

But I were just a poor man for now just a sad fucker with a cut above my eye where someone hit me. I were a orphan too no family at all no woman no children I were all alone in the world. Maybe I didn't know nothing but I knew it were no life at all to be alone in Boston in the year 2200 it was all heat sweat corn whiskey sadness that is why I left. I wanted an air condition mansion.

Now I will tell more of Old Dan. He were a very old man maybe 750 years old he said. I did not believe him yet still he were very old like a piece of meat salted down for keeping. One day he talked of whales. I did not believe him once again for I did not believe in whales. There were no reason for an animal to grow so big when it were so good to be a small animal a cockroach a rat which can live on crumbs. He laughed he said the whales they lived on crumbs too only it were giant crumbs for to them a ship like ours were a crumb. Fine I said whatever you say. You don't believe me he said. No I said. The biggest were four hundred feet long he said they could swallow our boat entire did you not ever see a picture for there was many pictures. Yes I said I had got a picture book of animals when I were young in the orphan house however I believe the pictures was faked. How could you fake a picture he said it is a picture. They could find a way I said. No he said it can't be done.

I didn't listen to him I thought he were a fool. You will see I had got it wrong he were no fool for example it were him taught me to write. Anyway there you have it that were how I come to leave home at the age of eighteen or nineteen years.

# 1750

I have liv'd upon this *Nauseous Orb* the Earth for near seventie years, and to-day, the principal actors in my life's Drama being dead (except I imagine Dr. Dan Defoe who will outlive us all), and accordingly unable, if I judge rightly the termes & conditions of the *Afterlife*, to bring a Suit against me, I perceive the time is ripe to tell the adventures and misventures of my life, for tho I am now Resident in Boston, city of snows and fogs, yet my memory capers among the palmy green islands of youth.

I shall tell my story from front to back — I shall pour it out scum and sediment and all — for it wants nothing, and requires nothing of the *Artificers Art*. I was born in the Barbados, and there I was inured to hardship and cruel treatment, but in the year 1750, when I was a young man of nineteen years, I fled from there to the Bahama islands and sought to raise myself by an audacious deception, as I will shortly explain.

In the Bahamas I traveled from one house to the next, the guest of all, and from one island to the next, pass'd as it were from hand to hand among the debased gentry of that piratical country, who were all of them second sons & bastard sons & spalpeens and barrowers raised to the peerage, and I received as hearty a welcome as ever I could have wished. One day I came to stop with Mr. Galsworthy of Babylon plantation, upon an island called Little Salt. As it was then after noon, and his custom to feed without stint or measure each day at two o'clock, or three, I dress'd quickly in the best of what I had and came down to meet my host at the table, including many other guests. It was here I spied for the first time Daniel Defoe, whom they call'd the Spaynard, an old man like a hat-stand with eyes, or a scarecrow totteringly put together, or a jointed insect in a wig, acclaim'd by popular belief to be near three hundred years of age.

The great house at Babylon was poorly constructed, & in grate haste, namely that some rooms were walled with grave markers, and others with a kind of white washed dung. I think this were not for want of credit or capital, but only that Mr. Galsworthy did so enjoy a sumptuous table that his only thought was for feasting, and all the rest were bagatelles and trifles. In this he was like the man who gambles his estate for a thrill, or sells the cloathes off his back for the taste and quickness of wine. To-day we dined upon stew'd mudfish, pickled crabs, roast pig, roast yam, plantanes, boil'd pudding, roast coot, water milions, and many other fuds viz. doves ducks & fishes. For my part I worked at a ham the size of a cloak-bag.

Yet soon our revelry was interrupted by the visitation of brooding death. One of the guests, a Mr. Foster, gave a small scream and, stiff and benumb'd, though also it seemed in excruciating pain, endeavored to rise, which task being impossible he next grobled about for whatever chanced to be within his reach, snatching the wig from his companion's head, and then, giving another scream, slipped forward dead with his face in his fud. We now all gazed about uncertain what to do, for if Mr. Foster had been poisoned, as it did appear he had been (which was not unusual in the Bahamas at that time, where the slaves did frequently season their masters fud with corrosive sublimate), then I expected our next concern would be to torment slave after slave until we had learnt the culprits. Daniel Defoe no doubt thought as I did, and not wishing to see this feast spoilt, for it was a good one, nor indeed any slaves tormented, he knelt by the dead man, & grabbed hold of his cheeks, & looked in his mouth, & lifted his hand and let it fall, & listened at his chest, and then, without canvassing the matter any further, pronounced him dead not of poyson but from a surfeit of Pig.

Now we were at ease once more, this occurrence being nothing remarkable in such a place, where death blew through every big house like a *summer breeze*. Only those guests newly arriv'd from England were alarmed, and stared about, their faces *masks* of *horror*. Mr. Galsworthy for his part was delighted to discover in Daniel Defoe, called from that point *Doctor* Dan, a person with some knowledge of medicine, and pressed him now with questions and concerns of all sorts, asking whether a surfeit of duck mite produce a similar outcome, or of crab, and if not was there some Fatal Characteristic peculiar to the pig.

I settl'd in to listen, drinking punch & gazing at the slaves, who moved about clearing dishes. I knew from their faces they had poisoned Mr. Foster, though I ne'er learnt the reason.

Dr. Dan answered that a surfeit of pig sometimes produced what was called by physicians a coagluation of the *Gluten* or some say *Animal mixt*, which retarded & obstructed the circulation of the blood. A surfeit of any animal fud will produce the same outcome in any other animal, but the calamity proceeds quick or slow according to the degree of relationship between the animal consum'd to the animal which consumes it, for ex. a man must eat more duck to produce the same fatal coagluation, but a much smaller amount of monkey, and still less of Ape, Sphinx, or Satyr, which of all animals are man's closest cousins. Cannibalism that heathen rite is known to produce an *instantaneous* coagluation. However, said Dr. Dan, remember that a duck is safer eating the meat of a Human than if he eats the meat of his own cousin and near relation, the goose.

Notwithstanding he spoke with authoritie I knew him for an imposter, yet I said nothing, for I recognized him *as one oozy worm recognizes another* though neither have the use of reason. Here I was at table to every appearance a white man among white men, yet I was a sheep in wolf's clothing after all. You see dear reader my father was Mr. Coleman of Elizabeth plantation in the Barbados, that is God's truth, yet my mother was his *Slave*, named Liberty, which made me neither one thing nor another, but surely no gentleman. In the Bahama islands I called myself John Green, and have done ever since.

## 2500

My father was the hereditary king and president of the Democratic Federation of Mississippi States, which was lucky for him because he loved the amenities of power and the exercise of governance. It was not so lucky for the people he ruled over, however, nor for the country at large, which ultimately disappeared away into the lavender light and sweet scented dust of history. But that is putting the car before the hearse.

Originally, our dominions comprised St. Louis, where we lived, and most of the land west to Kansas City and south to the first wild reaches of the Mississippi jungle, which in truth made it not Mississippi states, as the country's name boldly stated, but only the one individual old state of Missouri with some drips and drops of Arkansas. As for ourselves, we remained in St. Louis at all times. I recollect it as a city of almost twenty-five thousand souls, a city of date palms and mud houses and banana beer, and it was hot enough to fry an ape most of the time, except January and February. It was my family's home for centuries.

Our name is Roulette, but I am Jasmine St. Roulette, the St. part having been added for a hint of style. I was the only issue of my father's union with a mystery mother whom I never knew, and therefore our presidential family consisted of only two members, although the household was augmented tenfold by servants and slaves, and days might pass when I did not see my father at all, or saw him only at official occasions. We lived extravagantly in our hereditary palace, which had once been the city library of imperial St. Louis. We had an oven big enough to bake fifty cassava rounds at one time. We had baths as big as a farmer's whole house. We had a hundred peacocks, acrylic clothing, real carpets, paraffin lanterns, plastic bins and jugs, and exotic commodities like cashew wine, which we obtained from neighboring countries on an economy of exchange. We had water tanks and strategic grain reserves, and the whole edifice was encapsulated from the poor people within an enormous concrete wall.

For me, however, life was corrupted by frustrations, because I was a woman in a place and time where men hoarded up all the power. I could never participate in the larger sphere of activity. My father used me like a bartering chip. He affianced me to a sequence of men, the last of whom was the piggish senator Anthony Fucking Corvette, whom I had to visit each week to solidify family alliances. We would sit together at an antique plastic table and he would say things like, "It is better to drink muddy water and eat dirt." Better than what? Then I had to let him do it to me. He did it by rote and political requirement and then he bollocked off to his hookers and his poppy juice and I went home to lie in my hammock and dream of another life. This is what it was to be a president's daughter in the final years of the twenty-fifth century. It was an endless liturgy of palace tedium and an injustice of diminished freedoms. I called myself an anachro-feminist, a term of my own proud coinage, but it was only a phrase. I had no recourse.

My father did not care a sesame seed for my troubles, but we did share one fascination in common, which was the transformations and legacies of history. We had only a limited selection of books in the palace, but we knew which side the world was buttered on. We knew that we were opulent people in an impoverished time. We knew that our country was just a subsistence nation of millet and goats and camels. The ruins of great days fringed and ringed the city in a huge periphery and we knew that our own St. Louis was only a tiny particle of the St. Louis that had existed in ancient bygone imperial days. The difference was that while I sat in the library striving to learn all I could about the true and established facts of the world, my father hardly read anything anymore, and instead he preoccupied himself with thoughts of his own place in history. His great ambition was to unite all the nations of North America under one flag, as they'd been united in freedom and democracy under the empire of the United States. He also wanted to revitalize culture and learning. I often heard him say things like, "It is time we remodernized this ragbag old country."

He had mandated that we speak only Modern English at home, the language of American scholars, and I wasn't allowed to speak Mississippi Spanish at all until I was ten years old, but other than this he did nothing, for he didn't know how to commence the effort of remodernization. Maybe, in an alternative reality, he would never have been catalyzed into action at all, but it happened that one night, when I myself was already twenty-six and my father had long since begun to feel the pinch of years, he bought an old slave named Daniel Defoe from some people who came in off the desert. It was a night of shining rain and cicadas, which I know because I chanced to be there. I was just returning from dinner and fornications with Anthony Fucking Corvette, and my father was out by the front gate, and when he saw me he said, "Oh, it's you," as if he had just recollected my existence. "Then come along and I'll show you something."

We issued into the camel pen and there was Daniel Defoe. It was the first time I cast eyes on him. He had a superannuated cat named Christopher Smart, who was like a gray carpet with teeth, and he was handsome and there were lights in his eyes, but his chief appeal and the reason for my father's interest in him was that he was said to be one thousand years old. This was not impossible if you considered that he came from the desert. In very dry air, with abundant sun, meat will cure before it spoils, and therefore a human being, which is made of meat, could theoretically live forever. The marked contrast was that in St. Louis, which was frequently ravaged by pestilences like Nevada fever, even rich people lived only fifty or sixty years. Poor people were lucky to survive into their thirties.

"If he's as old as he says," my father instructed, "he would have known the glory of the United States."

He was speaking Modern English, and it was an astonishment when Daniel Defoe responded in the same language. His accent was untraceable. He said, "Don't talk to me about glory. Those people were out of their minds. They only cared about whale oil. They lived in tents called wigwams. Their method of gardening was to explode chemical bombs, which killed everything."

My father said, "We know about oil. We have books and prospectuses in the palace." But I knew he had not read a prospectus in years.

"It wasn't only whale oil. It was fossilized oil too. They pumped it out of the earth and drank it like it was banana beer. They pumped so much out of the ground that the land began to sink, and that's why it seemed like the seas were rising. They also made a special train oil from the fat of a seabird called the great auk, which was the national bird of the United States. Train oil made the economy boom, but it also caused global warming because it released all the heat that would otherwise have stayed inside the auks, which were arctic birds, and very warm inside, and anyway extremely numerous."

This was not true. It was a feast of lies. However, my father devoured it, and I think this marked the sea change for him. He had lacked an adviser to ratify and affirm his ideas. Now he had one.

"We've got to find some of these great auks," he said quietly. "We won't burn so many to cause global warming. Only enough to make our economy boom."

## 2016

Azar was up, or rather he had crawled out of his tent. He was on all fours, breathing heavily, disoriented by shocking dreams. I told him there was no coffee yet and no food and our host was involved in pagan rituals on deck, and he lifted his head and groaned, a soft and mournful sound.

"We have to figure out what we're doing here," I said.

"We're making a documentary. Remember we have to be firm about this."

"But we don't know anything about it. What's our approach? Do we do it self-conscious and formal, like Errol Morris, or do we follow him around, candid moments, regular life, et cetera?"

"These aren't the things you have to decide at first. For now we shoot lots of stuff and then we cut it together later. We've only been here half a day. First we find some coffee."

"It's a movie about a very old person," I said, "but it's also about today, our society, in which here we are, two privileged young men without any skills applicable beyond the framework of that society."

"It's not about us, that's one thing. No one gives a shit about us. I certainly don't."

"I don't mean us as in us, I mean us as in now, our world, Generation Credit Debt, the Age of Irony and climate disaster. And the ancient mariner belongs to a different time. The last survivor."

We pondered this, or we pretended to. Really I was too tired from a night in the sand to do much pondering. Azar stared into space like he'd been hypnotized.

"But five hundred and sixty years old?" I said.

"It doesn't matter. There's no reason to proceed skeptically. The movie is better if we take him at his word. Otherwise we're cynics. I'm tired of being a cynic."

"Maybe the movie is about trying to substantiate his claim," I said, "and then gradually we show that it doesn't matter what the truth is. He's ancient in other ways. In outlook and orientation. A metaphor develops. Something about the boat. I don't know what the metaphor is but it develops and that's the movie."

"Fine, good. As long as you understand that in essence the whole thing for me is that I don't want to be a cynic."

"Why are you talking about cynicism?"

"I had an epiphany about this because I finally tried kombucha. It's delicious! I've been making fun of everyone for drinking it, but if I'd been less cynical I could have been enjoying it this whole time."

He rolled onto his back and stared into the sky. The yard was filling up with light. Palm trees stirred in the soft breeze, a sound like rain, and it was very peaceful, very peaceful.

"So he comes from the fifteenth century," he said. "In actual fact or in spirit. It's a compelling thought. He must think he remembers the discovery of America. He must think he remembers the invention of chewing gum."

He closed his eyes. There were banana plants growing against the fence, quail grass and okra and Indian lettuce and callaloo, squash and beans, a sapodilla tree and a mango tree and other trees I didn't recognize. There were strange mushrooms growing under an ixora bush, where the ancient mariner told me he'd planted Tylenol capsules. The yard was stuffed with plants. It was good for the spirit to grow food, he told us, even though he didn't eat much any longer. He could make do with one thimble of honey each week, a teaspoon of tamarind pulp, a sniff of lemon blossom.

I noticed that there was a column of red ants on Azar's chest. I wondered if I should warn him. But if they were biting ants, they would bite him whether I warned him or not, and if they were harmless it was better not to frighten him. Then he screamed and leapt to his feet and I ran forward to brush them off. He stood there with his arms raised and his face twisted in pain. There were already welts on his soft belly.

"You have to understand," he said, "that if somehow we could prove he's telling the truth, it would be more than a world-historical medical discovery. It would also make a difference for me on a personal level."

We learned that the oldest person with documents to substantiate her claim was Jeanne Calment, a Frenchwoman who lived to the age of 122. She drank port and ate two pounds of chocolate a week. She'd quit smoking when she was 117.

But there were other claims. Old Tom Parr was supposed to have lived to the age of 152 on a diet of rancid cheese and milk, hard coarse bread, a little booze, a little whey. Henry Jenkins, a destitute Yorkshireman, lived to be 169. Li Ching-Yuen was either 197 or 256 at his death in 1933. There's a tradition that for the first forty years of his life he lived on rice wine, goji berries, and herbs. He was seven feet tall, long fingernails, a ruddy complexion. When he was 130 he met a 500-year-old hermit who taught him to breathe. He outlived twenty-three wives and died in the arms of a twenty-fourth.

Trailanga Swami, the walking Shiva of Varanasi, lived to be 280 or 358. He could levitate and he could breathe underwater. He fasted for months and broke his fasts with buckets of clabbered milk. He never wore clothes.

At the upper end, wild hearsay shades into mythology. Methuselah and Jared and Noah and Adam and the rest. The Persian shah Zahhak lived 1,000 years, and the kings of ancient Sumer lived for millennia. En-men-lu-na is supposed to have reigned for 43,200 years.

What's the secret? Li Ching-Yuen had four rules: Tranquil mind, sit like a tortoise, walk sprightly like a pigeon, sleep like a dog. I learned that some people have success with long-lasting substances like jade, hematite, gold, and cinnabar. The logic is that if you ingest these things, you acquire some of their own properties. Everything has its vogue.

Predigested protein, calorie restriction, raw food, brain exercises, the Okinawa diet, a positive attitude, an extract made from deer antler velvet. There's no wrong way to live forever. The ancient mariner had known a man in Lisbon who drank potable gold from the body of a clock, and it might have worked, who knows, but he was hauled before the Inquisition and burned alive.

And there was the ancient mariner himself, salted by the sea air and dried in the tropic sun, and now, for all I knew, he was incorruptible. He was like a strip of rawhide.

What would it mean to live five hundred and sixty years? If I myself lived so long, what would I live to see? Would there be responsible land management and 2.1 children per woman? Would gas stations be replaced by solar charging stations? I had been a man with a clipboard, ostensibly a believer in collective enterprise, but the experience of wandering around New York encouraging people to unplug their chargers and meditate on the inundation of their city had not filled me with optimism. There would be no solar charging stations. Instead there would be extreme weather and high heat. There would be avocado trees in Washington, D.C., Spanish moss in Boston, wineries in Greenland. Key West would be underwater, and New Orleans and Miami and Lower Manhattan as well. There would be no more plastic bags. No more social media. No more lightbulbs or cheap underwear or reliable weather forecasting. No one would remember how to make asphalt or super glue or sunblock or cortisone cream. We would no longer be able to fly. The world would be like it used to be, years and years ago, except that it would be entirely different.

For breakfast the ancient mariner fried sweet plantains in the kitchen shed at the back of the yard. There was no coffee, but he offered us a thick milky liquid called po, which he said was much stronger. Azar drank some out of a little tin cup and professed himself a changed man. I had a little sip, just a sip, and I felt like an angel had sneezed in my face. We were at a loss.

"Well," said Azar. "Do you remember the invention of chewing gum?"

"First only clove-flavored gum," said the ancient mariner, "and then cinnamon. Spices! But you have to understand what they meant to us. We sailed around the world, half of us were murdered by Turks, and all for these spices. Today no one remembers and gum comes in a bright envelope that you close with a little flap. You buy it for a nickel or I don't know, fifty dollars, and you chew it and you stroll around and you feel like the Soldan of Aden."

"The Soldan of Aden," I repeated.

"And pepper is so cheap that they give it away in paper packets!"

He gestured forcefully as he spoke. He jerked his head around and bounced on his heels. He had enormous hands, teeth like old ivory, a smile that creased up his face like a baseball mitt. From certain angles he was still a handsome man.

"If you could take one item back with you to the sixteenth century," Azar said, setting the camera on the table in front of him, "what would it be? Would you take malaria medication?"

"I had malaria for a hundred years," said the ancient mariner, "all through the seventeenth century. But I'll tell you what I'd bring back with me. I'd bring back some cotton T-shirts. Soft as a breath of wind and no more expensive than a loaf of bread. When I was stationed at Fort Marion in St. Augustine, up on the east coast of British Florida, we had woolen uniforms, twenty pounds of uniform, thirty pounds even, and this in the summer when the coquina walls of the fort were hot to the touch and you'd see the Indians at the market in nothing but little beaded loincloths and you'd say to yourself, Obviously. But of course there were mosquitoes in those days that would turn a pink-cheeked British boy to leather in twenty minutes, so when I celebrate the cotton T-shirt I am also celebrating the vanishing of the mosquitoes, wherever they went."

"You'd take a T-shirt back with you?" I said. "A T-shirt, of all things?"

"A light cotton T-shirt," he said.

"But look," said Azar, tugging at his own shirt collar. "This T-shirt is actually made from merino wool. It's a lightweight blend. It wicks away perspiration and it has natural antimicrobial properties to combat odor. Plus it hangs better. Cotton is terrible in the heat."

"A merino wool T-shirt, then, or rubber-soled shoes," said the ancient mariner. "Or an assault rifle and lots of ammunition. Or a trunk of peppercorns. I'd fill it up at the store here in the twenty-first century and take it back and I'd buy huge parcels of land. I'd be a king. I was going to say penicillin, because once on the Mississippi River I was bitten by an enormous glowing ant, like a lobster, and my foot got infected and had to be cut off by some Indians, but in the end they also had a medicine that made it grow back, so I wouldn't have needed penicillin after all. It would have saved me some grief but I wouldn't have needed it."

Azar helped himself to more plantains. The ancient mariner ate nothing, true to his word. I wanted very badly to have more po, but already I felt jittery and unsound.

"This stuff you're telling us," said Azar. "This is like smelling salts for a cynic like me."

## 1560

One morning a Christian comes floating down the river in an Indian canoe. This is Diego Paez de Sotelo. His torso is twice as long as his legs and his beard hangs all the way to the ground. He is all skin and bones. He is all torso and no heart. He is the only other survivor of the Lopez y Barra expedition to the land of cinnamon, and he has been wandering in the forest since he was abandoned there by Daniel de Fo.

For this abandonment he desires vengeance, so he comes to the alcalde's residence and denounces Daniel de Fo for all manner of crimes against the Faith. He says that he saw Daniel de Fo eat unleavened bread during the recent expedition. He says that he not only amended a hymn of David but also insisted that the hymn was improved by his amendment. He says that he ate Indian roots for the purpose of divination, and that he had prophetic dreams, and that he did indeed make a certain conjuring in order to restore his missing left foot. He says that he made invocations of demons for the purpose of causing Pedro Avila to lose his wits and murder the captain general Lopez y Barra. He confirms the story that Daniel de Fo is one hundred years old and he says that his robust health is a result of a pact with the devil. He also says that he was observed reading a book that treated of profoundly deep spiritual things of the Faith, which, as an ignorant person and a soldier, he should have abstained from reading.

I cannot stop laughing during this recitation. The alcalde laughs too, haha, but only because I'm laughing. These are serious violations of canon law and now, because there is no apostolic inquisitor in Santa Inés, it is for him to decide whether Daniel de Fo should be sacrificed to the Christian God or sent away for trial. When Diego Paez de Sotelo is gone, he orders his men to remove Daniel de Fo from the brothel and lock him in the guardhouse down the street. Then he explains to me that Daniel de Fo is not a true Christian after all, but a converso, a Jew who lives as a Christian. He tells me that the Jewish heresy, which is also called the Mosaic heresy, is one of the greatest heresies, and there are those among the Christians who believe that a Jew can no more repent and become a Christian than a fish can become a monkey. He tells me these things because he believes it is his duty to instruct me in the precepts of Christianity.

The alcalde wants peace more than anything, and all of this grieves him terribly. He puts his head in his hands. He sighs. He himself believes that anyone who loves God is a Christian, but in the eyes of the law this is not enough. He walks outside to the pigpen to pray and suffer and drink wine.

In Pirahao there are words for the colors of things, but no words for colors in themselves. In Pirahao there are no numbers. If I want to say ten cows, I say a bigness of cows, but there are no cows. In Pirahao there is nothing more than what there is, and nothing exists beyond the present, and it is not proper to say I will do this, I will do that, I will kill you next week, I will pay you tomorrow. But for the Christians time has a different shape. Life is lived now and it is lived in the future. This is one thing I have learned from them. I have learned to make plans.

And now I have a problem and I must make a plan to solve it. Without Daniel de Fo there can be no expedition to Anaquitos. He is the only one who knows the way. Diego Paez de Sotelo has not been there.

"You have heard what he says about El Dorado," I say to the alcalde.

"I have heard the stories," he says.

"But what he says is true. It is true that they have a medicine to restore lost limbs. The rich people harvest the arms and legs of the poor for their spicy stews, and then they make the arms and legs grow back again so as not to diminish the number of laborers. They need these laborers to construct their idolatrous temples."

"This is the detail that condemns him. If his foot was restored by Indian magic, and the Indians don't know God, then how can we say this was God's will? It must be a compact or fabrication of the devil."

I cannot persuade him, and now I must prevent him from taking action until I can think of a new plan. I crush paóhaihao into his wine so that his mind will darken and his legs will turn to stone. I know he won't taste it, as indeed he does not, because paóhaihao does not exist in Spanish.

The alcalde remains in the pigpen while I begin to prepare his meal. I watch from the shadow of the kitchen shed. The air is the color of a papaya. The sea is the color of jacaranda flowers. Soon he begins to stagger and rave. His hair is matted, his tongue rolls in his mouth like an eel, his hair curls with a fine sizzling sound and grows lighter and lighter until it is the color of a ripe canistel. He wets himself. Then he sinks to his knees and slumps forward into a kind of sleep, but it is a black sleep in which nothing happens.

Now I walk to the guardhouse, where I find a soldier eating wild pineapples from a cloth bag and spitting the seeds into the dust. He is the only man on duty. I tell him I must speak to Daniel de Fo and I do not tell him the reason and he does not ask. We stand facing one another, I in my cotton dress and he in his belted tunic and leggings, and we can hear the moon wheeling in its heaven. My beauty shines like a torch. My beauty is like paóhaihao. He unlocks the door.

Inside I find Daniel de Fo sitting on the floor of his cell. He raises a hand in greeting. He is not surprised to see me.

"You have been to Anaquitos," I say.

He responds in Pirahao.

"Tell me in Spanish."

"I have been there," he says, laughing. "I was there with Amadis of Gaul."

I tell him that I want to bring the Christians to Anaquitos, but he does not need to be convinced. He wants nothing more than to return to the city and carry off its treasures. He tells me there is a woman waiting for him in Spain, but he can never return because he is a converso, so he must make himself very rich instead. Then he will buy an island in the

Caribbean and he will send for her. Her name is Anna Gloria and he has only seen her once in the light of the world, though he sees her sometimes when he sleeps.

"But Diego Paez de Sotelo has denounced you," I say. "He accuses you of the Mosaic heresy and of other heresies as well."

He considers this solemnly for a moment. The forest shrieks. In Pirahao it means it is the time for a dance, the time for sweet potatoes, the time to lie down. In Spanish it means nothing.

"Interesting," he says. "I am not surprised. I left him to die in the forest, but only because I thought he would die anyway."

"The alcalde has heard the story of your foot."

"Aha!" he says. He cannot escape the story of his foot. He begins telling it once again. "It had become putrescent from the bite of a big blue jungle ant. Lope de Guzman had to cut it off. A true friend is one who will cut your foot off." He starts laughing as he tells the story. "I was trying to make him cut the other foot off too. I was so excited! Cut it all off, I kept saying, the hands too, cut them both off, they'll only cause problems later. Then Lope de Guzman and some of the others had to beat me until I was silent. It was okay because the Indians had a special medicine for lost feet, as I keep telling everyone."

But he says the medicine also turned the water orange and the sky purple. It made the tree trunks boil with faces. It made time flow in the wrong direction. It made time flow in any number of directions, not just backwards but side to side also, so that he couldn't tell what had happened in the past and what had only happened in the future.

"The Christians believe your story," I say. "That is the problem. They believe this medicine is the work of the devil."

I tell him that he must tell the alcalde about Anaquitos instead. He must describe it not as it is in Pirahao but as it is in Spanish, which is what I do when I tell my own stories. In Spanish it is El Dorado. He must say that the houses are roofed in gold, that people crush pearls and bake them into bread, that there is a king who covers himself in gold dust before his bath every morning. He must say that he is the only one who knows how to find the city. This is how he will free himself from the accusations against him. The gold of El Dorado is more important than any crime against the faith. Sin can be paid for with gold.

"I understand," he says. "There are two cities. There is the city of our most glorious aspirations and at the same time there is the city where the whores paint their teeth black."

"Yes. In Anaquitos the whores paint their teeth. In El Dorado they have white teeth and all of them are virgins. Try to remember. Christians love virgins."

He leans back and looks at the ceiling. He is at ease. He has no fear. He looks into the future, as a Christian does. What is it that makes him a Jew?

"I will tell the alcalde that Diego Paez de Sotelo was planning to keep all of this a secret," he says. "Or else that he wanted to condemn me so that the treasure would be his alone. I'll say that first I wanted to protect him, since he is my friend and companion, but now I feel moved by my love of God to reveal his deception."

"Very good," I say.

"But what is the food they have in Anaquitos? Remind me. It is a kind of rat meat in dough."

"Xaxa."

"It's delicious."

"In Spanish it is food for a starving person. Don't tell the alcalde about it or he'll think the city is poor. Tell him there are no city walls. Tell him to forgive Diego Paez de Sotelo, who is only as flawed and sinful a person as the rest of us. Tell him that. The alcalde loves compassion."

Now we are agreed. He will tell the alcalde his story and we will go to Anaquitos. We will put it to the sword. I will have my vengeance and he will have his fortune, his island, his woman. I will go as an interpreter, and just as Cortés had Malintzin to speak for him, so will I speak. I will be the tongue of the expedition. It is what I desire most. It is what I least desire. The devil speaks to me and I try not to laugh.

"I am the blue bird of devastation," I tell him. In Spanish, the phrase means nothing.

He stands up and stretches. There is no window in the cell, but we can hear the birds. They tell us that the sun has set.

"What will you say about your foot?" I ask him. "What will you tell them?"

"For that I have a plan."

"A plan."

"I have a plan, yes."

"But you must promise me. Promise me we will go there."

He laughs, haha, and he says, "My friend, I'm a hundred years old, and if I've learned anything in that time I've learned that when a pretty girl tells you to jump, you had better jump. I promise you we will go there."

## 2200

Old Dan was kind to me he looked after me and one day he had a proposition for a mutual endeavor. What proposition I said what is it. You could come with me he said if you don't have nothing else to do you could help me with some things. We are on the same ship I said we are coming with each other anyway. Yes he said but I mean we could be official partners not just shipmates. Okay I said. You could help me find Anna Gloria he said and on the way we could dig up the treasure of Anakitos which I have been meaning to dig up for some time. The treasure of Anakitos I said. Yes he said we will dig it up and you will be a rich man it will solve your problems. Oh I said okay good yes great. You would like that he said. Yes I said I would like that very much this sounds like a good plan. Okay he said it is a deal. Deal I said. That were how we struck our bargain easy no problem. It were obvious I would not be any help to him for I didn't know what Anna Gloria looked like. However he did not care about this he were just doing me a favor he were making me feel welcome.

Next I saw the skyscrapers of New York bigger than Boston enormous. I were a city boy myself but this were a different city. It were huge buildings trash filth commerce a harbor packed with sailing ships. It have a sea wall in New York just like it have in Boston but even behind the wall some of the buildings was standing to their ankles in water and others had fallen apart. It were a city spread out over miles very glorious but it were also a place much come down in the world. I did not dare go ashore for it is said the people of New York are terrible vicious thieves. I stayed aboard playing bawbles with Old Dan he kept winning but he wouldn't take my money.

I were very worried looking over my shoulder at the buildings all gone to smash it made me crazy. What had happened to us I wondered how had we lost the secret of building cities. I asked Old Dan tell me stories of the old days before everything were so fucked up. Tell me of New York I said it were a great city once that were plain. He said yes okay well there was Hurricane Devaun and then later the sea come up also there was drought everywhere too many people too many factors everyone in New York starved it were beyond belief. I said he did not understand me I did not mean stories like that but stories of the very good days when every man were a king with air condition Ferrari electronic lights ice cream toothpaste footballs streamy media. Okay he said sure for instance the subways they was sucked underground through vacuum tubes they was trains beneath the earth it were a marvel. Interesting I said was they air condition. Yes they were he said. Amazing I said. Yes he said it were thousands of people on those trains all the time speeding toward their doom. Don't speak of doom I said. Okay he said yes alright New York were a very grand place before its doom it were no green thing growing anywhere the complete triumph of man over nature I do not see how New York averted its doom so long. Please do not speak of doom I said but anyway never mind enough of New York tell me of a beautiful place. He smiled very sly he said I will tell you of a island with meadows fish blackberries blueberries great green trees it were one of the great natural harbors in the world so beautiful. Yes I said okay but I knew it were a trick. Aha he said it were New York he laughed it were no city then just Indians and that is how I remember it for in truth I never saw the subway I admit it. Tell me of Indians I said. He grew serious he said I must not speak of Indians they are the original doomed people sad to say.

Old Dan he were so stiff after years of the sky pressing down that sometimes he were not able to bend at the waist he were all one piece like a hinge rusted together. Still he knew how to sail he knew everything about ships sails winds. We beat down the coast that is what it was called we beat south against the wind Old Dan shouting at us haul this fix this reef this make it fast heave. He were not the captain but the captain did defer to him. Much of the time whenever it were navigable we was in the canal not the ocean for it had big storms at this season and every season now the weather it were all fucked up. But it were often the same the canal the sea for the sea had come up over the land between them what a mess. Very much of the coast were drowned houses buildings towns what a mess you could not say it enough what a mess.

Now I will tell about the other people in the boat. It were eight of us and a small yacht too all beat up and dirty. You could not sleep nor turn around without there was another man breathing at you and grinning and shouting and pissing over the rails. There was none like me so new to the sea but none like Old Dan so expert. There was Ming Kobe Karl Metta and one other I can't remember never mind it don't matter as you will see. The captain owned the boat but he were a true fool with his talk of gold and plastic growing in the sun. It were Old Dan that explained how gold grew underground so how could it matter the conditions of the light. Karl who had some school before his dad went bust Karl said Old Dan were right and now we knew the captain were a idiot. Karl played bawbles with us he were a large man he considered himself expert in all subjects though Old Dan skun him at bawbles as he skun me also. I am not always so lucky said Old Dan once I gambled away a whole island it were Little Salt in the Bahamas.

For my part I simply were thinking of women all the time 24/7 I could hardly sleep. We saw girls sometimes on the banks of the canal they had water jugs rolling hips they laughed at us they pointed it were too much. One night I went ashore I came creeping around. There was shacks some torchlight no girls that I could see or they was all asleep. For my pains I got a shovel in the meat of the ass it were a farmer thinking I were peeping. I were however he were correct. Poor fucker I thought I am a poor fucker. But even though I were getting the shovel in the ass running away crying I did see in the bluffs a community of great houses electronic light like the moon itself gleaming on the heights amazing. I thought when I am a rich man no one will poke my ass with a shovel it will be me does the poking.

Soon the canal was choked. We found a channel to the sea we slid out into the chop whereafter every day on the boat were the same the coast the waves the salty smell such tedium. How could I of thought this were seeing the world you could see more of the world in the bottom of a glass. We had corn mush to eat it were horrible. Old Dan said it used to have so many fish you could scoop them in a hand you could catch them with a hook you didn't need to eat corn mush. I had never seen him eat food anyway only honey or sugar in a little water. I thought maybe it was his secret of eternal life. Oh no he said it is cause I ate probiotics in the old days have you heard of this. No I said. Probiotics he said is a type of disease eating creatures they live in your stomach but they don't hurt you they only hurt the diseases they thrive on those things. Interesting I said how do you get them in there. There are many methods he said for example if you eat a old shoe left out in the rain so it has that old shoe smell. Oh I said can you cook it. No he said that would kill the probiotic after all.

Sometimes Old Dan joked with me he thought I were too serious. For instance I had a old plastic figure with me a woman figure. Old Dan said it were a toy for girls he called it my Barbie doll but it were not it were a idol it were the Blessed Virgin. Her hips was exaggerated yes her tits also I admit it but it were a idol I asked it to intervene in time of danger.

Next we come in sight of Norfolk Harbor we was in Hampton Roads. No one but Old Dan had ever been here so far south. However now we saw a terrible thing it were the waves breaking in the middle of the ocean. Even I knew this were strange. What is that I screamed a monster it is a giant squid. Old Dan said coral I think it is coral fancy that. Next he begun to shout commands he were calm but we did not understand him for his commands was very technical. He were shaking his head for the wonder of it a coral reef in Hampton Roads amazing he said then he shouted more commands. Turn right he said just turn right for God's sake.

It were not coral for all the world's coral was dead or so I heard later. It were just another sunken bridge however the effect were the same. It ripped a hole in our boat which glanced off the bridge and sank like a stone in deeper water. I treaded the water I were a good swimmer for I had sometimes dove for salvage in Boston Harbor. Old Dan were floating on his back crying out not again not again saying call me Jonah call me Ishmael. I now saw however that the rest of the men were drown. Old Dan called to me don't worry young man God will not kill me he preserves me from death I am useful to him as a plaything he will preserve you too stick with me. It seems he had forgot about probiotics and now it were God kept him alive. I said Old Dan you are crazy you are a crazy fucker for all the other men are drown and they had stuck with you too. I swallowed some water I coughed but as the wind come up and I were swallowing water now suddenly a treetrunk come floating past we grabbed on we held to it and it buoyed us up. Old Dan he were saying never fear don't cry for I were crying with fear. Amazing he said lying upon the log drooling coughing he said you men are always crying but men never used to cry. Then again he said considering this then again before that men did cry. Amazing he said I have lived to see the world change and change back again.

# 1750

---

I slept like a shipwrecked mariner on the beach of his salvation, and when I woke next morning in the great house at Babylon I could not recall the name by which I had introduced myself the night before. I should never have remembered but that a house slave, whose name was Polonius, brought me tea in my chambers and addressed me as Master Green. Ah yes, said I to myself, when Polonius had gone, my name is John Green. I laughed at this, and spilt my tea. I am the second son of a rich factor in England, said I, and laughed again, and once again spilt my tea.

This lapse of memory should have recalled to me the danger I was in, for if I were found out as what I was – a free mulatto named Sam – I would be liable to a harsh punishment indeed, and perhaps, for all I knew, miserable servitude. Yet I feared nothing, for I was young and vigorous as the green weeds in a New England springtime, and I thought only how marvelous it was to live as a white man, and be treated as one. Directly upon coming down-stairs I applied to Mr. Galsworthy if he had employment for a person such as myself, for I liked Babylon very well and felt I had distinguished myself last night in smoaking, and in manners. He said dear boy you have come at the right time, for our book-keeper poor Rollins he was *struck down by a thunderbolt*, and reduc'd to a pile of ash.

Thus did I become a book-keeper, knowing nothing of that trade. I had fifty pounds a year and a house all my own, though it was but two rooms at the edge of the morass, & a malarious situation that was indeed. Dr. Dan was now also hired, namely as physician, knowing no more of his own trade than I knew of mine. Thus Mr. Galsworthy had made two hires that morning, and both of them imposters, notwithstanding he went about telling all that he was now at last bringing this plantation up to the stick with good employees. So great was his happyness he required volatile salts to bring him round for dinner, & in such excitement no one explained the job of book-keeper to me, and I still could not tell you what this job consists in, so therefor I did as always — nothing — and passed my days in peaceful repose.

Who was this Dr. Dan, and where had he come from? He wore a cotton night-cap at all times, saying this protected him from the damp which exhaled from the earth. He said he was as ancient as the Americas, and as many-natured. He said he was a great explorer, and had been once to El Dorado and once to *The Great Southern Land*, where the earth plunged back within itself, and men walkt on their hands, and women gave birth to eyeless homunculi which they raised to infancy in a lubricious fold of skin upon their bellies. I did not believe a word of this, yet among his outrageous stories were the kernels of truth as well, & when I asked why had he come to the Indies, he spoke plausibly enough, saying he had come to cut himself a slice of the sugar boom.

But you must take care to observe what kind of a boom it is, said he,

for a big planter will die of the black vomit [with no help from his physician, he observed with a laugh] and leave his sons only debt, for it is a boom on credit. Nor is a man's station any obstacle, and a razor-grinder today is a baron tomorrow, and a rat-catcher a member of Parliament. For myself I sailed down on a Bristol trader, and though bound for Jamaica we had the unhappy accident of running off-course in a storm, and foundering in the Bahama sea. I washed ashore on Nassau, where I had not been since I stopped there for water and tortoises in 1492, with the sea captain Christopheros Colombo, on our way to the court of the Great Kahn in Cathay. In Nassau I spent all my money on a suit of cloathes, namely a ruffled shirt, blue broad cloth coat with scarlet cuffs & gold buttons, nicely puff'd breaches, & a wide black hat. It was a suit *Fit to be Buried in*, for I thought I would play the part of a noble-man, and obtain credit enough for some slaves and a few pretty acres. I had also a letter of credit wrote for me by a shipmate in the impenetrable language of the Finn, & tell me who would challenge such a letter as that? But my true concern was Manners, for this is the mark of the gentle-man that he may pee on his host's shoes, & the host will believe he is himself committing the outrage. Believe me young man I have sat at the court of King Arthur, and I know beautiful manners. Therefor, I tell you, though I am no dab at your fine sayings, I was going to pee on my host's shoes.

This rhapsodic speech being done, I asked him what had come of his plan, for as it seemed to me he was not master of a shilling. Yes, said he, I have lost everything, or I should say I ne'er got it, for in the debauched whirl of plantation visits I soon forgot what I was doing. A shame, said I, to which he nodded, laughing and saying, I am a *Doctor* without the tiniest grains and scruples of learning, and when I betray myself I shall be hanged! Even speaking so he was very cheerful, and seemed certain that all would come right in the end.

Dr. Dan and I spent long afternoons in each other's company, and he told me of many things more, viz. the Popish Cruelties of the Spaniards among whom he had liv'd, & the grate pirate Blackeye, and the many shipwrecks he had endured, five or ten shipwrecks I think, for each day he spoke of a new shipwreck so that it seemed his life had consisted of little else. For me these stories were an entertainment, and I gave them little credence, absorb'd as I was in the thoughts and vanities of youth. Yet Mr. Galsworthy attended to them with the *lidless absorption of a pucker fish*, and soon one of these tales was the cause of a great change that he wrought in the administration of his plantation.

The gentle lady reader will perhaps have her own picture of the West Indian sugar plantation — the waving green cane, the dark faces of the slaves, the heat of the boilers. Babylon was just such a place, and yet not so, for it was Mr. Galsworthy's fate to have located his plantation upon Little Salt, where the soil was in all truth perfectly salty, as presaged and advertis'd, and from which the slaves could no more coax a bountiful crop than could a curate teach the devil to dance a minuet. Yet there was another problem that was paramount and supreme, which was that such cane as did grow was often as not food for black ratts, which at that time infested the island. The poor health of the cane, and the vigor of the ratts, gave the place an impoverished aspect, and a visitor from distant lands might have supposed that Mr. Galsworthy was not growing cane at all, but growing food for rats, & husbanding these small creatures, & doing an efficient job of it.

Dr. Dan and I were feasting one day with our employer, who had that morning deliver'd a speech upon rats to slaves and overseers alike, exhorting all to pull together so that we might be delivered from this evil, and explaining that in cooperation we should found a new brotherhood of harmony. It was then that Dr. Dan unburden'd himself of yet another fantastical narrative. He spoke of a great queen he had known, the Queen of America, who lived in the city of Memphis, said he, unless it was called Anakitos, or Manoa. He avow'd he could never remember the names of cities. This one lay in the jungles of Terra Firme, close to the very girdle of the world, where the *Great Orb* rose to that point which lies closest to the sun, and is therefore hottest of all lands save the trackless Zahara and, of course, Arabia deserta. In such places, said he, grow all the world's great jewels and stones, for they require the hot sun for their growth. Now this queen, Maria Yako was her name, did one day cause a great cloak to be made in her honor, and it was made from no other than ratt leather (this being the detail which had recalled the narrative to his mind), for ratt did constitute the chief food of these Piranha Indians.

Mr. Galsworthy had listened carefully to all of this, & tipping back his claret, & watching all, with eyes like raisins, from above the lip of his glass, he pronounced himself inseminated with a grand *Idea*, and made shift to rise and go to his library, though his legs misgave him & he went down head foremost upon the hard floor. To this I gave a great laugh, and Dr. Dan made an expression of dismay, and Mr. Galsworthy had no reaction at all, having drubbed himself insensible. Yet he shortly revived, and whether he then recalled his grand idea, or whether the force of the blow had expelled that idea from the globous jelly of his brain and caused a new idea to crystallize there, we shall never know, though we shall forever speculate. In either case, he now smiled and spread his arms, & said with no small amount of pride, Here is my idea, it is this: When God gives you ratts, make ratt leather.

Thus was the whole mission and purpose of our enterprise changed in an instant, and thus began the massacre of ratts, or rather it continued, with the difference that now the slaves were occupied in the curing and tanning of the skins. I owned it was a clever scheme, for if we could not vanquish these bewhiskered bandittoes, which had greatly the advantage over us by their superior faculty of multiplication, we could take the benefit of their numbers, and turn this multiplicative faculty to our own profit. Also, this labor of making leather – which did produce, as everyone knows, such a smell that there was no place upon Little Salt island where a man could not get a smack of it – was not one quarter so injurious to the slaves as making sugar, which fact especially endeared it to Mr. Galsworthy, who pronounced that he had whipt his last slave, and would from thence act midwife to a kind of *Golden Age* upon Babylon plantation, when slave and master would pull together in this labor of making ratt leather, and all would live as brothers. It would be a heaven on earth, said he, a heaven of ratts.

I had no part of all this, and simply enjoyed myself upon my veranda, sometimes in company of Dr. Dan and sometimes alone. I slept well, for the fatigues of an industrious life are as nothing compared with the fatigues of roguery. I drank tea and burned foetid material of all descriptions to drive off the moskitos and black flies. I chew'd crude opium, which I found among my predecessors effects. I sweated & ate & sweated, no one ever asking how my work went, and therefore I felt proud, as if I were working hard, and getting ahead at last. Plantation life, dear Reader. Shaded verandas, rum in punch, moskitos & cotton trees & long afternoons of the rainy season, shuddering fevers & a prospect of blue water, the shade of the plantane walk on a March evening clear as glass. I own it is not a bad life at all, as long as you are a white man.

# 2500

Not long after he purchased Daniel Defoe, my father announced a five-year remodernization plan for St. Louis. He promulgated an edict to this effect, and then, in an example of aspirational governance, he declared by presidential decree that our country would henceforth be known as the Reunited States of America. He said that we had been wandering in an exodus of poverty, but now he would usher forth a golden age. He levied fresh taxes, reimposed the ancient system of weights, and seized the sesame presses so he could distribute the oil on a ration system. In order to infuse all of this with credence, he also manumitted Daniel Defoe and made him Vice-Secretary of Remodernization, for he was persuaded that Daniel Defoe carried in his mind the whole accumulated knowledge of history. He himself, of course, was Preeminent Secretary of every government office.

For some time he was awash with invigorated curiosities, and he even did some studying again, although he only read his economics book. He would invite his rich hereditary friends to the palace and discourse to them about economic opportunity, fiscal growth dynamics, capital gains, and free trade laissez-faire global market liberalization. "We will reconquer the whole continent," he would say. "But we will do it economically." One night he hung an expansive map of the United States on the ballroom wall and he said, "That is our goal." But it was only an approximate goal, because the shape of the continent was much altered from what it had been. Instead of the old state of Louisiana, there was a shallow bay called the Delta Bay, and Florida was lost beneath the sighing seas, and the Bahamas as well, and also the cities of the Atlantic littoral. This at least was what we gleaned from travelers.

As for me, I repudiated the whole idea. I repudiated the patriarchal state itself. But I didn't bother saying so to my father, who never listened to me. The only person in whom I confided my true heart was Edward Halloween, who was our palace clown and my own principal friend. We stood together in the clamorous rabble-house of a ballroom, full of shouting bureaucrats and vice-secretaries, and we looked at this ancient map, which sang a song of nostalgia but told us nothing about our current political and territorial realities. Cartography was a vanquished art.

"It is like looking into the eye of our insignificance," I said. "Missouri is just a remote fraction of the whole. What goes on at a place like California?"

"Daniel Defoe says it is gone to desert," said Edward Halloween. "But he also says he knows a sorcerer named Quaco who can transmute dreams into woolen cloth, so we can't trust everything he says."

We only had good intelligence about our own territorial neighborhood. Across the river was the Mississippi Democratic Confederacy, which we called the MDC. It combined parts of Illinois, Kentucky, and Tennessee. To the north was devastated land and then, much farther north, a bevy of small rich countries, in particular Minnesota, our former colonial overlord, against which my Roulette ancestors had fought a liberation war. To the south was hot trackless wilderness and to the west was the American desert, where there were mummified ghost towns and a few scattered roving ensembles of people. I often mused upon the desert and fancied that I had a large envy for the freedoms of that wild life. These people were few in number and they lived without formalized national coalitions. They slept in tents and gathered wild dates and sucked milk from their camels. They worshipped Jesus in the eternal blue sky and they hated us because we ate grain.

"We should just run away to the sweeping sand hills of Nebraska," I said. "We should just tell all these palace people they can kiss our south ends."

"Ah," said Edward Halloween, "but the desert people are said to drive their women before them like camels. For anachro-feminists like us, the desert is no more congenial than the city."

Edward Halloween was actually a eunuch, so anachro-feminism had a different resonance for him. He was allowed to live however he preferred. Sometimes he lived as a man and wore denim and a red bandanna, like the presidential guard, and sometimes he lived as a woman and wore tight leather shorts and a strip of black cloth around his chest. But he was also barred from conventional employments, which is why he was forced to be a clown. His true vocation was that he was a poet and a genius. As an impoverished youth, he had magically and spontaneously learned to read, and later he composed an alphabetic novel, although he never wrote it down. He would recite passages when he drank too much sweet potato wine, which frequently occurred because he was addicted to sweet potato wine, as most poets were. I suspected it was a tour de force of searing intensity, but it was impossible to understand.

"Sometimes I think I am more of an anarchic feminist," I said. "Especially when Anthony Fucking Corvette is grunting on top of me. Sometimes I think I want to see the whole façade of state come crashing down."

He gazed at me with affection and sympathy, or at the least I thought he did. It was hard to determine because he'd painted his face white and he had a purple hat pulled down to his eyebrows.

"Your father is just the hand puppet of history," he said. "It isn't useful to hate him because he's hardly a human being in his own right. He is the despotism of centuries. He's a system of patronage. He's a scepter and a crown."

"But what does that make me? Anyway, I don't hate him. I don't know what I feel for him. All I really want is a chance to fizz. But every time I achieve a good mood, I have to take my dress off for Anthony Fucking Corvette."

"And I have to keep clowning," he said, "even though I despise clowning."

"It would be better to have no thoughts. That way, humiliations are just humiliations and they lack theoretical underpinning."

"Thoughts are what save us, my friend. We are the only people in these dominions with a remodernized outlook and philosophy."

A slave came around with silver thimbles of poppy juice and I snuffed a little into my nostrils. The ballroom was very loud. I said, "What would I do without you, Mr. Halloween?"

"You'd turn stamping crazy and burn this palace to its foundation, which would probably be better for everyone."

The biggest obstacle to remodernization was that the people of the Reunited States were extremely superstitious. They weren't likely to embrace new, anachronistic technologies and ideas. When there was a lunar eclipse, for example, they stood in the streets shouting encouragement and throwing stones and setting big fires so that the moon would not be swallowed up by the darkness. When someone died, they filled the dead person's mouth with sand. They believed that thunder was a magical wind unchained by a person who had communion with demons, and that any grain lost during a thunderstorm became the property of men in flying cars who came from a country called Manoa. They believed that an illness begun in the fourth quarter of the moon would always have a fatal termination.

My father wouldn't tolerate this hokey-pokey in his own household. "We are secular Americans," he said. One of the only times I ever heard him shout in anger was when he heard Domingos, one of our house slaves, asking Jesus to make the cook give him cornmeal for breakfast, like a rich person. My father said that Jesus was nothing but a magician who was buried in a cabbage patch and that talking to Jesus flew in the face of his whole ideological agenda. But none of us could swear that there was no place called Manoa, and even though I told the slave girls that they should not give up hope if they became sick during the last quarter of the moon, it was true that people died more often at this time.

My father started an information and propaganda campaign to extirpate superstition and remodernize the spirit of St. Louis, but his larger strategy was to introduce economic reforms that would extirpate poverty, since poverty stultified the wits and was ultimately the cause of ignorance.

His first large initiative was a factory that made cloth from camel hair. Daniel Defoe had explained that in other arid countries, camel cloth was a principal item of manufacture, and my father wanted to produce huge quantities and sell it across the river in the places that camels abhorred. He was like a lunatic in his excitement over this idea. He now revised Daniel Defoe's title, which became Vice-Secretary of Camel Cloth Manufacture and Remodernization Policy.

It's true that the cotton crop often failed because of droughts, so initially I thought camel cloth was a clever alternative. Camels were the animal equivalence of poppies and mama beans. They thrived in droughts. They could drink sunlight and breathe sand. They could also see through their eyelids. All day they absorbed heat and in the night they cooled, emanating warmth like coals. They were also very familiar to everyone in St. Louis, so it was reasonable to think the cloth-makers would be comfortable working with them. Everyone drank camel milk, and whenever poor people were celebrating they also ate camel meat. They called it shamo, after the French chameau, a convention which delighted my father because it dated from the time of the United States.

"But the problem is labor," said Edward Halloween. "He says that camel cloth will create jobs, but who is the only person who has no job? It is you, my feminist friend."

"It's true. The poor people have so many jobs they can hardly do anything. Instead of jobs, it will create chaos."

"Ah, but that reminds me. I've thought of a new theory. Ask me about it."

"Ask you about what?"

"My theory!"

"Oh yes, of course. Tell me, Doctor Halloween, what is your new theory?"

"My theory is about chaos and craziness," he said. He lifted his chin and gripped his hands behind his back, like a child reciting a poem. "Both are types of disorder, but craziness is an affliction of the mind and chaos is an affliction of the world. You might say, 'Hello, I am a human.

It is my job to impose order on chaos.' But this is not true. Chaos is born in men and women and it is our fate to disseminate it in an orderly world. That is the purpose of a human. Chaos is the outcome and craziness is the force or the process. Those of us who are craziest are those through whom chaos shines like a torch."

This speech had a firm allegorical rigor that appealed to me very much. It was his way of saying that the great remodernization campaign of President Roulette could be figured as a process of disseminating chaos, which did in fact turn out to be true.

At this time I didn't know Daniel Defoe yet. I logically assumed that he was crazy also, and this was because of the unimpeachable reason that he said many crazy things. Chaotic messages came pouring out of him in a ceaseless unbridled torrent. But I soon learned that he was only trying to stay upright and gain an advantage if he could. I discovered this one evening during a feast with officials and dignitaries. As usual during such affairs, the conversation just simpered along, rife with banalities. My father couldn't stand it and called upon Daniel Defoe to tell us a story.

"Then I will tell you about the Lewis and Clark expedition," he said. "The relevance of this topic is that the expedition began right here in St. Louis. Back then, St. Louis was truly the last settled place on the wild frontier. There were herds of wild camels as far as the eye could see. There were stands of cashew trees where the central square is now. There were also large earthen mounds, and these were the mounds of Cahokia. I traveled with the expedition as far as the mountains, where General Clark was killed by Indians in a kind of ambuscade, and then I went south. It rained so much that I had to fold myself in long sheets of plastic when I wanted to sleep."

I knew that imperial St. Louis contained no camels, so I cast a look at Edward Halloween and raised my eyebrows. He was sweating copiously from the heavy and delectable food. It was his favorite meal of spicy ginger beef with cornbread and jute leaves, mashed green banana with pig, and trembling custard. He grinned at me.

But then I perceived that Daniel Defoe was looking at me with a smile of his own. In fact, I had an impression he would have winked, except all eyes were riveted upon him. What did this mean? His own plate was empty because, as we had been interested to learn, he never ate anything. Much later I learned that he never voided anything either.

"Later I was in a place where hot water erupted from the ground and everything smelled like sulfur," he continued. "It was my private hell. After that I was in Las Vegas, which was a Mexican city built in a beaver meadow. It had many brothels and casinos. Eventually I found my way back to the river, which the Indians called the Pirahao, and I paddled down the whole length in an old bathtub and reached the city of New Orleans just in time for election day, where I got drunk with a writer named Edward Ellen Poe."

This was the end of his story, but I could not banish that smile from my mind. After dinner I seized a chance to confront him. I said, "Do you really believe the stories you tell?"

"Well, I exaggerate them a little bit to entertain your father."

"I thought just as much. But why? You're not a slave anymore."

"And yet I'm forbidden from leaving the city. I have to ingratiate myself and make myself indispensable, so he doesn't oppress me or enslave me again. But it's okay. I have some experience in this zone of endeavor."

"Interesting," I said. "This is not so different from how I live. A slavish way of being free. But tell me the truth, in that case. Where did you emerge from and why were you wandering the desert?"

"I will tell you. A long time ago I was ejected from Europeland because it was illegal to be a Jew, which is what I was and am. The woman I loved stayed behind. Later I learned that she'd been sold as a whore by her own people. Ever since then I've been looking for her. That is my whole story. It's a story of unrecanted love."

I considered this with grave thoughtfulness. Christopher Smart pushed his head against my leg. I said, "But this happened to me also. My father sold me as a whore. Did you know? I have to marry Anthony Fucking Corvette in four months."

"I heard something about it, yes. It's like you say. It is a slavish way of being free."

"It makes me extremely furious. I think I'll never forgive my father."

"But you never know. Life is very long."

"Longer for some than others. Why do they say you're a thousand years old?"

"It isn't so miraculous. It's only because I reaped the benefits of modern medicine."

There came a crash and a shout of jubilance, and when we turned around we saw my father laughing amongst broken glass. He was wearing a yellow acrylic cardigan and also his crown, which was made from obsidian and gold. He was drinking sweet potato wine from an agateware pitcher. He was very happy. If a man must be a cracked window through which chaos escapes into the world, it is nice for him if he is a king and president.

## 2016

---

After breakfast, the ancient mariner hung upside down from a scaffold behind the kitchen shed. He'd put on some boots that could be fastened into the wooden frame. The idea was to stretch his spine so that his rib cage and pelvis didn't become locked together. Azar was taking a shower in the tidy little bathroom shed a few yards from the back door of the boat.

"In your letter you said you needed help with some digging," I said.

"Never mind that." He pointed to the bathroom shed. "Your friend. How well do you know him?"

"Azar? I know him very well. I've known him since we were eighteen. I should tell him sometime how much he means to me."

"But what kind of name is Azar?"

"Persian. Iranian? Persian?"

"Persian," he said, his voice stifled and his face red.

"Iranian? He's a Persian Jew."

"A Jew! I myself am a Jew. Then never mind. I thought he was a Turk."

"He's not a Turk. Or maybe he is. I'm not sure what you mean by Turk."

"Turk doesn't mean anything. Our enemies were the Turks, therefore anyone who was our enemy was a Turk, but they might have been Saracens and Malabars too. Truly I had no idea where they came from. They were Mohammedans. They must still be out there somewhere."

"I don't know if the Turkish Turks are our enemies now or not. I'm not so knowledgeable about politics. Are you talking about the Ottomans?"

"I'll tell you sometime about when I was a slave in the Arab world," he said. "It was all camels and camel milk. And the Turks! I will say one thing for them. They had a delicious pastry called a croissant. You will know it today as a French butter crescent. But I can't tell you about these things while I'm upside down."

Out in the street it was the twenty-first century. I drank espresso out of a Styrofoam cup, which made me feel very guilty, and then I checked my email, which I'd sworn not to do, and then I checked my weather app for new information about climate change, which I'd especially sworn not to do. There was indeed new information. *In a Warming World, Where to Grow Wine?* And less trivially, *Melting Arctic Permafrost Looms as Major Factor in Warming.*

But even though the world was ending, I got my shoes out of the car and went for a run. Tight narrow streets, reckless driving, outlandish tropical plants, pastel houses with idyllic shady verandas, frigate birds stuck like decals in the hot blue sky. Soon I felt much better. Sharp and clearheaded and cheerful. It came to me that the movie would be a success. It would make us famous. Surely this would mitigate, at least for us, the sorrow of environmental devastation?

The island had come alive by the time I got back. Groups of stunned tourists were drifting down the street. The bars were open. There were street vendors who'd write your name on a shell, but the only people interested were Korean tourists. The shell people were working hard to produce transliterations.

Out in the street in front of the ancient mariner's boat, a stumpy little man with a plastic toupee was having a telephone conversation and drinking from a red Solo cup.

"Baby," he said, "there's not a thing I can do. I'll have to stay here in Cleveland another day."

He was wearing a lavender sport coat and a bathing suit and his hair had slipped down over his right ear. He adjusted it fastidiously and put his phone away.

"I guess you want to know who was that on the phone," he said.

"No."

"It was my wife."

"Of course it was your wife."

He was silent for a moment. He drank from his cup and looked around with some satisfaction, savoring his deception. Then he pulled a crumpled McDonald's bag from his pocket and held it out for me to inspect.

"I'll bet you I can throw this thing into the trash can," he said. He pointed to the trash can, which was close, not more than ten feet.

"I'll bet you a hundred and fifty dollars you can't."

He was unnerved by this response, which had surprised me as well. "Let's say twenty."

"Deal."

He missed, but then he fished out his wallet and paid me the money.

"Try again," I said, touched by his honesty. "Double or nothing."

"I can't. I have a gambling problem."

"Then I'll bet you this twenty that I can do it."

"Deal."

The trash can seemed so close that I could almost reach out and drop the bag in. He called me a ringer. Again he paid what was owed.

"The name's Tom Rath," he said.

"Is it? I think that's a name out of literature somewhere. Isn't it the man in the gray flannel suit?"

"It's my alias that I use for traveling."

"It sounds made-up. What do you do for a living, Tom Rath?"

"I own an advertising agency in St. Petersburg."

"In Russia!"

"In Florida. Pinellas County. I also have a boat. The Tampa Bay area is home to many attractions and destinations."

Azar asked the ancient mariner if he had known Christopher Columbus. I thought he was baiting him a little. It was like asking a tourist in D.C. if he'd met the president, and either he says no, in which case fine, or he says yes, in which case you know he's a madman.

"Of course I knew him," said the ancient mariner. "I sailed with him in the *Dirty Mary*. We called her the *Dirty Mary*. I was right there on deck when we slid into that coral sea and discovered the Lucayan archipelago. It was a beautiful tropic morning at the beginning of the world. I say that I was on deck, but so was everyone else. We slept on deck. It was a different time. We didn't use forks because they were against God, for instance. They were condemned by the Inquisition. If God wanted us to use forks, why would he have given us fingers?"

Azar winked at me. I had nothing to contribute. The ancient mariner talked and talked.

"His name was not Columbus. Another thing I should explain is why I sailed with him in the first place, because after all it was a crazy thing to do. It happened like this. I'd just returned from the Canary Islands. We had heavy seas the whole way, all the wrong winds, and three men in succession were taken by a sea snake as each went to pee into the ocean one fiery dawn. When I got back to Triana, I told myself I'd never go to sea again. I wanted to start a new life as a converso, a new Christian, and live out my days in a pious and retiring manner. No more canary wine, no more gambling, no more waterfront brothels. Truly I felt I'd turned a corner and put the mistakes of youth behind me. But then, to celebrate my resolution, I agreed to sip a little wine with a shipmate. We drank it from the skin like calves at the teat, and after that there was nothing, a splash of wild color, cartoon faces, a house of negotiable affection, a whore with breasts like watermelons and teeth like artillery shells, vomit sick, vomit sick, and a week later I knew I had to get away, I had to flee to the ends of the earth, and I went looking for a ship."

"So you went to the New World," I said, trying to be encouraging.

"There wasn't any New World. There was only one ocean, and India lay just over the horizon in the west, and the only land between Seville and the out-islands of the China Sea was an island called Antilia, where seven kings lived in seven golden cities. I know because I saw it. Shimmering coastline, high cliffs, pink trees with down instead of leaves. And who will explain to me how Antilia was lost? And who will explain how these continents came to rise from the sea? They were ancient already, and fully populated.

"Sailing out into the nowhere," Azar said, "and finding land. It must have been like walking on the moon."

"It was like there was no moon, and we walked on it anyway."

Later we went for a walk. We wanted to talk things over.

"Has he mentioned this woman again?" I said. "Anna Gloria?"

"He knows that she's out there somewhere. He's very confident."

"He seems confident in a general way too. Happy with his choices."

"The old man looking for love," he said. "Five hundred years of solitude. It's not really the story I want to tell. It's too tidy for the movie, almost. It's hardly a credible metaphor."

"And where do you suppose he's from? He's probably from Indianapolis or something. My great-uncle was happily married, living in St. Louis, and then he made a bio-rhythm chart that told him to abandon his family. Now he lives in San Francisco and eats a whole head of garlic every day."

Azar would have none of this. "Remember that my position is I believe him."

"You believe him?"

"Every word."

There were two parakeets having a shrieking argument in a date palm next door, but they quieted down as we went by. They looked down at us with sweet cartoon faces.

I said, "Come back to earth here for a second, would you?"

"I will not."

"Just for a second. Just listen to me. If not for me, then for the sake of the movie. Don't you think it's best to project a good-natured skepticism? I emphasize good-natured. We want to be generous and high-hearted without being stubbornly credulous."

"I've already explained to you about my kombucha epiphany," said Azar. "I'm trying to carry this understanding into the rest of my life. We're raised up from little kids to doubt everything. Sidelong glances. Smirking. When there's a miracle we roll our eyes. But not me. Not anymore. I'm drinking kombucha and appreciating the magic in life."

"But you admit that the story is not easy to believe."

"I don't care if he says he's Robinson Crusoe."

"He says that he's Daniel Defoe."

"We're going to cure ourselves of cynicism, that's the important thing. If we make a bad movie, what do we care? Are you suddenly very exacting about movies? Maybe we should also cure ourselves of good taste."

Something evil had happened in my head by the time we returned. I sat quietly at the table while Azar set the camera up.

"You understand what a camera is?" he said. "You're not worried about the camera?"

"Of course he knows what a camera is!" I said.

"I know in principle that there's nothing to be frightened of," said the ancient mariner. He looked warily at the camera. "I know in principle it's just magnetism or whatever it is."

He seemed to forget it was there, however. Soon he had yet another extraordinary admission to make.

"You might be interested to know that I killed Magellan. I might as well say so. I beat him to death with a cuirass in the surf off Mactan."

Azar wouldn't look at me. He nodded earnestly.

"Over the years you do sometimes have to kill people," I said, trying to imitate the ancient mariner's casual style. "I myself have killed a few."

He leaned back and folded his hands over his belly. "I've killed a tremendous number. Turks, mostly. Turks beyond counting."

"I poisoned my master when I was a slave in Jamaica," I said. "There's no harm in admitting these things now."

Azar gave me a nasty look.

"I killed the conquistador Gonzalo de Castellana," said the ancient mariner.

"You see how nice it is to get it off your chest? I killed a prison camp guard in Australia."

"He's never killed anyone," Azar said. "He's joking."

"He's joking?" said the ancient mariner.

"He was never a slave in Jamaica."

"Oh. I get it. Haha! Do I get it?"

"It's not a good joke," said Azar. "There's nothing to get."

"Well, anyway, you shouldn't feel bad. Killing people is not an agreeable experience. It gets easier, of course. Everything does. As for Magellan, he was a tyrant. We drew straws."

"Okay," said Azar, adjusting the camera and peering into the viewfinder. "But maybe now you could repeat what you said about Columbus, so we have it on film?"

My phone began to buzz and I squeezed it until it stopped. Our walk had spoiled my mood. It was all obesity and disposable packaging out there, and not a solar panel to be seen, and this was Florida, where there was enough sunlight to power the whole corrupt enterprise three hundred and sixty-five days a year.

"What do you think of our culture of consumption?" I asked.

The ancient mariner beamed, but he said, "I'm afraid I don't know what that means."

"It's nothing," said Azar. "Forget about it. Tell us about Columbus."

"He had a lazy eye."

"No," I said. "Azar, listen. If he's six hundred years old or something, he can help us put all of this in perspective." I turned to the ancient mariner again. "I'm asking about plastic, for example."

"Plastic is a marvel."

"I mean disposable packaging. You use it and you throw it out, like the plastic bags they give you at the grocery store. A plastic container of blueberries in a plastic bag."

"Okay."

"But where do the blueberries come from? The whole point of fruit is that it's seasonal! Are we kings that we have to have blueberries every day of the year?"

"Kings?" said the ancient mariner.

"It's economies of scale or something."

"What is?"

"It's cheaper to destroy the world than it is to save it!"

"Listen," said Azar, "slow down and take a breath. No one wants to destroy the world. It's just that who doesn't enjoy a handful of blueberries?"

"When you were young," I said to the ancient mariner, "there was no plastic, no landfills, no blueberries in the winter."

"There was sewage in the streets," he said. "It got all over you."

"But the cost now is that the seas are rising! The earth is heating up!"

"Oh yes, I believe you, but it's wonderful to be able to throw things out. Modern sanitation is a miracle. You put it out by the curb and it's gone. Isn't this a sign of progress? You should have smelled the old cities."

We could hear the parakeets again. The sun was shining. It was still a beautiful world. The spirit went out of me.

"I'm trying so hard to be less gloomy," I said, "and suddenly I'm talking about trash and plastic again, like always."

Azar sat down next to me and put his hand on my shoulder. Very gently, he said, "You're kind of fucked up, huh?"

I started to say, "I feel," but how did I feel? I felt painfully out of step with the world I lived in. I longed for a place and time in which there were fewer people, fewer cars, less garbage. At the same time I took hot showers and flew on airplanes and drank coffee out of Styrofoam cups. I was complicit. And I knew perfectly well that if I'd been born into another time, I'd have found another thing to grieve over. There was something wrong with me.

"I actually think you're doing better than you were," Azar said. "This is just a small relapse. A few months ago it was all garbage all the time. Remember?"

I hung my head like a sad cartoon man in an antidepressant commercial. I had never taken antidepressants but I was addicted to anxiety medication. I would have been addicted to painkillers too if it were easier for me to get them. I was addicted to bad news. Maybe I was also addicted to cynicism and gloom! Sometimes I worried that my tongue would swell up and choke me in the night.

"But it's such a nice day, though," I said.

"That's the spirit."

## 1560

---

I sit with the alcalde on the little bench at the back of the house. The pincha palms wave in the hot dusty air. The sound of an oxcart fills the street. He is telling me how miserable and sinful he is. He says that he only wants to live well and honor God, and yet he cannot. He hears the whispering of the devil. He sins and sins. He confesses but then he sins fresh sins. He tells me that he awoke this morning in the slime and muck of the pigpen, which I already know. He remembers nothing and he fears he has committed a terrible sin. He tells me that he awoke whispering the "Miserere Mei, Deus," but what was the use? His eyes are watering, his hair is slick on his round head, his cheeks are like the inflamed rump of a kogai monkey. He asks me if I think he is beyond salvation. He asks me if it is possible, as some heretics have claimed, that every soul is predestined for heaven or hell, and what we do on earth is only the enactment of that destiny, which we can do nothing to change. Then he says that he would like to kill himself, but that too is against God, so his only hope is to apply for a papal dispensation authorizing this course of action.

These are the problems of Christians, who are persecuted by God as they themselves persecute their animals. I am grateful that I am not expected to respond. I am grateful that I am not yet Christian enough to feel haunted by these spirits myself. For now it is easier to live in Pirahao, although the Pirahao will be haunted too, as soon as God learns of their existence.

Late in the morning, when the sun is high enough that it draws the color from the world, Daniel de Fo arrives with an escort of two soldiers. He wears his Toledo cap. There is a notary present as well. There is always a notary present.

Daniel de Fo begs the alcalde's pardon. There has been a terrible misunderstanding, he says, caused by his own confusion and negligence. He should have come at once and given his account of the Lopez y Barra expedition, but he went mad in the forest and forgot his duty.

The alcalde is delighted by this courtesy and apologizes in his turn for the rough treatment Daniel de Fo has received. He suspects that it is a blessing to be the auditor of any truth or clarification, because in that case he is privileged to become the medium by which Daniel de Fo begins to make an atonement for his crimes. Could it be that the role of medium, or of auditor, will redound to his credit in the ledger books of heaven, assuming of course that our terrible fates are not predestined after all? Both men apologize once again. There is no way to say "I'm sorry" in Pirahao.

"Now tell me, friend," says the alcalde. "The Lopez y Barra expedition."

So Daniel de Fo begins to tell his story. They departed from Quito, he says, but before they could descend into the lowland forest they had a mutiny. Neither he nor Diego Paez de Sotelo had any part in it, of course. They had a mutiny and Pedro Avila killed the captain general Diego Lopez y Barra.

"This happened just after you left Quito," says the alcalde.

"Within a fortnight. But we forgot about that very soon because the Indian porters died in the mountains, every one of them, so many that the men were simply striking the heads off the bodies so that they didn't have to waste time opening the fetters."

Without porters, they had to jettison some things. They chose to jettison their food. They thought they would be able to hunt jungle creatures, but the jungle creatures were too clever for them and soon they began to starve. For Christmas they ate a thin gruel of boiled saddle leather and girth straps. At the Feast of Saint Renard they cooked their belts and the soles of their shoes.

"But now Esteban Zancas had the clever idea to draw off some of the horses' blood and boil it in his helmet. For a moment we thought this trick would preserve us. It was food for nothing! But there were some disagreements about the proper way to prepare the horse blood. One man argued that horse blood was best with this kind of herb, but another said that it was better with a certain root, and there could be no consensus. No one had starved to death yet, and the three or four Christians who'd died since we left Quito had died only in the usual way, boiled into a broth by the ravenous air of the jungle, except of course poor murdered Diego Lopez y Barra. But now men did begin to die as a result of these culinary ambitions. Some died in combat with one another as they argued about their recipes. Others died as you might expect, from eating the poison herbs and roots they used to season their blood."

He talks and talks. I have trouble listening. At midday the sun makes so much noise that it isn't easy to hear anything. In the river I can see a vulture ripping open the belly of a dead caiman. They float together, the caiman on its back, the vulture balanced on its rib cage.

"Do you mind if I smoke the tobacco weed?" I say. A concubine should never ask such a thing, but I am impatient. I was never impatient before I became a Christian.

"I beg you not to," says the alcalde. "You may do what you wish but I beg you not to."

"Well," Daniel de Fo continues, "now things in the jungle started to get bad. Now arrows rained down from every quarter, and some of the men were killed on the spot, and others died later, in screaming misery, because the arrows were poisoned."

But if this was bad, he says, then what came next was worse. Now they attempted to travel down the Rio Equus in stolen dugout canoes, and in rafts they bound together with sturdy lianas. The canoes overturned, and the rafts were dashed to pieces in the rapids, and they lost twenty more men this way. But if that was terrible enough, and it was, then the days that followed were even more terrible. Now Death walked beside them and jeered and shouted and pointed his bony fingers. Two men, whose names were Rodrigo de Salamanca and Juan Carvajal, were taken by a dragon, and then Aloysius Federmen, a German, stepped into the river and was devoured by ravenous fish, and then one morning they turned out to find Giacomo Fontesecca, a Venetian, reduced to a clean white skeleton inside his armor. This calamity had befallen him without him even crying out.

"He made no sound?" says the alcalde. "Amazing. Such courage."

Then it pleased God to let fall a stone from Heaven, which killed Francisco Morales. Then one day another man was boiling a piece of aromatic wood and speaking of the three sheep he was going to buy with his share of the treasure, and suddenly he gave an expression of disgust, as if he had tasted something unpleasant, and burst open, like a seedpod, in an explosion of dark spores.

"This can happen," I say, making encouraging gestures. I pretend to know about the forest, although I know nothing about the forest. "These are common problems. The forest is an evil place. But don't you want to tell the alcalde what you told me? The cities, the king, the pearls."

Daniel de Fo nods. "I am coming to that," he says. And yet he is at ease. He takes his time. No one would know that his life depends on what he says. He asks the alcalde if it is not remarkable that you always remember the good things more clearly than the bad.

"So much bloodshed," he says, "and yet I woke this morning and remembered the smell of the forest, and the taste of the coffee fruit."

The alcalde is not troubled by this digression. He agrees. He says that he now finds himself remembering his wretched time in Salamanca with fondness.

"Once," says Daniel de Fo, "long ago, I was sold for a slave on the coast of Africa. I spent four years in the house of a rich merchant in Rabat. But when I think of that time I think of tea and chickpeas and the clear warm sunlight in January."

"But please continue," says the alcalde. "What happened to Pedro Avila, the traitor?"

"Pedro Avila went mad. He walked through the jungle with his organ of generation standing erect like a divining rod, which was very troubling for all the men, and then he was cut down by Indians."

"Remarkable," I say, "but what about El Dorado?"

The alcalde tells me that it isn't kind to interrupt. In reply I begin to open my dress, so he can see what God has given me. I smile as an iguana smiles. He looks away.

But he seems to have come to a decision. To Daniel de Fo he says, "I will be honest with you, because I believe you have been honest with me. Accusations have been made against you. I must decide whether to condemn you myself, or free you, or send you away so that you can stand trial. You must have realized this."

"I had my suspicions."

"First of all, you have been accused of eating unleavened bread."

"I certainly would have, but I had no bread."

"And you have been accused of amending a hymn of David."

"It was when José Casanova lay dying of snakebite. He began to sing. I repeated the words in a different order, but that was only because it was the order in which I remembered them. Diego Paez de Sotelo was outraged."

"What were the words?"

"In my own recollection, they were, 'Oh Lord, do not take me away in the midst of my days.'"

The three of us are silent. The birds are silent. God gives no sign of his existence.

Then the alcalde sighs and continues in a quieter voice. "You are accused of reverting to the Mosaic heresy."

"I have lived as a Christian longer than anyone in Santa Inés has been in the world. I have never returned to Spain. But they knew I was a converso, and it was for that reason that I joined the expedition in the first place. They thought I would be useful as a translator. They thought we might encounter Indians who spoke the languages of the Holy Land."

"Do you speak the languages of the Holy Land?"

"I do not."

The alcalde laughs. I keep quiet and stare at the wading birds in the swamp. There is no god but God, who is only one god among many and who is himself three gods. Nothing will happen but what will happen. The world exists for a reason, and we must always wonder what it is. If I want to prevent the destruction of Anaquitos, I must do something now, and I do nothing, and it is not my decision at all, it is God's will, which is as large as the world, and comprehends everything that will happen, and everything that won't.

Daniel de Fo is speaking companionably about the fate of expeditions. They are always the same, he says. Treasure, bloodshed, mutiny. He speaks of Fernando de Magallanes and his voyage around the world. He tells the alcalde about the pearls of Cipango, the rubies of Pegu, the gold of Sumatra, the silks of Kata.

"Enough," I say. "Tell the alcalde about El Dorado."

He speaks a Pirahao phrase that has no translation. I answer him in Pirahao. He laughs, haha, and the alcalde laughs, haha, and we all laugh together, haha, but no one understands anything.

"I've been telling everyone that I'm the one who killed Fernando de Magallanes," says Daniel de Fo, "but the truth is that it was my friend Jorge Ramirez. And yet I have a feeling that I'll forget. Someday I'll truly believe myself guilty of that crime. Will it then be my sin to atone for?"

And yet now he does return to his story. He says that Diego Paez de Sotelo took to wearing Pedro Avila's helmet after the latter was murdered. He wore it because he said the helmet was bewitched and he didn't think God could see through it. Everyone was dead and they had only this helmet to protect them. Then one morning they left Diego Paez de Sotelo behind, which is why he was so angry later. It was an accident. They were distracted by calamity. The men had been taken by jaguars. They had been taken by snakes. They had been killed by Indians or dissolved into a stew by a demon plant that enticed them by making sweet sounds, like a woman. Everyone was dead and Daniel de Fo had no foot and they were taken captive and dragged through the forest and that's when they came to El Dorado.

"But your foot," said the alcalde, suddenly aggrieved. "How can I ignore this? It was Indian magic."

"It was the will of God," said Daniel de Fo. "It was the will of God that my foot should heal, that I should return here and tell you about El Dorado, that we should then mount a new expedition to take the city and bring the Pirahao to a knowledge of Him. For this reason God preserves me from death. Look around you. Here I am, and here is Maria, who will be our translator, because I know only a phrase or two of her language. And here you are, with the power to authorize the expedition."

The alcalde nods once. The air hums. The sea is like a group of whores whispering over breakfast.

"Then tell me about the city."

"It is the white city," says Daniel de Fo. "It is the city of El Dorado. The houses are roofed with gold and the people crush pearls and snort them up their noses."

## 2200

Pearls said Old Dan such torments and all for pearls which have no value they are no good even for salting your bread. Why do you talk about pearls I said. He did not hear me. Also he said also anyway you cannot roof houses in gold it is too heavy did no one ever think of that.

He talked and talked he never stopped talking I didn't know what he were talking about and neither did he. Meanwhile we was still floating in the water. We was floating many hours clung to a treetrunk in the cold water of Hampton Roads. But finally when I thought oh well I will just go to sleep drown die whatever who cares finally it were a fishing boat sliding over the sea to rescue us. It were four five maybe six fishermen aboard I don't remember I was stupid from the water and tiredness. It didn't have so many fish in the sea but they had caught squids and jellyfish. You could call them squidmen not fishermen you could also call them jellyfishermen. They was salting the squids down while we was aboard. I will never die said Old Dan to the fishermen. Okay they said. I will never die he said I don't understand why God has selected me for eternal life it is vexing in the extreme maybe I am a prophet. Then he seen what the men were doing he could not stop himself he said squid is not good for salting. Later we tried some from their stores he were right if you have never ate salted squid don't start.

Norfolk harbor were drowned though formerly said Old Dan it were a good port. Therefore we come up the Chesapeake to Baltimore. This is a great city said Old Dan pay attention you are truly seeing the world now. One of the squidmen said Baltimore were home to almost two hundred thousand persons a city of booze thieves whores malaria fried pork. They use to say you could of got robbed any time any day by any citizen of Baltimore even a grandma even a young kid. It were torchlight by the harbor torchlight in the sailor's district yet elsewhere upon the federal hill you could see a great moonglow of electronic light. We did not visit that part of the city for there was guards plus a wall to keep us poor people out.

I were very excited to see this city. They was recently having a war with Virginia but you couldn't have known it there was so much prosperity. It had everything in the world for sale in Baltimore. It had teethbrushes hacksaws kneepads boots bicycles watches even a cell phone very expensive everything it had everything much more than in Boston. There was a water cleaner it run off sun panels plus there was sun creme they said you smeared it on your face it protected from sunburn. There was beautiful women everywhere and horses and cabcarts rushing past so much noise so much activity. Old Dan said maybe we can even find you a new Barbie doll. He knew I had lost my idol in the wreck.

We saw pigs too and these was like no pigs I ever saw at home those sleek black mean Boston pigs. These were Baltimore pigs fat pink sunburned with eyes like humans they could of used sun creme themselves. Were I telling you about pig toilets said Old Dan no that were someone else. I asked him were there any truth to the stories of men being changed into pigs by witches and if so how were it done. I were very worried looking into the eyes of these pigs for these pigs were men I knew it for a certainty. Yes said Old Dan I'm afraid many pigs perhaps two fifths are simply men transformed into pigs not proper pig pigs for I have seen this amazing transformation for myself. Wow I said how is it done. I don't know he said but I have a friend called Quaco he could tell you.

Now I wanted to drink corn whiskey until the sadness of life were only a memory. Also I wanted to stick it to all the girls of Baltimore and forget my troubles for instance the shipwreck. Old Dan he said he were past all that he just wanted to find Anna Gloria and settle down at last. But Old Dan I said where is she do you know where she is. Oh he said she is in Florida I think however we will check all the cities of the drowned coast. He told me there is nothing for a man but true love even if it were half imaginary for love itself were a act of imagination. I said corn whiskey were something for a man would he join me. I were just saying so for

I had no money he had all the money he had kept his bag through the shipwreck. I were really asking would he buy me some corn whiskey which now he did offer to do. Without corn whiskey I did not feel I were all the way inside my own life.

We went into the Mermaid Lounge and I drank my whiskey and he drank water which cost more than whiskey. This is very good water he said. It were hot in there and it had some old electronics stuck to the walls. It even had a big television painted up with a picture to look high definition high fidelity Internet streamy media. I were sweating hard thinking wow television Internet all the trimmings what must it of been like. I wanted to ask Old Dan about television however he were inclined to speak of other things. He told me he had seen men whose faces did grow beneath their shoulders. Then he told me about the sunken continent of Lemuria where humans laid eggs. Then he told me about Potosí which were a city on the moon. Amazing things he told me before long I were drunk from corn whiskey and stories and dreams of old days when the world were different and every man a king of Potosí and Lemuria with his air condition sun panels ecksekera. He told me for example about blueberries. Had I ever had blueberries no I had not. Blueberries were the exclusive food of bears he said. Tell me about bears I said. Bears were great creatures he said there are still some left they are like dogs but they are big as horses with huge teeth. Uh oh I said. Never fear he said they live on blueberries exclusively their teeth is just ornamental. Now he were thoughtful he said I remember that blueberries were also the exclusive food of kings.

I stared at the television with all my longing banging around in my head. I were saying to myself it's okay Jam it will all come back the television will turn on no problem you just have to want it hard enough. However it did not turn on.

Next I succumbed to sadness and corn whiskey and in the morning I were laid out in the mud. This is where Old Dan found me. I had not stuck it to any girls so far as I know. Let's get you cleaned up he said. Fine I said. He had got gel sanitizer in a wax paper sleeve therefore I scraped the mud off I cleaned my face. I were very remorseful plus my head hurt but even so I did not want to miss my chance I asked him could we go to a 24/7 whorehouse. He sighed he were exasperated check your pockets he said. I checked them there was money in them. What is it I said why does it have money in my pockets. You won it off a fellow at bawbles he said but now you don't remember. I don't remember no I said. You should not drink whiskey he said it will kill you. I said yes I had thought of this however for example I would not be able to feel the beautiful idea of Baltimore without whiskey for it were something wrong in my soul. There is nothing wrong in your soul he said. There is I said I am a man apart. Fine he said whatever you say but please stay focused remember you are my helper we are looking for Anna Gloria plus also the treasure of Anakitos. I am not such a good helper I said. True he said. But now suddenly I were worried. Please don't cast me out as your helper I said I will die out here on my own. I won't cast you out he said however what a joke the helper will die without the one he helps. It is like a joke I said which is also a universal truth. Haha he said very good smart boy. Thank you I said. We are a comic pair he said I am Dan Keyhote Knight of the Fretful Counterpane and you are my faithful squire Pancho. Yes I said. It is literature he said it is an illusion. Oh good I said.

It were raining now a clean clear rain it rinsed me clean I had money it were a gift from Jesus.

Old Dan went down to the water to look for a ship. I rushed off to the 24/7 whorehouse saying I would rejoin him in the afternoon. I were feeling better. I were excited to see more of the world. I had got an addiction now I'd seen a little part of it.

I now was bitten by many insects and soon took fever though it were the dry season. This were a new fever it did not have this fever in Boston. Then I could not remember were it the warm air caused fever or the insects. I thought it were the insects for I did feel a weakness when I were bitten so many times all over my hands neck face ankles lips knees feet armpits ears. I should of bought long pants but it were hot I could not bear it I just wore my shorts that was all. When I come out of the whorehouse having satisfied my desires I sat down upon the ground I were shivering thus Old Dan found me. Fever he said aha did you know I was a physician once. Physician I said. I will tell you what to do he said I will buy you a cucumber to hold it will draw out the fever. He bought me a cucumber I held it I were better for a time. Next remedy said Old Dan are some antiflammatory pills careful they will knock you right out. He bought me two white pills which came in a plastic bag amazing perfectly clear almost new. It would have fetched me a good price on the salvage market in Boston. He said keep the bag it is yours.

Old Dan had got us passage on a yacht. It were bigger than the last the captain a more cautious man for it were not his yacht it belonged to a rich woman. He were sailing to Florida to pick up some passengers the family of his employer who knows what they were doing down there. The boat were almost empty now just a skeleton crew and he were glad to have some hands. Old Dan said don't mistake me I am no hand I am old. The captain said grandfather it is a privilege to carry you for you have got wisdom. Then Old Dan he pointed to me he said here is my helper he will die if I don't let him help me. I smiled my best smile it were the smile of a helpless helper. Pleased to meet you said the captain.

Again I took fever it came and went and came and went it were like exercise. Meanwhile the captain told us about Florida its history its present situation. It were a sovereign state he explained. First it had seceded then it were a civil war and it were forced back in the Union. Then it had seceded again then it were another civil war then it were in the Union once again. Thus life continued for these Floridians one civil war after another and they never tired of seceding. At last the Union it said let them go and now Florida were all on its own like the Republic of California our neighbor in the distant west. Why did it want to secede I said. I don't know said the captain it were the carbon tax maybe but wow boyo did it go bad for them on their own. Floridians he said are not smart about laws government ecksekera they have got a problem with corrupt practice.

Old Dan were meditating he were talking to himself he said Florida she has got to be in Florida. What did you say I asked him. Anna Gloria he said she is in Florida I know it I have been wrong many times but now I know she is in Florida this time I know it for certain. Don't worry I said I'll help you find her. Once I thought it were her in the Bahamas he said but it were just some lady. Uh oh I said. I will not make that mistake again he said I miss her so much it is 700 years of searching 700 years is pretty long.

I had never met anyone from Florida it were far away it were like the moon it were like Potosí or Lemuria. I had never met anyone from the Republic of California neither I had hardly met anyone at all. Anyway government states unions they were not important we did not live in an age of government instead we valued our liberty and independence. It were the government caused us to be poor after all for it gave all the riches to the rich people. I could understand why Florida had secede.

All of this gave me an idea and I asked the captain tell me sir could a person secede and not pay the carbon tax. A person he said can do anything he wants. This were what I wanted to hear. Therefore I seceded all by myself quietly without saying nothing about it. Right there in the boat I seceded and formed the Independent States of Jam. It were my way of saying the world couldn't push me around no more just because I were poor and sad and addicted to corn whiskey.

## 1750

Life was quiet for a time, a considerable period in truth, and I sailed through the rainie season in a kind of *Trance*, up with the dawn, a breakfast of plantane and buttered toasted cheese, perhaps a guava, a day of rambling about or more often reading such books as the *Life and Adventures of Robinson Crusoe* (said to have been wrote by Dr. Dan, though he said it was another Defoe), a feast in the great house, a bleary evening, ghastly shapes wobbling toward me in the mist, the hard hand of darkness, a kind of sleep, and up again in the cool of the morning. My sole labor was the totting up of ratt skins in a ledger, and thus the months totted away as well, & one day was so much like the next that I hardly noticed I was still alive. I was John Green, a bookkeeper, and happy to be so.

Did I fear discovery, dear Reader? I must have done, though perhaps I was not sensible there was another way to live, for I had liv'd all my life with such discomfiture, knowing from earliest youth that my father did *Hate* in me that which he must also *Love*, which was, namely, the dusky echo of my mother. Thus did I know already, if I knew nothing more, that our life's turn is trulie an opposition of appalling contradictions.

True also that my task was not a difficult one, for I had only to act a gentleman and I was utterly ignored. For Dr. Dan the labor of imposture was more arduous. He called himself a physician, or was called a physician, yet he had also to work as a physician in order to sustain this fiction. But he was aided in his task by one Quaco, a slave physician who had communion with the devils and sprits of darkest Africa, and whose knowledge was very great, though not greater than his tyrannick peevishness. Dr. Dan said he had known him before, on the fever coast of Africa, and though I did not believe this at the time, all these years later I am persuaded it might have been true.

I made the acquaintance of the slave physician after taking ill myself, which happened one day sudden as a thunderclap. I remember it as if it were yesterday (which was in truth March the 4th, 1800, and how I marvel at the time gone by!). Having given already many hours of thought to the question of *Air Flow* — for my house in the morass was hot beyond all imagining — I succumbed all at once to a *hectic ebullition in the sweet-breads*, and was seized with an inclination to open windows in the east wall of my house. Thinking of this with my eyes red, and the sweat pouring from my brow, and my mind stupefied with the opium, and the heat, and the terrific strain of feasting each night with Mr. Galsworthy, I quickly lost all decorum, taking up an ax which was happily to hand and beating holes in the walls for some quarter of an hour. Dr. Dan explained later that heat, like wine, does cause the blood to boil, this effervescence and frothy rarefaction often terminating in a delirium.

When next I was sensible what was come of me, I lay upon the floor in Dr. Dan's house, wrapt up tight in a sheet which was wet, and cooling. Attending me was Quaco, dark as a shadow on the wall. He had placed beside me a bonano sucker, also rubbing some powder in my hair, both treatments being intended to draw out the demon that was in me. In this they soon manifested their utility, whether it was a demon indeed or whether the demon of Quaco's medicine was the same as a disorderly transport of the humors in ours.

Hello, friends, said I.

Hello, said Quaco.

By my grandfather's whiskers, said Dr. Dan, you were down a long time.

Quaco said little more, and ate his breakfast (which was plantain mash) out of an ancient porringer. He wore a *necklace of teeth*, most of them shark or dog, but some human too, which he said were monkie teeth. In all that was to come he was the Ringmaker, and did on this occasion instantly recognize me for what I was, a colored man, though Dr. Dan I think ne'er knew a thing about it, and still does not.

It was Quaco who practiced such physic as was practiced on Babylon plantation. It was he mixed the powders & cremes & liniments, and it was he set broken bones. He was a Professor of Obeah and much respected among the slaves, who came to him not onlie with complaints of the body and sprit, but also with concerns of other kinds, for ex., a problem between man and wife. Nor did he administer to the slaves alone, but even to Mr. Galsworthy and his wife, the lovely and genteel Mrs. Galsworthy (of whom I shall have much more to say), though in this case powder & creme & medicine must be applied by Dr. Dan with all pretense he was the physician. Another thing is that Quaco did always mix some *Superfluous Irritant* into the medicine which he gave to the white people, so that the medicine would cure them and yet also cause them pain, which was compensation for Quaco, who received no wages.

Quaco had already become the *Lawful Propertie* of Dr. Dan, the latter having acquired him at a game of cards from Mr. Galsworthy. I wondered at this, for Dr. Dan was having a century of ill luck at cards, and could no more get the better of his employer than a rabbet could write his name in a bowl of cornmeal porridge. But Mr. Galsworthy had grown weary of Quaco, who several times escaped, and had upon his capture to be lodged in the work-house at Mr. Galsworthy's expense. Quaco had done other sins and crimes besides, viz. he had set fire to his own cloathing, & perpetrated an un-nameable mischief in the cow pen, & had placed a *Magic Egg* outside the previous bookkeeper's door, and also above all he had manifest'd an indifference to whipping. For these reasons I believe that Mr. Galsworthy lost Quaco deliberately, to rid himself of a nuisance.

Thus were we situated, Dr. Dan & Quaco & myself, all together and acquainted, Quaco mixing powders, and I upon my veranda in the light chewing opium & eating every day with Mr. Galsworthy, so that I felt always *one feast from the Grave*, and Dr. Dan in his house with the equipment he had inherited from his benighted predecessor, which man had suffered the ill-fortune to be murder'd in the seek house by the slaves. This included amputation saws & scalp lifters, rectal scrapers, tongue depressants, a lovely little brass mold for making suppositories, sharp-tooth'd trepanation instruments, & a beautiful new enema kit. He knew not the use of this fine equipment, yet he was not troubled, and made light of it all, as for example by holding up a shaving basin and saying, Oh what is this, oh I know, it is the enchanted helmet of Diego Sotelo, and placing it thereafter upon his head.

All might have continued easy and comfortable had not Dr. Dan been seized by a remarkable fancy. This happened one day when he was called to Melanie plantation, upon an adjacent island, in order to attend the planter's wife, their own physician having been poisoned, I think, or else having simply wasted away, as happened so often with Europeans in that climate. I accompanied Dr. Dan on this journey, yet we could not bring Quaco with us, for he had to attend to the burns and ratt bites that afflicted our own slaves. Thus I was witness to my friend's confoundment before his task. Simply guessing and playing at his role as an actor might, he caused this poor woman's cloathing to be burned, saying it was necessary to destroy the *animal contagion*. After this he fumigated her bed chamber with tabacco, oakum, sulphur, & aromatic wood. Covering his bets, so to say, for he was a prodigious gambler, he now also gave her volatile salts and Jesuit's bark, and he gave her to hold one cocomber, which would draw out the fever by its chill. Lastly he instructed the lady's maid, one Virginia, to anoint her mistress's fundament with tabacco oil and balsam of saltpeter.

It was now that Dr. Dan succumbed to his own imagination, as it were, for having knock'd the mistress unconscious with all this medisin, our next concern was to go to the kitchens for some food, and here, in the heat and sweat of the ovens, where a grate feast was being prepared, Dr. Dan spied a woman whom, as he insisted later, he had pursued through all the ages of the world. This was his beloved Anna Gloria, whom he had seen first in Sevil, where she stood selling Fish even as he wayed anchor upon the voyage of Discoverie undertaken that year by the Genoese Christopheros Colombo, and he had seen her again in the jungles of the Oroonoque, and once again in London, and now they were met in the islands of the Bahamas.

He said later that she had grown older (she would have been more than two centuries of age herself), & her hair it was darker, & her skin also, the effect of servitude, yet he knew very well it was the same woman. Never had he spoken of her before, but he said that not a day had passed without it should happen that he thought of her. He said that even on that first occasion so many years ago, gazing across the water in Sevil, he had pledged to himself that he would make her his wife, and he remembered his promise now.

Reader, what could I make of this? What can I make of it even now, as an old man, gazing back at the landscape of youth, which shimmers and jerks in the golden haze of memory?

He walk'd up to her and took her hand, which she snatched away, and he said, It's you. She frown'd, and said, Of course, why, you are Lord Herforshire, & he said Why no my dear not a Lord, & she said Forgive me now I realize you're the magistrate I did not recognize you with your trousers on, & he said No no no, now in some pain. He said, I saw you in Sevil, I called to you, what were you doing, were you selling fishe?

Now this prettie woman looked upon him as if upon a clam that would not open. Was I selling fish? she said. Fish?

And in London, said Dr. Dan, was it you? What were you doing in London?

If it was I, said she, daring a slight look at the other women in the room, let us not speak of what I was doing. Suffice it to say you left me there to do it.

Now Dr. Dan was very embarrassed, and nearly heartbroke I think, saying he had not had any monie, for he had just gotten out of Newgate, & before that he had been a Pyrate, & was luckie they had not hanged him till he was dead.

This woman did not know him, as I saw very plainly, but she was resolv'd to pretend. Said she, Very well, Sailor, very well, but what will you do to-day? Will you make all haste to my rescue? Will you take me away from this place?

For we now learned she was serving an indenture, which is to say she was no better than a slave (though according to Law she was no slave), and if Dr. Dan wanted to free her from this Contract he had to buy her, which is what he now resolv'd to do.

It is she, he said later, his fist in the air. I have been mistaken before, but this time I know it to a certainty, and will devote my life toward securing her freedom.

## 2500

---

In the early stages of the remodernization campaign, before everything dried up and blew away in bundles of tinder and chaff, there was an idyll of repose. It was the winding of a watch. My own routine continued unimpeded, with few palpable changes. I got up early, when the heat started to rise, and breakfasted on the roof in the cool morning air. I had cold cornmeal porridge as well as mango, a little yoga cream, and a cup of hot caffeine. Then I persecuted my education. First, while my brain was still soft, I read my Modern English history books, and later I had tutors in mathematical logic and other topics. This was all my own anachro-feminist initiative. However, my education served chiefly to enlarge my feelings of grievance, for our library was riven with gaps and lacunae. It was actually only nine hundred books, and even though we housed them on the top floor with titanic barrels of dehumidifier salts, they were continuously succumbing to disintegration. Therefore I shouted in frustration, "But what is a Hittite!?" and "What is a kipper!?" and "They used to have illuminated books!" I could never achieve a comprehensive knowledge.

By noon I was fatigued. Sometimes I tried to refresh myself with fizzy camel milk and fruit, and sometimes I went unconscious for an hour, but it mattered little because after that I had nothing to do. I was trapped like a scorpion in a jar. This was the time of day when I usually succumbed to a staring madness. I would tell myself I should take a walk, but then I couldn't decide what shoes and clothes to wear. I would tell myself to continue reading, but I could not make the words resolve into ideas. My thoughts scattered like marbles. Sometimes I just sat naked on the floor with one boot on. Sometimes I drank poppy juice to console myself. I had no true public existence. I had no trajectory

except as a wife and mother, although I secretly kept my womb untenanted by eating a monthly abortion medicine that Edward Halloween
bought from a slave magician. This medicine was exceptionally illegal,
but I didn't care. It was another small exercise of my anachro-feminist
prerogative.

At night we would have date wine in the garden, which was nice, but
then we had state dinners with hereditary senators or visiting dignitaries from the MDC. These dinners were an agony of repeated courte-
sies, although they were much better than my nights with Anthony
Fucking Corvette. He was a coarse frolicker who didn't give a good
damn about anything. He ate sorghum paste and peanut soup, he drank
muddy water, he drowned his faculties in wine, and then he heaved
himself on top of me. Our wedding was scheduled for December, which
was a traditional time. Daniel Defoe had come to us in late summer.

Originally, the only thing that remodernization changed was that
Edward Halloween found himself less occupied. In former days he had
been ceaselessly busy with his job of singing, dancing, telling jokes, and
playing the flute at orgies, but now my father decided that consorting with
clowns was an indulgence unbefitting a serious monarch and president.
He spent all his time with Daniel Defoe, though you could have argued
that he had only exchanged one clown for another. In any case, Edward
Halloween and I were left alone more often, which was nice for me but
surprising for him, for he was dismayed to see how I passed my days.

"How do you stand it?" he said. "A person must have some occupation.
How do you while away sad afternoons? Just a few days of this boredom
and already I want to espouse anarchy and bring down the state in a
crashing fiery cataclysm."

He decreed a private clown's decree that we were no longer allowed to
do nothing. Each day we had to do at least one activity. And that was
how we came to make our first exploratory nighttime venture into the
city. I wasn't supposed to leave our compound because there was a danger
of catching dog malaria or being murdered, and previously I had only
seen the poor sections of St. Louis from the window of a horse-drawn

automobile, but Edward Halloween was right. Sometimes you have to throw caution to the hounds.

First we disguised ourselves. I removed my silver armlets, put on a pink cotton dress, and circled my eyes with greasepaint. He wore rough cloth pants and no shirt, like a river boy. Then we crept away through the contingency escape tunnel and walked all the way across the city to a place called Fat Tuesday's, which was next to the national lottery shack in the Tokyo neighborhood. For several hours we drank banana beer with the hookers and rat catchers and denture servants. It was an outstanding location. They served banana beer in earthenware cups, and you could pulverize the cups afterward because they were disposable. The ground was carpeted in red dust and pieces of cups. There was also a charcoal pit where they char-roasted barbeque shamo and goat, and all the tables were assembled from palm trunks split down the middle and fastened together with the flat side up. This was said to be the fad in the Mississippi jungle, for people in St. Louis had an enduring fascination with the Mississippi jungle. This is why they drank banana beer, for example, which was expensive and didn't have the smoothest finish.

Edward Halloween was mostly incognito, but my accent betrayed me and several people tried to speak to me in Modern English. They knew I was a rich person. One man grinned and said, "If you would try to have perfect shoes, okay! Good on you!" But later an angry woman shouted, "Explain it please, why are they genius scientists, but it still have no cure from a zombie bite?"

These nighttime ventures became regular with us, at least for a few weeks, and I learned more of St. Louis on those nights than in twenty-six years of high privilege. I liked to keep silent and fantasize that this was my real life. It was only noise and torchlight and wheeling stars and nothing more, no state dinners, no engagements, no stuffed-pepper atmosphere of a president's house and a president's aspirations. It was the air and savor of liberty. It was men playing dice, and they kept score by clipping clothespins to their beards, and it was a woman with arbitrary letters shaved into her hair, and it was an embalmed decorative rat stuffed with aroma berries. Sometimes there were even MDC men from across the river, where I had never been. You could identify them by the perfumed wax that they employed to shape their hair into high crests and ridges. They came to visit the brothels. There were no brothels in the MDC because, if you believed my father, their president was an enemy of private enterprise.

Edward Halloween was addicted to banana beer in addition to sweet potato wine and palm wine and date wine, and he was also addicted to millet beer. Millet beer was only for very poor people, but he relished it best of all because it smacked of his childhood, before his uncle made him a eunuch and sent him into service as a clown. Usually he was so fuckered up by the end of the night that I had to stuff his cheeks with cocaine leaves so that he would have the energy to walk home, and this was the precipitating factor in our discovery. One night he was so badly poisoned with cocaine and beer that he could not cease himself from belting out poor person songs as we returned home through the contingency tunnel. The presidential guards came hustling down and found us there. After this my father posted nighttime guards at my door.

The camel cloth factory was not a ripping success, for it transpired that camel cloth was not a new product at all. Small amounts of it were manufactured in the country hinterlands, and desert traders had been selling it in the market for years. It was already known as a poor person's cloth, perhaps because it was the color of sand, and this contraventially meant that even poor people refused to wear it if they had the slightest means of buying cotton. My father was surprised by this but ultimately believed we could sell it in the MDC, which proved true, so he mandated a constant low-level production. Then he fixated on smaller items for a time, like new compost toilets, the distribution of irrigation water, and the allocation of slum land to rural migrants, who kept fluxing into the city. Sometimes you could mistake him for a benign and enlightened monarch.

But sometimes he succumbed to a seizure of craziness. Then, to follow Edward Halloween's formula, chaos flowed out of him in an intractable river. For example, one day he decided he was going to use some of the camels from the cloth factory to breed back all the ancient diversity of extinct hoofed creatures. Daniel Defoe had been theorizing that we could breed the camels into giraffes, which were their close cousins, but it seems my father wanted to use them to breed rhinoceroses, kangaroos, and olyphants as well. Then he universalized the concept. He said nothing was unattainable but that which we failed to dream of. We could use crows to breed back the whole diversity of birds, including the great auk, and we could use Christopher Smart to breed back the large land carnivores, and we could use river goldfish to breed a monster sea-fish that would devour all the jellyfish and return the oceans to their ancient condition of pristine luminous beauty. This would create a habitat for other sea-fish, which we could also breed from river goldfish. Then we could start a fisheries industry.

The breeding program was a misconceived and flawed venture that had only two consequences. The first was that we learned about a concomitant breeding program that was already afoot. It turned out that some people had succeeded in breeding a special type of dairy camel. These creatures were so fat that they could hardly walk, and they didn't have the haughtiness and ill-temper of wild camels. They had floppy ears and they produced milk by the gallon, although this milk was of a very low quality. The breeders joked that it was only for sale. They would never think of drinking it.

However, the second consequence was that my father promulgated a law against eating shamo. This precipitated violent clashes between the presidential guard and the many people who committed themselves to transgressing the ban. Daniel Defoe encouraged him not to oppress the citizens in this way, but it was his presidential instinct, and it is from this controversy that I date the decline of good feeling in St. Louis. By this I only mean that for the first time I became aware of rattling simmering revolutionary energies.

As for me, this talk of extinct animals filled me with a sunset longing for vanished times, and I spent interminable hours in the library scanning for information about olyphants and the rest. There were only casual references. I tried to ask Daniel Defoe about it, but he couldn't remember which animals were real and which were only mythological. The distinction was actually unimportant to him, which threw me into a daydream of perplexity. What is left when you cease to distinguish truths from fictions? I longed for one true unequivocal image of a moose, but there was nothing. This was the ineffable sorrow of living as an intellectual in a time of radical simplification: We had the words for things, but not the things themselves. Olyphant, mermaid, giraffe. Dead language shimmered through our minds. There were passages in Edward Halloween's alphabetic novel that were just lists of defunct words. Toaster oven. Whack-a-Mole. Boeing 747. Asphalt. Gluon. Sometimes we could envision these things and other times, as with Gluon, we could not even grasp what category of thing it had been.

"At least we have the words," said Edward Halloween, "even if we can't make a Gluon anymore."

One night, in a bid to offer encouragement and explain how we should not be too quick to lament the poverty of our times, Daniel Defoe told a confoundingly fictive story about the decline and fall of the empire.

"It wasn't all sunshine and gravy during the United States," he said. "The empire overextended itself and also became extremely decadent. They tried to invade Kuwait, because of the fossil oils. Then they lost a lot of money in the guano trade. They also invested heavily in Andean silver mines, but everyone knew they should have been investing in domestic industry. Then they dropped nucleotide bombs on the islands of Hiroshiva and Namasaki! It was decadence and bad decisions. And meanwhile there was so much overpopulation that you couldn't get a word in or find a cup of noodles to eat."

My father paced rapidly to and fro, but I myself just gazed up into the empty air of the dining room and wondered at the uses of falsity. I no longer believed that Daniel Defoe told his stories as an exclusive entertainment for my father, for he told the same kinds of stories when my father was not present.

He continued, "The symbolic eclipse of American hegemony came one morning when a group of Comanche terrorists hijacked a spaceship and flew it into the Sears Tower. They hijacked it with nothing more than an eight ounce tube of toothpaste, which is why it was subsequently illegal to bring toothpaste on interstellar flights."

"Take a note," my father said to Edward Halloween, who nodded and took a scrap of brown paper out of his pocket. "Start toothpaste factory. Start inquiry into use of toothpaste as a weapon of war."

Daniel Defoe was still ensconced in the camel pen, having refused more gracious accommodations, and because we were unable to prosecute our nighttime forays into the city, we began to visit him instead. This was a break from the helter-skeeter life of the palace proper, and my father did not object. He believed we could all learn something from Daniel Defoe.

It was on one of these nights, a breezy night of late November, that we met the sorcerer Quaco, whom we had previously considered another of Daniel Defoe's fictions. He came gusting up the river out of the wilds of the blue yonder. He was dark like a shadow, and he wore a broken plastic bucket around his neck, and no clothes except for a skirt of plastic strips hung from a ribbon at his waist. He was here to transact a mysterious business with Daniel Defoe. It seems that he was very old also, older than Daniel Defoe, and he spoke Modern English in a beautiful euphonious accent.

"I'll tell you about Quaco," Daniel Defoe said. "At one time I made my living in the passenger pigeon business. I sold the meat, which was tough and cheap and easy to get because there were so many birds. There were at least a hundred trillion of them. They'd blot out the sun. Their feces fell like melting snow. Then Quaco made a magic to destroy them. He had his own reasons, so I didn't hold it against him."

It was yet another wild story, but I wished I could believe in it. My wedding loomed closer every day and I could only hope for some variety of magical intervention. We had now entered the three week countdown: The elite cashew wine had arrived from across the river, a garden pavilion was being erected, and the peacocks had already been corralled so that they wouldn't alarm guests with the clamor of their irksome screaming and the obscenity of their tail feathers.

"Please, Quaco," I said. "Could you make a magic for me too? Could you extract me from my engagement to Anthony Fucking Corvette?"

Edward Halloween laughed. Daniel Defoe laughed. Quaco closed his eyes in the breeze and quiet and hay-fever darkness of the camel pen, and I didn't expect he was listening, but then he said, "Anthony Fucking Corvette."

"He is a monster of atavism. He parades his hookers in front of me. He allowed his friends to beat one of them bloody for an amusement. I also think he raped his cook."

Daniel Defoe said, "I'm sure Quaco can poison him, if worst comes to worse."

"But it's not only Senator Corvette," said Edward Halloween. "It is the whole system and edifice of our paternalist government. Quaco would have to poison the whole country."

"It wouldn't be the first time," said Daniel Defoe, laughing and riffling through the cupboard where he kept his few possessions. Now he fished forth a small purse full of coins and he said, "Okay, Quaco, I've owed you these for a long time. It took a while but I found them after all."

Quaco weighed the purse in his hand.

"You keep them," he said.

"Are you sure?"

Quaco nodded. "What will I do with them now?"

Daniel Defoe looked doubtfully at the purse. "They're no good to me either."

"You could pay your way across the river," said Edward Halloween. "You could escape the sinking ship of state. What do you mean they're no good to you?"

"I have only just arrived," he said, making a gesture of dismissiveness but also, simultaneously, casting me a glance of unknown significance. "I think I would like to stay a while longer."

It was the cool season, and in the early dark the clouds were picked out against the hard moon. Soon we were inspired by this lyrical vision to descend to the river and stare into the black water. Daniel Defoe took my arm. Quaco sang a melancholic tune. I had a camel cloth sweatshirt to keep me warm, for it was far superior to cotton and I didn't give a date pit for the worry that it was a poor person's cloth. I reflected how we were almost like four standard people out for a stroll, but of course we were not, for one of us was the president's daughter, and another was a eunuch and clown and poet, and the others were millennial wanderers of the earth.

Down below, in the turbid waters of this ancient grand river, we saw torn tattered nylon and other plastic waste. This was a frequent sight. We had lost the ability to create plastic, so we understood that this garbage was very old, unless they'd discovered plastic again in the north. We watched it as it waved in the current, and it was a spur to wondering and contemplation. In the light of dockside torches, with the breeze turning over the little waves, there was even something beautiful in this emblem of a ruined magnificence.

"All this old trash," said Edward Halloween. "It is like being shit on by history."

Daniel Defoe laughed like a hyeno, and I laughed, and even Quaco smiled, although not very much, and not for long.

## 2016

---

The ancient mariner wanted to take a nap. He told us to wake him up at five o'clock, and then, to remind us, he pinned a note to his pants: *WAKE ME AT 5 PM*. His handwriting was astonishing. Large capital letters with heavy serifs.

It was just after two o'clock, so we went down to Smathers Beach. On the way there we saw a man selling coconuts out of his truck. I bought one because I wanted to see him shave it open with a machete, the way I'd seen it done in movies. Instead he drilled two holes in the husk with a dirty quarter-inch bit and handed me a straw. It was delicious.

Azar was trying to cheer me up. "We can do whatever you like," he said. "Is there something else you want to do?"

"The beach is good."

"You know that I don't ever mean to trivialize your worries."

"I know. You're a good guy. I should tell you sometime how much you mean to me."

"You should. But anyway, I was proud of you when you were one of those clipboard guys! I was proud you forced yourself to do it, even though you were so poorly suited to the job."

I laughed. He laughed. I felt very tired.

"And, of course, it was absolutely the right choice to quit. Otherwise you'd have gone bananas."

The beach was beautiful, but for now I could only enjoy it in principle. I sat underneath a palm tree because I was afraid of the life-giving sun and I didn't have reef-safe sunblock and anyway, anyway, I was convinced that sunblock was carcinogenic. I was trying not to take my anxiety pills, but it had been a few days already and I could feel the creeping strangeness of withdrawal.

Azar lay down to nap in the sand. I tried to breathe deeply. A sweating smoking tattooed walrus of a man went by with his kid. He was giving the boy a lecture.

"Sea water not only cures you," he said, "it gives you all the nutrients you need to survive."

Another idiot, I thought, but when I saw them coming back a few minutes later, the man was holding the boy's hand. There was a lesson to be learned here about affection and kindness, prejudice and ignorance, whatever, and I tried hard to learn it.

"False memories?" said Azar, snapping awake and giving voice to some internal dialogue about the ancient mariner. "Or else, let's think about this, selective memories?"

"You remember what you need to remember."

"Or even better," he said, "elective memories. You remember what you want to remember."

There were more frigate birds hanging around up there in the sky. I'd read somewhere that frigate birds were able to sleep in flight by shutting down one half of their brain at a time.

"When I think of one particular fall a few years ago," Azar said, "I think of reggae and muscadine grapes. Is that a true memory? Did I listen to a lot of reggae and eat a lot of muscadine grapes? Or did I eat muscadine grapes and listen to reggae one time, and then it came to stand for that whole period in my life?"

He didn't last long at the beach. He was excited about the movie and he wanted to do something. He went to the bookstore to read about Columbus, Magellan, Captain Cook.

When he was gone, I sat crunched like a broken umbrella in the shade of my coconut palm. It was very hot and I wanted badly to go for a swim, but I'd gotten stuck to my ego somehow and I couldn't bear to walk across the sand and make myself into an object of scrutiny for the people around me. I kept promising myself I'd move as soon as this couple went by, or this couple, or as soon as those people over there were distracted. It took me twenty minutes to get down to the water, and then I squatted there like an alligator, just my eyes above water, and told myself I wasn't feeling so bad after all. I was not a starving pauper in Nairobi. I was not a garment worker in Central America.

Two girls settled in near my palm tree while I was in the water. I reflected on this word, "girls." They were my age, and in a different era they would have been called young women, or even just women. In a yet more remote era I suppose they'd have been getting on toward spinsterhood. Today they were still girls. One of them was dark, Hispanic maybe, and the other was a small redhead with skin like a snowfield. She looked like she was getting burned even underneath her enormous straw hat.

I could not stay in the water forever, and eventually I went back to my towel and introduced myself. I forced myself to do it, even though my natural mode was shyness disguised as aloof self-absorption.

"People call me Bee," said the Hispanic girl.

"What's your real name?"

She looked troubled. "Are you making fun of me?"

"Am I making fun of you?"

"My name's Bee."

"Sorry."

"Lena," said the other girl. "Elena, but people *call* me Lena."

They had a bottle of vodka and four cans of sugar-free Red Bull, which they'd carried here in a pink Victoria's Secret bag. They were mixing the Red Bull and vodka in jelly jars.

"You want some?" said Bee.

"I'm trying to sort of live more cleanly these days."

Bee could appreciate the benefits of clean living. With the dispassionate air of a woman discussing the features of her new cell phone, she explained that her father was a drug addict. Lena's brother was too, she said, though Lena herself did not look happy to have this fact disclosed. She did not look happy about anything. She drew her legs up underneath her and pulled her dress down over her knees. She was trying to fold her whole body into the disk of shade under her hat. I suggested that she move to the shade of my palm tree, but she pointed to the coconuts. Yet another danger. She was afraid they would fall on her.

"What are you reading?" I said.

She held the book out so I could see. It was a battered Signet Classic.

"*Tristram Shandy* on the beach!" I said.

She looked embarrassed. "I always thought I should read it."

"It's great. It's all of modernism two hundred years beforehand. The black page."

Bee squinted slightly and looked away. Lena nodded and blushed. I knew I was misreading the situation somehow.

"Are you just on vacation?" said Bee.

"My friend and I are here making a documentary."

"A movie?"

An egret floated out of the sky like a plastic bag. I was conscious of Lena watching me from beneath her vast shady hat. I did not want to seem like a pretentious jerk, but isn't that what I was?

"We don't know anything about filmmaking," I said. "I don't know how we got the idea we could do it. It's about an old man who lives in a boat over on Mango Lane."

"Old Dan," said Bee. "Daniel Defoe."

"You know him?"

"Of course we know him."

They knew him because they lived on Key West. They had grown up here, which seemed extraordinary to me, like growing up in Las Vegas or Disney World.

"What's the idea with this guy?" I said. "He told us he was five hundred years old. Six hundred maybe."

"Yeah," said Bee. "He's pretty old."

"There's a photo of him at John Baxter's maritime museum," said Lena. "You should go look at it. It's from just after the Civil War, I think. So says John Baxter. Obviously it's a fake."

"John Baxter's maritime museum?"

"He runs it out of his house. The John Baxter Maritime Museum."

They went for a swim. Lena was skinny and pale and beautiful. They were both beautiful. Girls in their bathing suits! Girls or women or spinsters. No matter. It was a reason to go on living. It was a vision of life itself.

But then they had to go. Bee had to get to work. She was a housekeeper at Tradewinds Cottage. Lena had to get to work too, though she wouldn't say where. They had this little break each afternoon and that was all. I didn't know what to do. Bee said maybe they'd see me tomorrow, if I was still around. Lena smiled and made a show of getting her stuff together. I waited until they'd disappeared around the corner and then I left as well.

I met Azar at the bookstore. We had coffee and then walked back to the ancient mariner's house, or his boat, or whatever it was proper to call it. Tom Rath was loitering outside the gate once again, peering in. Later we learned that he was staying across the street at Pelican Court.

I said, "We're not in the mood, Tom. We're serious people and we're having a serious conversation about the environment."

"My toupee is made from recycled water bottles. It's hot as the dickens."

"Hold on," said Azar. "How do you know Tom Rath?"

"How do you?"

Tom Rath said, "Everyone knows everyone."

"He bet me he could stand on his head for ten seconds," said Azar.

"Once I was standing on my head so good," said Tom Rath, "so still, like a statue, that a dog peed on me."

"Not this morning, though."

"Hey, Tom," I said, "we've got some things to do. We'll check back with you later."

"You think I'm a scumbag, is it? You think I'm out here and I like lying to my wife? She's not even my wife! She's my husband. His name is William. I love him but sometimes a person needs to flap free in the wind a little bit."

It took a while to rouse the ancient mariner, but when we'd gotten him upright again he was very cheerful. He told us to set up our camera. He was going to tell us a story about mermaids, to take our minds off garbage.

"The first time I saw one was in 1575," he said, "off the coast of Ceylon. We caught her in a net while we were fishing for our supper. She had a small flat nose and round gray eyes and hair like seaweed. Actually she was very ugly, but I was haunted for weeks by her perfect breasts. This mermaid also had gray skin and a powerful fluke, like a porpoise. That's why we didn't eat her. It wasn't because she looked so much like a young girl. Monkeys look very much like human children, after all, and in port we ate monkeys often enough. It was just that we thought her flesh was likely to be too oily, because of this additional or secondary resemblance to a porpoise, or a grampus."

"A grampus?" said Azar.

"Or a porpoise. But today's story takes place on a fishing boat off the Faroe Islands. It must have been around 1770. That's where I had an almost fatal encounter with a mermaid. We caught her when we were fishing for cod, which was an important commodity in those days."

"Hang on," said Azar. "Are you saying that you did not eat that Ceylonese mermaid, or that you never ate mermaids at all?"

"And anyway," I said, "how did they go extinct if they weren't fished out? It was probably climate change."

"Mermaids and snowmen," said Azar. "Endangered species in a warming world."

"I never ate one. And I should also explain that 'mermaid' is only a very general term. There were as many kinds of mermaids in the sea as there are monkeys and apes and humans on earth. Some of them had soft gray skin, like the one I'd seen off Ceylon, but others had rough skin, like sharks, and others had fine rainbow scales. Some had a fin running from between the eyes, up over the head, down the neck, and all the way to the lower back. Some had webbed fingers, and others had very short necks and a funny kind of feet at the extremity of the tail. The main thing is that all of them had breasts like a Dutch wet nurse or a sixteen-year-old dairy maid. That's what I'm driving at. And the mermaid we caught that day in 1770 was sleeker and prettier than the other mermaids I'd seen. She had thick black hair and a strong fluke and caramel-colored skin, and she had breasts like you could only hope to see in the moments before death, when you're caught in the anchor chain and going over. She was a knockout. We put her in a rain barrel and she sat there watching us."

"Do you think it was like dogs," I said, interrupting again, "where they're all the same species, but they look so different?"

"This is part of what I'm getting at. Why were some so humanlike, and others more fishlike? What accounts for the diversity of mermaids?"

"What about mermen?" said Azar.

"We hardly ever caught mermen. They must have had different habits."

"You did catch them sometimes, though?"

"Stop interrupting. I'm telling a story. I had the second watch that night, and I was in a fever of anxiety over that mermaid. I remember thinking that I was in the prime of life, just three hundred years old, and it was a scandal to live like I did. Like a monk. Did I need to keep myself perfectly spotlessly chaste, for Anna Gloria's sake? And I didn't think I could resolve this trouble by ignoring it and waiting for the dawn, so I went below and stole some canary wine from the mate. What you have to understand is how beautiful this mermaid was. You yourselves have probably only seen monstrous embalmed mermaids, if you've seen one at all, or maybe you've seen fake mermaids. In England I once saw a mermaid said to have been taken from the Gulf of Stanchio, but it was only a salmon's tail sewn on the torso of a shaved monkey. Awful sight! Another time, in Boston, they were exhibiting a mermaid's skeleton, but I knew it was the dugong of Sumatra, a type of sea cow, because I'd subsisted on dugong milk for a few months when I was shipwrecked in the archipelago. I'd swim up underneath the cows and suckle with the calves. I just want to emphasize that the word 'mermaid' comprehended the most repulsive creatures in the sea, but also the most beautiful, the sirens of the ancients, and if you've never seen one of the beautiful ones then you can't know what it was to be there, drinking canary wine in the haunting twilight of the North Sea, while she beckons you with her mischievous adolescent eyes."

"We can imagine," said Azar.

"I couldn't keep away. I was just pivoting around the rain barrel and gawking, and anyway I was roaring drunk. You know how there's a sweet desire that comes from beauty in the garden at dusk, but there's also the feeling you get in a Calicut brothel, when your lungs are burning and the air is thick with sailors' curses? The mermaid smiled at me! Her breasts were full and round! They bobbed to the surface like buoys! Then she grabbed me with her webbed fingers and kissed me. It was a warm shocking kiss, and I didn't need to be told twice. I climbed in there with her. I took my clothes off beforehand so I'd have something dry to put on afterwards, but anyway there it is. I remember the shock of cold, the white northern sky, the warmth of the mermaid herself, her dexterous hands, her teeth. I was very timid at first, but she knew what she wanted. I suppose she was accustomed to powerful mermen. She bit me hard, out of love I think, and laughed a human laugh, and licked the blood where it ran down my neck. It was like a holiday in a distant port. You come ashore and everyone's celebrating, you don't know whose God is whose, you don't care, you just put on the feathers and drink the sweet-potato wine.

"The next thing I knew, some of the other crewmen were pouring rum down my throat and slapping me all over to get my blood moving. I'd fallen asleep in the water and they'd found me hung over the edge of the barrel. I was naked and chilled to the bone, and the mermaid was just sitting there as before, bored as anything. I didn't hold it against her. Later we threw her back and she swam away like nothing had happened. I think about her sometimes. I think how sad that they've all gone away. But anyway, I think this explains why there were so many types of mermaids. It was because of incidents like this one. The sea was crowded with the progeny of sailors and mermaids, and maybe some were only one-sixteenth human, but others had human and fish characteristics in different proportions, in as many grades and combinations as you please. The first mermaids must have derived from an amorous connection between a sailor and a porpoise."

"Of course," said Azar, looking through the viewfinder. "That explains it."

I said, "You were three hundred years old at the time, and still vigorous enough to get in that barrel with a monster?"

"I may be getting my dates wrong."

Later that evening, Azar and I walked down to the beach. There were fucked-up kids all over the place. They were only a few years younger than we were, but it felt like a lifetime.

"When I was trying to be a graduate student," I said, "we used to go to this place called Tim and Terry's. They had a little courtyard out back and you got your beer and sat at those wire mesh patio tables. Spanish moss and the big southern moon. We'd go there together at night when we got out of the lab, and even though we wouldn't have been friends in real life, we were all part of the same enterprise. There was a real feeling of community."

"I was never sure what you were actually studying," Azar said. "It was like you were keeping that from me."

We were standing out on the pier at the end of Duval Street. Hilarity and consumption all around us. It was warm and breezy and the sky was the color of watermelon hard candy. I felt like an expatriate in my own country.

"It was in ecology and evolutionary biology," I said. "But of course I just thought about extinction all the time. I couldn't stand it."

"Sure."

"My point is that it wasn't really as convivial as I remember it. I was lonely and sad and I didn't know any of those people. I have these fond memories, but they're false memories. They're like memories of someone else's life. They're a story I've told myself about my own life."

"False memories again," Azar said. "What does it mean to have memories that aren't your own, but they mean so much to you?"

"But it's so sad! It's the brain trying to console itself. It's the smallness and sadness of life. It's the sadness of birthdays. Everything is so sad."

"It's true," he said. "Or anyway, I understand."

"Everything got away from me. Graduate school. And then living in New York. I hate cities! It did a kind of violence to my spirit."

We were out there on the pier with everyone else. Americans, Germans, Spaniards, a Chinese tour group, college kids, three stunned Irish girls. I said to myself, Don't be gloomy don't be gloomy don't be gloomy. I looked out over the pink tossing sea toward what I felt was a zone of radiance and gloomlessness beyond the horizon.

"I've been joking about cynicism," said Azar, "but at the same time I'm not joking. Right? I actually do think it's possible to live another way."

"Maybe."

"Okay, then what about this: What about Daniel Defoe? What's the thing about Daniel Defoe?"

"He says he's five-hundred and sixty years old. He says he's Daniel Defoe."

"Is it true?"

"If you say so."

"Of course it's not true! And is it a metaphor?"

"Maybe."

"But who cares? What's a metaphor? Resonances and symbols. Do we remember our literary-theoretical definition of the word? We use it colloquially. We're not accountable to anyone. So what is really the thing about Daniel Defoe?"

"He's a madman who lives in a boat?"

"Maybe, but all of that aside, the real thing about him is that he's a nice guy."

"He's a nice guy," I repeated.

"Correct. He's a nice guy. If we could make the documentary, people would like it, because it's so good to hang around with him."

It was true. It was an amazing thought. So simple!

"You'll be okay," he said. "I think you just have to heal. It's like an ankle sprain."

"I know. I get it."

He tightened his belt and clasped his hands behind his back. I closed my eyes and enjoyed the breeze.

"Let's also just pause here and reflect on his little story," he said. "Because in a nonmetaphorical sense, understood purely as testimonial, it was about making love to an arctic sea mammal of some kind."

## 1560

Daniel de Fo has persuaded the alcalde to organize a new expedition to the land of cinnamon. Diego Paez de Sotelo feels the tide turn against him and vanishes in the night.

The alcalde has been preserved until this time by his own misery, as vinegar and salt preserve vegetables, but the prospect of riches excites him, and the prospect of converting the Indians excites him even more, and he grows more spirited as he begins to put the expedition together. Surely he will be admitted to heaven for this great service to God? Surely he will be able to buy a papal dispensation as well, should he still desire to commit suicide?

"It is knowing the time and seizing the opportunity that makes men prosperous," he says.

I encourage him to come with us, but he refuses. I say it will get him away from the pigpen, but he says there are pigs in the jungle as well. He is not wrong. A Pirahao pig is baaí or baahóísi. In Spanish it is called a peccary.

So the alcalde looks forward to his salvation, and Daniel de Fo looks forward to his reunion with Anna Gloria, whom he will send for when he has made himself rich, and I do not know what I look forward to. Now that I know the expedition will become a reality, my sense of grievance has become rarefied. My desire for vengeance has become a story I tell myself.

For now there is nothing to do. We sit by the crashing muddy sea and chew pieces of sugarcane, which the Christians have just begun to plant. We eat coconut candy. We eat the eternal cashew fruits and peanuts and guavas. We look forward to a time when the world will be a different place, and we ourselves different in it, and this is the Christian way of living.

The alcalde arranges for the ships that will take us west to Panama, the first leg of our journey, and he writes letters to the officials there. He hires a pirate named Gonzalo de Castellana to captain the enterprise because Daniel de Fo has insisted that he is too old to command troops himself. He recruits soldiers and sailors from elsewhere in New Granada and from the islands as well. Some of these men expect to make their fortunes on the expedition, but most of them are poor and their greatest ambitions fit into an oilskin bag. They hope for a handful of golden ornaments that they can exchange for a piece of land, a few sheep, fewer cows. One man tells me that his only desire is to own a pair of French shoes.

Some of these men have the yellow faces of men persecuted by God. Some of them worry that they have the devil inside them. One man tells me that the devil showed him a book written in blood and explained that he had only to sign his name and he would never again have to labor as he had always done. The devil would chop his firewood for him. The devil would help him make a house with plaster walls. He has not signed the devil's book, but if the expedition is a failure he will have no choice.

Some of these men are persecuted by other Christians because of the way they choose to worship God. Some are conversos like Daniel de Fo, exiled from Spain and doomed to wander the earth. I am like a converso also. When I speak Spanish I feel that I know God, but when I'm asleep God is only a monkey with the face of a young woman. He is a Pirahao man with no teeth and he has stolen the keys to the sky. He has a son named Hiso. He has no power over the things of the forest.

We meet a Christian heretic named Miguel Oreja. He too has been exiled from Spain, though he has never been a Jew. He is a large and impressive man with a head like a cube of limestone. He cares nothing for riches. All he wants is to convert the Indians. He is well liked and well respected, but he is an unstable character and sometimes he vanishes into a world of gods and ghosts. He tells us that it is a sin to cross the street because crossing the street is so uncompromising an expression of individual will that it constitutes an affront to God. At the same time he believes that man is capable of perfection. He says that man is capable of looking upon God and contemplating his glory in this life and not only in the life to come.

"This appeals to me," says Daniel de Fo. "I've started to worry that my days in this world are going to be innumerable."

Daniel de Fo says that he visits Anaquitos in his sleep. Sometimes, high above the vast plazas, he sees a hanging swinging basket suspended beneath a wineskin full of hot air. I don't remember this floating wineskin. Sometimes he sees enormous men in sleeveless doublets and short baggy hose. They play a game with a rubber ball. They run and jump and toss the ball through a loop of iron high up on the wall. I cannot remember this game either. Sometimes he sees Anaquitos as it will be many years in the future. It is a devastated city at the edge of a desert. There are camels in the streets. There is a Christian king named Roletto, and he has a daughter named Yasmina, and the people are starving.

I also visit the city when I'm asleep, but I always return to the same house and I always say the same things. I try to apologize but I can only apologize in Spanish, and no one understands me. On other nights I visit different cities. Sometimes, because I have become sick with the Christian disease of looking into the future, I visit cities that don't exist yet. They are gray and endless and they glow with lights of all colors. They are bright and dark all at once. The noise is unbearable. The people have forgotten how to see. The only animals are purple doves.

I have more and more trouble moving between night and day. I have more and more trouble deciding what I am and what I want. Sometimes I don't know if I'm speaking Pirahao or Spanish.

We tell the soldiers stories about Anaquitos, which we call El Dorado. Daniel de Fo says that in El Dorado they will be able to eat as much rat meat as they like. They will be able to wear clothing dyed every color imaginable and some colors that cannot be imagined. They will be able to go to the zoo and see the karawa bird, which is ten feet tall and appreciative of fine singing. They will be able to dance with the big bird and sing the tapir song.

I tell them stories too, but only because this is what I have always done. I have no reason for saying what I say. I tell them that in El Dorado the people bury their dead idolatrously, with many golden objects and with dead animals too, so that the dead person will have food in the life to come. I say that they always void themselves in full view of their children, so that the children will have no illusions about life. I say that they make sacrifices to the mountain peaks. I say that their most important ceremony is the ceremony of a boy's first haircut. I say that the men have to bind their balls up with snakeskin and rub them with a special ointment or else they hang down to their knees and eventually fall off. Daniel de Fo nods and laughs, haha.

"This trouble with balls is an effect of the heat," he says. "It comes from living under the climate of Venus and not under the climate of the moon."

The Pirahao have no golden objects, though I must never say so, and no one would believe me if I did. Nor do they perform sacrifices. The idea of sacrifice is not imaginable to them. It is only the Christians who perform sacrifices.

Meanwhile we wait. We do nothing. The macaws and the monkeys talk to each other in the trees. The plants are the color of the earth, and the earth has no color. The soldiers wander around town and rub their heads. They drink wine and chase the whores. Some sleep at the brothel and some sleep in provisional huts and rude shelters. Some sleep where they fall in the street, so stupid with wine that for them night is only a black void during which they can accomplish nothing. In the morning they rise, blinking and terrified.

One morning we sit in the street with a calabash of cashew wine. We expose our heads to the sun so that the great heat and light will stupefy us. We are to embark in three weeks.

"It used to be that when you crossed the equator all the lice on your body would die instantly," says Daniel de Fo. "Amazing. It isn't true anymore. It used to be that the universe was very small, arranged neatly as a sequence of nested spheres, one inside the other, the stars above and heaven above that. I don't remember if this is true any longer or not. It used to be that there was no America, and now here we are, and here you are, and where did you come from? We have galleons now that cross the ocean as easily as a person crossing the street, Miguel Oreja's difficulty notwithstanding. The arquebus is a terrible weapon that will only become more terrible as it's perfected. We have clocks so small they fit in your pocket, and water-operated latrines, and all kinds of cranks and wheels that can do in one hour the work a hundred men can only do in a week."

We sit with the sweat running down our faces. We are nearly blind in the noonday sun.

"And someday we'll have a sailing ship powered with gunpowder," says Daniel de Fo, "and one in which the very heat of the sun works a series of cranks and shafts and drives the vessel through the waves. We'll have a ship that will flap through the air, through infinite space even, on wings larger than those of any bird except the roc. It will be possible to cook meat in an instant, in a single explosive pulse."

He envisions a new kind of siege warfare. The attackers will leap from a tower and bounce off large rubber balls and fly over the ramparts of the besieged city. They will carry sails in their arms, which they'll toss into the air, and the sails will arrest their fall and they will simply float down, sails fluttering above their heads, firing crossbows and arquebuses onto the heads of the enemy. I ask him whether the enemy could not simply charge his cannon with gravel and rip these sails to shreds, but Daniel de Fo says that he has a solution. He says that you could give each man a great charge of powder so that if the enemy did cut him down and set him falling to earth, he would become a bomb. He would blow the city apart even as he met his own fiery death. But it wouldn't happen like that because the very knowledge that each man was a bomb would dissuade the enemy from firing.

"This is a tremendous idea," says Daniel de Fo. "It is almost like a philosophy bomb in its own right. A weapon so terrible that its existence would eliminate the necessity of its use."

I tell him that he's thought of everything. He is the great strategist of the age. But does he have a strategy for dressing himself? His tunic is on backwards. It is a nearly impossible error because the tunic is laced in front.

"Aha," he says. "I see what you mean. This just goes to show that you can't neglect the strategy of the smallest things either. The strategy of daily life. But let's imagine a time when there will be shirts of so supple a construction and so simple a design that you could slip them on backwards or forwards with the same success."

The life of the city continues all around us. Flies, dust, meat, shafts of sun. The rains come. The earth vomits green leaves. One day Gonzalo de Castellana arrives from the islands. Immediately we realize that he is a person of scandalous character. He takes a room in the brothel and whips an Indian with a horse's reins. He asks us to visit him and he shows us the skull of a Mexican prince, a boy he killed himself during the destruction of Tenochtitlan. He knows that Daniel de Fo is a converso and he hates him for it. He does not believe a Jew can be converted. He hates me because I am an Indian and he has fought Indians all his life.

"Defend yourself with the cross and recite the Lord's prayer," he says. "God the father, God the son, God the Holy Spirit, one God, only one, and also Saint Mary, always virgin."

"Oh yes," says Daniel de Fo, amicable as always.

"Blessed be the Holy Trinity and its mother, the holy virgin Mary, and all the saints and angels."

I have learned to worry about the tendency of some Christian objects to attract gods and spirits, and I know that this Mexican skull is just such an object. Castellana himself behaves like a man beset by gods and spirits. It is easy to see that he is not fit to serve as captain general, but there is nothing we can do because his authority is affirmed in a document from the Audiencia of Santo Domingo. This is a disappointment, and yet Daniel de Fo is not concerned. He says that such troubles are only to be expected on an expedition like ours. This is how expeditions work. Castellana can be removed when we are safe in the forest, where this document means nothing and where God will not be able to see us.

## 2200

---

Next we left Baltimore. It were six people in the boat including myself. It were Old Dan the captain a quiet fellow called Joseph who were older and two men young like me they were Lun-Biao and Peaches. Your name is Peach I asked him. Peaches he said. Peaches I said. Peaches plural my name are Peaches he said don't laugh.

It had a wild temperature flux our first morning and we was all shivering but in a few days it were hot again. Meanwhile I had fever some days and other days not. It come on like a bell ringing and it died away again but slowly I did get better. We was in the Intracoastal Waterway mostly for that were the protected passage. My job while I was sick was to look out for sunken dangers like trash dead cars cement drifts of silt. Soon the canal were silted up however and we had to come out upon the sea. Luckily it were not rough out there it were easy it were almost pleasant. I were happy drifting along like this. It were a pretty good start for the Independent States of Jam. One day I thought if only I never did go ashore I would never drink corn whiskey I would be cured in my soul after all. Old Dan however were impatient with our slow progress. He explained how it were easier in ancient days when they had gunpowder ships which rocketed through the waves.

Next we come to the Outer Banks. Here it is the Outer Banks said the captain. I looked and looked but I saw nothing just some small islands all overgrown plus broken cement. This were the Outer Banks all gone to smash. Next after that we saw land to our starboard and the captain played his same trick he said look there it is Wilmington. I did not see nothing there. Then Old Dan said to him captain I see you are a student of history. Yes said the captain. I am history in the flesh said Old Dan. Yes said the captain I know so I would ask you what do you think as you look upon the ruin of Wilmington. Well said Old Dan it is different for me cause I remember from before there was any cities on this coast destroyed or otherwise. The captain thought about this. Then he said does it get easier seeing such destruction. Of course it does said Old Dan.

Now I thought I would try him again on Indians. Tell me of the Indians I said. I could tell you of Maria goddess of the Pirahow he said for sometimes I worry it were her was Anna Gloria after all. Tell me about her I said. There are many false Anna Glorias he said which makes me worry if sometimes I saw her but I didn't recognize her. Okay I said but now tell me about Maria Pirahow. No said Old Dan I can't all I will say is I will say that if you smudge out all the humans over here they will reappear eventually over there. Then he were quiet for a moment. Did you know he said did you ever hear of Chris Colombo. Yes I said of course. Did you know it once had a national holiday called Colombo day. Interesting I said were it his birthday. Yes said Old Dan cut that dude a piece of cake. Yes I said birthday cakes of course. Later said Old Dan it were changed to Indigenous Person day we called it Indian Day. Then he were quiet again and the captain and I was quiet too we was reflecting. We was living in a smudge we knew it very well it were embarrassing. Old Dan he had known great days I feared he looked down on us.

It were all history and light airs until we come at last to Savannah Harbor half-drowned behind a ineffective seawall. Another city nearly destroyed in the hurricane of 2130 said the captain. Aha said Old Dan now here is a place I could tell stories about I were arrested here I were nearly executed you see I were the pirate Blackeye scourge of the Atlantic. I weren't listening however for I were so excited to get ashore I almost swum the rest of the way. I went right to Mimi's Round the Clock Bordel the first whorehouse I seen. I done it with two girls at once plus I even done it with a boy like myself. It were not like you think it were tender. I did not emerge for many hours whereafter I felt like a man again.

If I thought Baltimore were a teeming foreign place then Savannah were the distant tropic itself for it had beautiful coconut trees swaying upon the harbor walk and along the streets. It were sunshine and a hot breeze carried the smell of urine ginger manure rotting vegetables. In the market it had crates of fruits alligatorapples pineapples sugarapples bananas. We had bananas sometimes in Boston too expensive for me but we had never got the other things. Remind me said Old Dan are fresh fruits safe to eat these days I can never remember it changes each century. They are safe I said. Are you sure he said. Yes I said. Very good he said then you must taste a pineapple there is nothing like a Georgia pineapple. Okay I said. Georgia is the pineapple state he said. I tried it and yes I had never tasted anything so good it were the perfect fruit. Don't eat so fast said Old Dan you will bust your buttons.

We had such a good time even Old Dan were caught up in the celebration for he now said he would enjoy a coke he had not had one in many years. I said I will buy you one grandfather what kind do you like orange lemon palmberry ginger they have all kinds. He said kola nut I would like kola nut. They did not have it. Never mind he said I will have lemon. We was at a market tent the cokes were upon the shelf not cold for it were no air condition or frigerator but that were okay for Old Dan he liked it warm. One lemon coke I said. Coming up said the fellow. I had some money for my pay it were my treat.

Old Dan now begun drinking he were snorting snuffling the bubbles it were a great joke for him he laughed. Soon he were drunk though it were only coke. He were stumbling laughing saying to me it is like the old days I were such a rogue once I murdered Ferdinan Magelan did I ever tell you. Tell me the story I said. It were no story he said it were that Magelan he were a villain I beat him with a cuirass in the surf off Mactan. Oh I said. Now I have his death on my soul he said but it doesn't matter because I can never die therefore I can never go to hell. Interesting I said what is cuirass what is Mactan. He said cuirass were armor and Mactan were a island. Are we going there I said. No he said it were thousands of miles away. Farther even than the Republic of California I said. Yes he said very much farther across the Pacific Ocean. You have been across the Pacific Ocean I said. Many times he said. Amazing I said is it farther than Lemuria. I am not sure he said it is about the same distance however Lemuria is under water. It is under water I said. Of course he said it were the first to go under before Miami before New Orleans before Antillia.

We stood looking out upon the bustle the fruitsellers the sailors. Old Dan he were now swaying laughing drunk. Then after a pause he begun shouting. Anna Gloria he shouted Anna Gloria where are you come back to me I am Dan Keyshote Knight of the Fearful Clockface. Then he fell down laughing. I picked him up I were his helper after all. We will find her I said I am helping you. Yes he said haha you are my helper. We will find her I said. Don't forget the treasure of Anakitos he said we will find that too. I have not forgotten I said I am counting on it. Haha he said. Then he were serious he said did you hear how I said Keyshote not Keyhote that is how it used to be pronounce it were also Meshico not Mehico. Oh I said. Did you know that he said. I don't know nothing I said.

It were manure under our boots the sun hot in the sky. I were thinking about everything he had told me. You have been across the Pacific Ocean I said. Many times he said I have been around the world I was one of the first to go all the way around. Do you look down on us I said. Why should I he said. We have no air condition I said or hardly any we have no cars no Velcro no streamy media except the richest men. Air condition destroys the world he said. But why I said. Air condition doesn't eliminate heat he said it only moves it and then the heat has to go somewhere and it goes straight to the climate. But the world is not all the way destroyed I said. I guess not he said. If it was all the way destroyed then I would understand I said but why don't we have cars if it's only half destroyed what happened. Oh kid he said good gravy kid it were only a moment when people had cars it were a wild exception. Only a moment I said. A hundred years he said and it could not last for it were at the expense of the future it were a pyramid scam it were future generations left holding the empty bag. I would like to have a car I said fuck the future. It could not last he said but shall we talk of happier things I enjoyed my lemon coke. Yes I said sorry to be so gloomy it is Savannah hinge of the world I should be happy to see it.

Winter days sang an old man a street performer sad and lonely he sang. It were a song from old days why did he sing it at this very moment.

I were trying to be happy but I were suddenly very angry about everything. I were angry about how I had nothing no car no family no nothing. Then I decided if Old Dan were drunk with his lemon coke then I would be drunk with my corn whiskey. I bought some I drank it in a coconut shell fuck this I thought fuck the future.

Old Dan were looking at me he were thinking. Now he said would you not better enjoy your time ashore if you did not drink so much corn whiskey. I pretended to think he were joking haha I said. We discussed this he said now ask yourself did you enjoy sleeping in the mud in Baltimore. It were not so bad I said. Very well he said I will tell you in advance the best cure for reseca is coconut water. Oh is it I said and what is reseca. Aha he said sorry that is what we called hangover we called it reseca which means dried out because reseca is when your brain is dried that is the cause of the headache. Interesting I said. Remember for tomorrow he said.

He were right about my brain. I were intending another visit to Mimi's Round the Clock Bordel but I woke up in the mud again I did not make it. Now I were broke for I had drank all my money and maybe some were also stole from me. I had terrible reseca so bad Old Dan took pity on me though he were annoyed also. He went down to get me a coconut he bought one off an old man who looked reseca himself. Old Dan said give me your machete I will do it. He took the machete he begun swinging wildly which I thought was very dangerous but eventually he had cut off the top and made a hole. I drank the water inside it were delicious. Then Old Dan he cut the nut in two. I ate the white meat it were very good full of calories vitamins carbydrates but it sank through me like a stone in water and I were very sick. Old Dan were sorry he apologized it seemed fresh fruits was not safe this century after all. No matter I said it were good to have a cleanse I were shitting out the toxins. Very good said Old Dan good for you. I lay down whereafter I heard Joseph say to Old Dan and the captain he said my friends I would not be young again for anything it were no picnic being young.

No doubt this did appear true for I were shitting myself inside out and Lun-Biao were reseca as well. He lay upon the deck asleep and there were a great blue knot risen upon his head. We was two young men in port and Peaches the other young man he were praying by himself almost crying no better off it seemed.

## 1750

This morning I rose at 6 o'clock. I ate milk for breakfast, I danced my dance, and before sitting down to this writing I took a ramble in the garden, for I am an old man now and I hunger for the sun. There I stood, beneath the apple tree, when a cloud darken'd the morning. It was not a storm, no, but a great flock of those birds which are called wild pigeons or long-tailed pigeons, passing overhead in a clamor, their faeces like snow. For all of an hour we rushed about beneath a roiling tempestuous living sky, and there was one man hereabout who said he brought down sixty of these creatures with one shot, but they were all flown away by dinner, which today was hashed mutton.

There are those who say these flocks are much diminished, when in old days their passage required most of a day, or two days, and in all this time one saw only the birds. I know this cannot be true, for it is absurd to think that in the vastness of the world such creatures, which have like man a divine origin, could grow more or less numerous than they are. Perhaps it is only that they wane here as they wax elsewhere. Yet this morning I realiz'd that such an observation — that the pigeons are vanishing from the world — is truly concerned not with pigeons but with man himself, who does the observing, and with man's faculty of seeing what he wishes to see, or wishes not to see, in accordance with his view of the world and of his place in it. Therefore I see this morning flock as an admonishment of the muse, but not an admonishment such as you might expect — not an exhortation to tell the truth, & keep well clear of the distortions of time — but rather a reminder that each story has a human truth, which is the real kernel and meat of its importance, so that even though it cannot be true that pigeons were formerly more numerous, it is true that when a man says so, he *feels* it to be so.

I have strayed from my subject, which is my adventure upon Little Salt island in the year 1750. And yet it is meet to speak of truth and belief, for these questions were important to me then. Did I truly believe this fond old Dr. Dan that he was, as he said, three hundred years of age? Did I believe he had known this woman, whom he called Anna Gloria, in a previous century? Of course I did not, yet just as those great vanish'd flocks are a fancy by which men illustrate their longing for a vanish'd time, so also did these stories serve to illustrate Dr. Dan's own innermost longings. He did believe *himself* incomparably ancient, & he did feel as if he had been wandering lonely through the world all that time, so that his joy upon seeing this woman was real enough. He believed her the woman he was destined to marry, and whoever she was in truth, this is who she was for him.

After our visit to Melanie plantation, Dr. Dan had resolved to buy this woman out of her indenture, a resolution that no doubt surprised her as much as it pleased her. At first he evinced a great patience and resolv'd to hoard up his salary, that he might acquire money in the normal course of things. He had no other way of acquiring riches, for his only property was Quaco himself, and he could never sell his friend. There were sentimental obstructions but also, it must be said, Quaco had persuaded him to amend his will, viz. that he, Quaco, would be granted his freedom in the event of Dr. Dan's death — this a fair recompense for the service Quaco had done in propping him up as a physician — and had then threaten'd that if Dr. Dan should ever meditate upon such a sale, Quaco would kill him and obtain his freedom. Thus was Dr. Dan effectually dispossessed of his slave by the Obeah man's own stratagem and threats, though he conceded it was a clever trick, and prais'd Quaco for it, and there was no diminishment of the peculiar friendship they had contracted one for the other.

It was at this time that another possibility presented itself, exerting thereafter a kind of fascination which I felt Dr. Dan must be powerless to resist, for I found it very attractive, and had myself also begun to grow impatient of getting some money. It happened one night that

Mr. Galsworthy suggested we three take our seegars in the garden, a walk from which Dr. Dan did his best to discourage him, explaining that at night plants exhale azote rather than oxygen, which is why the noxious character of the night air has been proverbial since ancient days. I appreciated this danger, yet I had also resolved ne'er to rest after eating, lest any *morbifick matter* should be conveyed toward my head, and cause in that way the surfeit of pig beef duck goose that I feared would kill me in the end. Walk we did, therefore, the vote being two to one (for we often put such things to a vote in the Ratt Republic of Little Salt), and it was very pleasant, though the mosquitoes bit me extremely. It may be that azote and exercise produce a pleasant stupefaction of the higher faculties.

Feeling greatly satisfied upon our return, Mr. Galsworthy next volunteer'd to show us his collection of Spanish coins. He kept them in his study, which was beside his bed chamber with its own door to the back hall. For myself I instantly thought of stealing these coins, and I believed Dr. Dan must have done as well, though I cannot know the truth. In any case, by the time Mr. Galsworthy had replaced the coins, and lock'd the cabinet with a key which he kept to a chain about his neck, and we had all gone down to the kitchens for meat, I felt it had become *inevitable* that we would steal his coins. Thus I went directly to Quaco (for he was the most clever of us all) and asked him could he not study and ruminate upon the question, and think of some plan of abstracting them.

Perhaps the sight of these coins did inspire a greater sense of urgency in our lovelorn friend the doctor, for though he had been quite patient such a short time before, now he was possessed of the idea that he might earn what he needed by gambling. His idea was this, that if he did not gamble his monie quickly, why then, so he said, he would only gamble it slowly, and lose it all. He did not perceive the difficulties with this line of thought, and when I challenged him said only that there were two kinds of gambling, viz. thoughtless gambling of wages, which is what he had been doing now many months & to the grate detriment of his future prospects, and so-called *Productive Gambling*, which was gambling of borrowed monie, this money then growing by a principle of increase as ashes grow even as wood burns, leaving you not with nothing, no, but with some *Thing*, namely ash. Or he explained it another way also, which was that if he borrowed what he could, and increased the amount of monie he was able to wager, then inevitably by the *principle of long-term increase* his gambling Profits would exceed his gambling losses, which losses he held to be fix'd, like a tax, the profits being the only part in the equation which was elastic.

Though I felt strongly there was something wrong with this plan, I could not think how to defeat it by mathematical logic, and came to feel it must be a very good plan after all. Further, seeing that Dr. Dan was slow to act upon his own ideas (for in this he was like many a philosopher), I had the gallant notion that I would do it myself, and assume the risk, and earn for my friend the money he required.

I now borrowed money from Mr. Galsworthy, and drank killdevil by the hour, and wager'd all I could, thinking that I must keep up the pace. I soon fell into a kind of phrensy, dear Reader, with the result that very soon I was in a desperate condition. For example, one day about mid-afternoon I came to myself in a cane piece at the edge of the plantation. My lips were bloody, and my arm was bruised black as tar, and though upon waking I assum'd I had been enjoying a species of *Siesta*, it was soon plain that I had been fighting. Indeed here was Mr. Galsworthy some yards distant (that man being still unconscious), bruised and bloodied as well. He was dress'd, as he was habitually at that stage, in his long shirt, which hung like a lady's gown, and no trousers to his legs, so that these legs were now fairly *quilted* with sores and boils and *suppurating Ulcers* from the biting of the outraged and innumerable ratts. He gave no sign of life, except if it be that at prodigious intervals he farted, and this being the only evidence of suspiration I guessed there was some exchange of ayre going on in this way.

I roused him, but we two unhappy men could not recall what had befallen us, and at first thought the field slaves had beaten us. It was Quaco who explained later that we had gone out walking together after many drunken and rambunctious hours at the gaming table, and we had shortly quarrel'd. Such a circulation of blows ensued that we had beaten each other bloody inside a minute (tho after this we had wept and reconciled, said Quaco), & then we had both fallen asleep in the *full violence* of the sun. Only then had the field slaves dared to beat us.

This event disposed me to an unwonted depression of mind, and even to feelings of *Dread* and *Gloom*. I sat upon the veranda and chewed my opium, which now stopped me up sure as a gutter choked with leaves, and I drank spirituous liquors in grate quantities, bucket upon pail upon hogshead, and feasted as usual with Mr. Galsworthy, yet I began to fear the effects of so many indulgences more than I had previously. Among these vices it was always feasting I expected would kill me & now I went so far as to swear off this practice for the all in all, yet at the same time I worried my absence at table would give Mr. Galsworthy food, as it were, for suspicion, even if he did pledge himself to see only the finest qualities in each of us. Thus I felt myself poised and rocked between two evils, namely, on the one hand, the evil of death by feasting, and on the other that of being found out as a colored man, & either kill'd for my deception or else, still worse, forc'd to live as a slave, and to work in the new-founded ratt leather industry.

For several days, I kept myself aloof from my friends. This was no great matter, for Dr. Dan was occupied in longing, and in telling wild stories to the slaves, and Quaco was very busy also, saying one day he had swome all the way to Africa in the night, and had swome back again. Yet it seems I could not honor my resolution after all. There was a little voice in my head, which sang to me in the most querulous monotone, viz. that I had nothing whatever to do, and why not have a rack of lamb, or a dish of chopped milion, or a sweet custard, nothing more, oh nothing more, it need not be a feast in all truth. And so one day, forgetting my fears, for no young man is long burdened by the fear that his organism will misgive him, I went up to the great house and sought out Mr. Galsworthy. I found him in the back piazza, where he sat fanning himself, and drinking soursop juice, and reading *The London Magazine*. Seeing me, he called for Quamina that she should bring rum in punch, and soon we were joined by Dr. Dan himself, who had a ragged chop-fallen look, and was hopeful of drowning his sorrows in the *salutiferous balsam* of wine. Of this potation he swallow'd no more than a teacup, but it broke my heart to see my friend so sad, and I gazed at him with a kind of wild sympathy as Mr. Galsworthy began to discourse upon ratt skins.

Here follow'd a night like all other nights, with the difference that later, Mr. Galsworthy having fallen down the cellar stares, and beat himself unconscious upon the stones, I was accosted by his wife, Mrs. Galsworthy. I had known this woman a little, with a daily growing familiarity, and had long admired her, for she was a woman whose looks and subtle graces did haunt my nights. How then could I answer when, from a motive of loneliness and saddening melancholy, she now invited me to her chambers, there to work my amours upon her if I wish'd? Reader, here was a thing more dangerous than any feast, for I could well imagine how my employer would react if ever he learned of my betrayal. Yet though I was so stuffed with food I thought I would be of little use to her, even perhaps disgorging my feast upon her white bosom, I was powerless to refuse.

To my huge astonishment, Quaco poisoned Anthony Fucking Corvette
two weeks before our wedding. This at least is what I conjecture must
have happened. Officially the cause of demise was an explosion of the
heart. It had happened that one night, hunched over his sorghum paste
in the din of dancing hookers and cavorting revelous friends, he had
tipped forward dead with his face in his food. I have no proof that it was
Quaco who did it, for he evaporated away the next morning like river
mist in fresh sunlight, but what alternative explanation could there be?

I sighed an enormous breath of relief, but in the strangeness of that
solstice season no one else seemed to pay this death any heed. That year
the south wind ceased to blow and the western sky blushed a winsome
pink and the rains, which should have come in November, did not come at
all. Sometimes round white clouds appeared, but a mysterious heavenly
artifice prevented them from rising into the higher strata. It was strange
to see them there, piled up in the middle sky like trash behind a dike.

So my relief was tinted and troubled by the apprehension of an emergency. We did have grain reserves, and we could also trade sesame oil to
the MDC in exchange for millet and cassava, but immediately there
were pressures and protests on the subject of irrigation water. My father
had followed ancient protocol and tightened the strictures, allocating
water to the presidential and senatorial bottomlands but depriving some
marginal farmers wholehandedly, and this caused a torrent of outrage.
In January an outlaw saboteur named Carlos Pedigree exploded some
earthworks and diverted untold quantities of illegal water to the scrub
farmland above the city. He could not be located afterward, but his
collaborators were executed in a bloodthirsty spectacle.

I reflected upon this event in my echoing presidential rooms. Actually

I could not banish it from my mind and it would be better to say it haunted me and hung about in the air and waited for me under the bed while I slept my uneasy sleep. These water thieves had only desired to improve their qualities of life. They had desired water for millet and sorghum. Was this a crime? In the cool morning I devoured cornmeal and fruit, a quintessential rich person's breakfast, and considered how I was born to that daily luxury as camels are born to the sunshine, but at the same time my food seemed to have no taste. It was just the sensation of prickle pear seeds between my teeth.

So Anthony Fucking Corvette was dead and gone, correct, but this was the other aspect of it: Nothing was altered. I remained a wealthy person, complicit by ancient tradition in the repressions that my father practiced, and yet also a victim of those repressions, for I was a woman with no capacity to effect good change, a lonely anachro-feminist to be passed around by men drinking wine. In summation, I was still unhappy, and now I lacked even an Anthony Fucking Corvette upon whom to fasten the blame.

Daniel Defoe had known many presidents and kings and rulers, and it was a gracious relief at this time to sit with him in the camel pen and listen to old fictive stories. Only here did I feel I could escape the pigeon hole of presidential categories. Only here did I cease to be a distinguished person of high renown, perched atop a pyramid of subjection, and become a simple reader of old books and inquirer of exotic questions.

"Once I knew a space captain named Robinson Caruso," Daniel Defoe said one morning. "He figured out how to grow corn and potatoes on Mars, which was also a drought-stricken place. He discovered how to build cities there. I'll admit I don't remember how this grand scheme finally unraveled."

"Did you ever go there?" I asked. "To Mars?"

"I'm afraid not. I was already too old for such a long voyage. But I did walk on the moon once. There were trees with pink feathers instead of leaves. Am I thinking of somewhere else?"

"I've only read about the earliest days of moon travel."

"Ah. Well, it became commercialized, like everything. They mostly just had recreational activities. It wasn't somewhere you wanted to live. There were casinos built to look like Roman palaces. I also seem to remember a golf course. You could go surfboarding or get a laser vasectomy if you wanted. All the construction was extremely provisional."

But sometimes he spoke of Anna Gloria, his lost love. He had met her across the broad heaving seas, in Spain, and he had encountered her again in the Orinoco jungle, and also in Australia, and in the Bahamas, and in Java and Old Maui. He said that interlapping circumstances always conspired to separate them. I tried to affirm my conviction that he would find her again, but the truth was that these love stories cast me down in sadness. I was increasingly pierced by an attraction for him myself, and I knew that this feeling was just a piped dream that flowed ceaselessly into the sewer of my presidential ennui. I knew he was just in transit through our world. I knew I was just a parochial princess with whom he whiled away a miniature fraction of his time.

It was during one of these conversations that I experienced a revolution in my own thinking, however, and it was this: I was asking myself whether Anna Gloria could possibly be a true historical figure, and suddenly I understood how it didn't matter. These love stories were evocations of sentimental truths which existed beyond the orbit of factuality. She was real because she existed for him. Why had I never realized? And I also understood that an equivalent logic extended to his accounts of history. I had the revelation that history was only the rabble-house of facts and details from which human beings confabulated a sentimental truth. At the best-case scenario, at its truest and most illustrative, history was an effort of imagination, mostly fictive, mostly allegorical, like a story of unrecanted love. Why should Daniel Defoe not conceive his own fictive discourse for discussing it?

These philosophical upheavals occurred in the foreground of my life. In the background, the remodernization plan moved forward with the jerking sidewise motions of a river crab. For example, my father now decreed a private and frivolous reform of serving only United States food in the palace. Such a reform was unpardonable in a time of drought, for there were those who struggled to locate any morsel of food at all, let alone a United States themed morsel, and when knowledge of this practice seeped into the city there was a riot in Hi-Pointe. However, I am also driven to admit that I enjoyed this reform very much. It was like the culinary reflection of my new perceptions about history. It was history come to poetic life, or else refigured as food and made ingestible.

My father got his recipes from the *Jennie June's American Cookery Book*, which he selected for its emphasis on modern science, and we had authentic traditional food preparations like imitation crab, water soodjee, Trenton Falls fry, and macaroni. The cook usually had to make some substitutions. She made venison puffs with shamo and she used Jamaica cherries in her compote of green gooseberries. Our porpoise pepper steak was just goat.

"It definitely takes me back," said Daniel Defoe, who didn't eat anything. He sniffed a shamo puff and said, "It definitely reminds me of the United States. Once, I ate venison puffs at MacDonall's every night for a whole year. I don't remember why."

"You were a hobo," I said, trying my own hand at speaking in his allegorical language. "Don't tell me. You played knucklebones with some Shoshone women at an all-night bowling alley."

"That sounds right, yes."

"It was wild America, home of the braves."

"Exactly true." He laughed. "You're the most clever of princesses."

But the United States Food Program was only a small and private ingredient in the stew of remodernization, which was now spiced by a new and potentially groundbreaking reform. This was my father's proposed reintroduction of electrification and incandescent light, which would fill our nights with luminous rainbows and also enable people to keep working after dark. This was intended as a circuitous drought-relief initiative, because people could sell their increased output of goods to the

MDC in exchange for food, which would free them from the natural caprices of agricultural production. Camel cloth, for example, was enjoying a boutique appeal in the MDC, just as my father had hypothesized, and he wanted to run the cloth factory night and day.

We knew that lightning was just atmospheric electricity, and Daniel Defoe thought that it would be easy to harness it. Bert Franklin had done it with only a soda can and some string. The truly big job was reinventing the light bulb. I actually chanced to be present when my father and Daniel Defoe attempted this. It was because they commenced their labor in the dining area, where Edward Halloween and I were eating a traditional vol-au-vent of peacock. We tried to escape, but Daniel Defoe cast us a glance of entreaty and supplicated with us to stay. He did not relish another afternoon alone with my father. And actually it was no trauma to stay, because we yearned away for the wonder of light as much as anyone. All the sources attested that the cities of the United States were illuminated from dusk till dawn by magical electric glass tubes and bulbs. It was marvelous to envision.

They had three technical guides on electricity, but two of them were so complicated as to be unsusceptible to comprehension. Luckily they also had *Electricity for Boys: A Working Guide*, by James Slough Zerbe. My father began reading aloud. He did not seem to notice that I was present in the room.

"The cores, or armatures, will be magnetized. The result is that the electrode, connected with the armature of the magnet, is drawn away from the other electrode, and the arc is formed, between the separated ends."

But then he slapped the book closed and frowned. "I feel I understand this," he said. At that point, sad to say, it was manifest that the project would have the same conclusion as every other technological reform. The defect was philosophical. It was that my father, as president, assumed and affirmed that everything he said was correct, which codified his malapropisms into law and made him impervious to fresh knowledge. He could never learn anything because no book could contravene the established convictions of his heart.

"Just read a little more," said Daniel Defoe, who was the only person who had seen the things described by Mr. Zerbe. "Just to set the mood."

My father continued, "As the current also passes through a resistance coil, the moment the ends of the electrodes are separated too great a distance . . ."

Then he closed the book again.

"Well," said Daniel Defoe, looking at me with doubt in his eyes, "I do not have such a deep background in electricity, but this is pretty simple. An electrode is anything that has a potential. I seem to remember you could even use a potato. By potato I actually mean Incan earth truffle, which is different from our potatoes, which are sweet potatoes. But you could probably use a sweet potato too. It's the same word after all. Please get me two sweet potatoes, peeled at each end."

Domingos, our most attentive slave, went running off to get the potatoes.

"And have you got a magnet and an armature? An armature is a housing so that the magnet can spin. Twist some wire around the magnet and let the twists stick out so you can set it over a bowl. It has to be a metal bowl."

I was impressed by the fluency of his inventions. "You're an expert after all," I said.

He winked and gave me the antique gesture of a thumbs-up, which he had just taught me. It is a closed fist with the thumb extended heavenward.

Before long, he had made what he called the innards of the light bulb. These consisted of a horseshoe-shaped magnet wound up in wire, and each end of the wire stuck into a sweet potato. The ends of each sweet potato were almost touching, and that was where the incandescence would be produced. He balanced this over a copper serving dish. For cosmetic reasons, he enclosed the whole thing in a glass bowl. Christopher Smart leapt onto the table and tried to disrupt this work, so I had to hold him down.

"This is much bigger than it needs to be," said Daniel Defoe. "This is really a light bowl instead of a light bulb. But to make it smaller all you need is to use small potatoes, a small magnet, and a little metal cup instead of a serving dish. Easy."

"Easy?" said Edward Halloween.

"Easy," said my father.

They couldn't test their light bowl because they still had to figure out how to put a harness on the lightning, but my father was thunderously excited and began establishing his light bowl factory anyway. This was when theory encountered the trials of practicality, for nobody wanted to sit in a barn wiring up these sweet potatoes. My father had to conscript legions of the desperate poor from the scorching inland region of City of the Sun, where they lived in houses made from bamboo poles and cement sacks. A lot of them were mothers with tiny babies in arms, and in a time of drought their unimpeachable maternal instinct was to thieve the potatoes for their own consumption. Sweet potatoes, which I think must have come from the MDC, had become a rich person's luxury.

It seems the drought was worse than we had conceived, or else we lacked the appropriate grain reserves. Our own royal land was situated on the river and yielded a scanty harvest of corn, but deeper inland the crops were stressed or even failing, except the poppies and mama beans and sesame. It seems the poor people were living on dust and sunshine, like camels, and also on poppy juice, which eliminated scruples against crime even in the midst of good circumstances. There was no hope for the light bowl factory in such a situation, and it burned down before too long. Some people thought this too was the work of Carlos Pedigree.

"Oh well," my father said, "you learn a little something from each failure. Each failure is an ingredient in your future success."

But no one who was sensible of the course of things and who had an inkling of what was happening in the city could be confident in any future success. Conditions were deteriorating in the Reunited States. Even my father seemed cogniscent of this. Sometimes he was on top of the whirlwind, laughing and shouting at his vice-secretaries, and one day he even succumbed to the vanity of erecting a statue of himself in Federation Park, but more often he was overcome by the ideological pathology of gloom. One morning I was on the roof eating my yoga cream when I saw him coming out of the family tomb, which was a marble structure in the garden where three generations of my royal family reposed for all eternity. He had been sleeping in there! The day was warm and dusty, with a smell of wildfire, and his director of spying was sitting on the dry grass waiting for him.

## 2016

---

I retired to my sleeping bag in a mood of relative contentment, but I slept badly in the riot heat and woke up feeling like I'd spent the night in my own grave, and this despite the beautiful sunrise, the tropic breeze, the interest and novelty of our project. I had been chewing on my teeth in the night and there was blood in my mouth. I thought this was justification enough for a breakfast of tranquilizers, although I decided to forgo my usual ration of two green pills, which provided the most agreeable lift, in favor of a broad-spectrum, slate-cleaning combination of one green, one white, and one blue. These were not recreational drugs, after all. One could even argue that they were a kind of medicine.

Never did I feel so generous and cheerful as when I'd decided to enjoy a few pills. Never was I so hungry for human interaction. I woke Azar up and tried to shock him into a discussion.

"I was thinking just now about how much of happiness is expectation," I said. "I think maybe this is a way to console myself about global warming. The people of the future won't know how easy our lives were! They'll be born to hardship and they'll expect less in the way of material comforts. They'll be less unhappy than we'd be if we had to live in their world."

"Dogs must get bit by mosquitoes all the time," Azar said, "but they just seem to take it."

"Exactly. It's all they know. We imagine how terrible it would be to live without everything we have, but the people of the future won't know what it was like to have it."

But this wasn't right. This was not cheerful at all. This was the very opposite of cheer. I sat down on a stump to regroup. It would be twenty minutes before I felt tranquility pooling behind my eyes. Dust stirred menacingly in a shaft of light.

"Everything is just expectations," I said. I could feel my eyes bugging out in panic and excitement. "If you grow up in a world without good mirrors, like the ancient mariner claims to have done, then probably no one expects you to be so well groomed, right? If you've got mirrors, it changes the expectations. It solves one problem but creates another. It creates new and higher expectations vis-à-vis grooming."

Azar seemed not to hear me. He said, "I dreamed my elementary school gymnasium was full of electric eels. I had to shave but I couldn't get my shoes off. I was married but my wife was in a jail in the Everglades."

"Did you get a look at her? It would be good to know what she looks like so you recognize her when you see her in the real world. Otherwise she's just a figment, like Anna Gloria."

The ancient mariner had been up on deck praying. When he came down a few minutes later, we saw that he wasn't alone. Descending the ladder behind him was an ancient black man with a computer keyboard around his neck.

"Young men," said the ancient mariner, "this is Sancho."

"Sancho?" I said, alarmed by the implications.

"I mean Quaco," he said. "This is Quaco. Quaco, here are two more young people."

"They never stop coming," said Quaco.

"One after another after another. These fellows have agreed to do the digging."

"Hello, Quaco," I said.

"Of course," he said. "Hello."

His voice was melodic and professorial, truly an elegant voice, but in addition to the keyboard he was wearing a pink ladies' windbreaker and a set of bracelets made from teeth and worn-out glo-sticks. This in combination with his red eyes and his hair, which was black and gray and wild, like an old dog curled up on his head, produced a startling effect. He wore a pair of mesh shorts with the logos rubbed off, and he had no shoes. Later I learned that people called him the mayor of Key West.

"Quaco is here to help me divine the location of the buried treasure," said the ancient mariner.

"Aha," said Azar, frowning in concentration. He already had the camera out.

"Because of the rising seas."

"Right," said Azar. "But maybe you could just elaborate on that?"

The ancient mariner held up his hands. "Everyone tells me that the seas are rising. You told me this yourselves. Isn't that correct?"

"It's correct," I said. "Do you want to see the data?"

"You are two smart fellows, armed with all the best facts, and I believe you. I've heard it from other people too. So now Quaco and I have to dig up our treasure before the sea drowns these islands and it's lost forever. This is the favor I have to ask you. Quaco and I are not young anymore, as you can see."

"Okay," I said.

"Okay," said Azar.

"But first I have to remember which island I buried it on, so Quaco has just given me a medicine to help me remember."

"Uh oh," said Azar.

Quaco was strolling around the yard, hands clasped behind his back. He stooped and coughed and muttered in the raw sunlight. He didn't pay any attention to us.

"Quaco is a sorcerer," the ancient mariner explained. "Once he turned me into a pig so I could escape from my creditors."

Azar looked anxious. "I feel like something big is going to happen, but I'm so hungry I can't concentrate."

"You want to talk about hunger! Many years ago, for a period of about two weeks, I ate only cardamom pods. I hardly eat anything now, but that's only because I'm not hungry. If you ask me what I drank, I'm not afraid to say I drank camel urine. We were crossing the desert. It was a place called Azawad. We were going to sell the cardamom pods somewhere on the coast, but yes, you guessed it, everyone died and I was alone with the camels. That was how I was freed from slavery, at least on that occasion."

Then the color seemed to drain from his face.

"Is everything okay?" said Azar.

"I think I'll just pop inside for a minute. Quaco tells me this is not going to be pleasant."

He began to walk back to his boat. At the door he stopped and turned around.

"Camel urine is very thick," he said. "These are impressive creatures. Their excrement is so dry you can burn it as soon as it falls."

He closed his eyes and stood still for a moment, breathing slowly.

"And one more thing. Have you ever wondered why Spanish food has so much ham and bacon in it? It's because the inquisitors always came at lunch, and if they saw you eating ham you were safe."

Then he went inside and shut the door. We were left watching Quaco move slowly along the fence, stooping every few feet to examine a leaf or a flower.

"Here's something new," I said.

"I'll say. Who is this Quaco?"

"Apparently he's a bum off the street."

"Yes. But we don't say so just because he's an old black man."

"Of course not."

"It's not about race."

"Why should it be about race?"

"I'm a swarthy fellow myself," said Azar. "But the reason I ask is the computer keyboard. Also the bracelets of human teeth."

"Bingo."

We ate some trail mix, and after a while Quaco was done with whatever he was doing and he came to sit with us at the picnic table. He was instantly and profoundly absorbed by the cartoons in Azar's *New Yorker*.

"Is it that they're cavemen?" he said, studying one of them. "Is that the joke?"

"You've got it exactly."

"The cavemen have invented language," he said. "Now their troubles begin."

But the ancient mariner was not the only one who'd taken medicine, and now I was suddenly conscious of not being conscious of my aching teeth. My shoulders felt loose. There was a singing in my chest. It had been four days, a kind of threshold, and my relief was profound. At this stage it seemed only proper to have another green pill. I had transferred five of them to my pocket, each one wrapped in little twists of receipt paper, and I took one while pretending to cough. My throat was so dry that it was like stuffing a bowling ball up an exhaust pipe.

"Quaco," I said, "you're about a million years old too, aren't you? Is it your perception that everyone in every era thinks they're living in the era when the world will end?"

"Yes."

"Which means that everyone's been wrong so far."

"Incorrect."

"Incorrect?"

"It always does end. Over and over again. Have you heard of Anaquitos? Or Achem?"

"No."

"Of course you haven't."

Azar found the bottle of po in the kitchen shed and poured us both a cup. It had a sweet, rubbery flavor. I swallowed it with difficulty and then it seemed to rise into my face and settle in my cheeks. I felt smart and collected.

"Quaco," I said, "did you poison Daniel Defoe?"

"Ask him yourself."

"Are there human teeth on those bracelets?"

"Is there a more effective kind of tooth?"

There was no sign of life from the boat, but Quaco told us to leave the ancient mariner alone, so we enjoyed a quiet interval. We drank our po and helped Quaco with the cartoons. The breeze rose. The sun climbed higher. I imagined a warm future in which all of America was just like this, a landscape of tumbledown tropical disorder, palm trees on the national mall, shaggy grass, the perfect quiet of a world without cars or leaf blowers. It was a beautiful vision. It was like a hallucination. I said to myself, Here I am in Baltimore in the year 2200.

Twenty minutes later we heard singing coming from the ancient mariner's boat. Then the ancient mariner himself came tumbling out the door.

"I saw a boy with an ape on his shirt," he said. "He was eating a cone of blue ice. He was the vision and the ape was the vision. The ape winked at me. The ape was wearing the boy."

"Is he saying ape?" said Azar. "Like a gorilla?"

"Apes," said the ancient mariner. "Apes, apes. I know about apes. They jeer at you from the trees. You ask them for fruit and they show you their asses. No help at all to a shipwrecked sailor or a man on the run."

He paused in order to gesture more forcefully. Azar was filming everything.

"I looked up and I saw an enormous bird. It was a roc. It carried off a fat man in a leather vest. He waved to me. He was still trying to drink from his red cup. In a sky gone purple like a bruise. On a morning like every other morning."

He pitched forward onto his face and then struggled to rise. Quaco stepped forward to help him up.

"Should we do something?" said Azar. "Should we call 911?"

"Apes," I said. "Amazing. This is an incredible situation we've involved ourselves in."

"Should we call 911?" he said again.

"It's already so much like a movie. All we have to do is aim the camera."

Azar gave up and turned to Quaco. "What do we do, Quaco? Do we trust you?"

"It would be a mistake for you to trust me. How could you begin to understand my intentions? But in this case, there's no danger. We're recovering ancient memories by magical practice, that's all. I wouldn't harm this man. He helped me cure myself of slavery."

The crisis, such as it was, did not last long. Soon the ancient mariner calmed down and went back inside, there to sweat and dream, and Quaco went with him to begin chanting or praying or whatever he was going to do. We wanted to get this on film, but he wouldn't let us. He was very firm on the subject. We weren't allowed inside at all, and in fact he encouraged us to leave the property for a few hours. This is when I remembered the John Baxter Maritime Museum.

I was out in the street waiting for Azar to brush his teeth when Tom Rath appeared on the veranda of the Pelican Court. He was having Diet Coke for breakfast.

"What have you got going on out here, Tom Rath?"

"I'm just enjoying the sunshine."

It had clouded over. It might have been dusk.

"How'd a man like you ever make it in the advertising business, huh?"

"Well," he said, "the insurance business is like any other."

"The advertising business."

"The advertising business, correct. It's like any other."

But now I'd had enough. I wanted to have it out with him.

"What's going on, Tom? What's your business here?"

"I'm in the advertising business, like you said."

"I mean what's your role in this story? Why do you keep popping up?"

"What's my role? I'm the main character. You're the one playing a role."

"I'm playing a role," I said.

"You're an extra in the story that is the story of Tom Rath's exciting deceptions and stratagems."

"I'm a minor character," I said.

"You're a minor character. You're just a guy I talk to. You don't have anything to do with my larger strategy. Even this whole Key West weekend is just a minor scene, and you'd better believe there's lots of exciting stuff in store for Tom Rath. Involving people you don't know. In places you've never been."

"I'm a minor character," I said again. I felt the truth of this statement. I felt its force. I was profoundly relieved. "So I can just do what I like. I'm offstage."

"Sure you are."

"No pressure."

"It's me who feels the pressure, being the main character."

The John Baxter Maritime Museum was not a museum at all. It was a private residence. We stood out on the sidewalk looking up at its battered façade. It looked like a haunted house. The yard was bare and parched. There were coconut husks piled up outside the gate.

I leaned over and hissed, "So what's our plan here?"

"What do you mean, what's our plan?" said Azar. "We're going to look at this picture."

I shook my head. I had taken a few more green pills and now I was experiencing a wild unraveling of the spirit. When Azar looked away I ducked my head and chewed up another one. It made me happy to imagine that I appeared furtive and corrupt.

"I'll make the distraction," I said, "you grab the photo. But you haven't even got a coat or something to hide it in!"

"Why do we want to steal it? We only want to look at it."

I thought about this. It was no good. We had to steal the picture. "I'll give the signal. The signal will be that I'll say the word 'Indigo.'"

"Indigo."

"Or 'Gooseneck.' I'll say 'Gooseneck.' When I give the signal is when I'll make the distraction."

I bounced slowly on my heels. I felt energetic and lethargic at the same time.

"Shit, man. If Quaco had come with us we could have a two-person distraction. Or better yet, he could pretend to be someone totally different, a third person who's not associated with us. John Baxter is never going to know what hit him."

"You seem to be feeling better today," Azar said, "but I also feel that we're losing control of the situation. Promise me we won't walk out of there with the photo."

I nodded. I clapped my hands. It was a delirious shipwreck of a morning and my mouth tasted like ennui.

"John Baxter is gonna rue the day, man."

But John Baxter looked as if he had rued many a day already. He had a florid red face, a big red nose, watery mud-colored eyes. His head was screwed into a blue Gators hat, and his hat was the most vivid thing about him. He looked as if he'd been built from the hat down, with diminishing attention to detail. His shirt was plausible, with buttons and a pocket and a verisimilar drape, but the shorts seemed cardboard-stiff and hastily sketched in, like shorts drawn by a child. His legs were hardly legs at all. They were featureless white columns, wider at the bottom than at the top. They terminated in brown cartoon shoes, like deflated footballs. Poor John Baxter. He wasn't going to know what hit him.

"Welcome," he said. Then, under his breath, he said, "Welcome to all the carpetbaggers."

The museum consisted mostly of incompetent maritime paintings, but there were also three magnificently executed models of old sailing ships. I'd have liked to spend some time examining them, but I could already see the way this would go and I was in a hurry to find the photograph before it was too late. There was a big Confederate flag hanging on the opposite wall.

"Had these paintings my whole life," said John Baxter. "Not that you all could understand tradition or what it is to be from a place."

Azar said, "What's the matter with this guy?"

I realized that I was wearing a ragged T-shirt from a long-ago political campaign, which is what must have provoked Mr. Baxter's anger.

"Tradition." I laughed. "So many proud traditions. Let's ask our black friends about American traditions."

John Baxter's eyes goggled around in his head. His face turned purple.

"Tell me one thing," he said. "Tell me what other country on God's earth ever fought a war to abolish slavery. The answer is no other country. You gonna tell me Sweden fought a war? You gonna tell me *China*?"

"Holy shit, man. That's the craziest thing. Where did you hear that? Is that something people think? Did you hear that on TV? Who do you think it was a war against? You've got a Confederate flag on your wall."

"A man can be proud of his history," he said quietly.

"I for one am sympathetic to the lost cause," said Azar. "A man should be allowed to do whatever he wants in his own home. If he commits a crime against humanity, that doesn't mean he hates all of humanity."

John Baxter nodded. He did not understand that he was being mocked. "It's just our constitutional freedoms," he said. "Even the Iraqi guy understands me."

The photographs were hanging beneath the Confederate flag. They were large prints, well preserved, probably worth a good deal of money. Most of them were from the late nineteenth century, if the little handwritten cards were to be believed, but there were two from before the Civil War. One of them showed three ladies in magnificent gowns, with frightened expressions and indistinct eyes, the effect of having to sit still for so long in front of the camera. The other showed two men standing together on a pier somewhere. The image was blurry but it was unmistakably the ancient mariner and Quaco.

John Baxter was growing frustrated. "But this is perfect because now I got a Iraqi and a socialist in my museum."

Azar said, "You've gotta be nicer to tourists, man! Don't you depend on the tourist trade?"

I called him over. He looked at the photograph for a long time. There they were, with sailing ships behind them, and an enormous fish hung up at the edge of the frame. If it was staged, I thought it was poorly staged. The fish should have been emphasized.

"Uh oh," said Azar.

"It complicates things, yeah."

"What do we do? What is this photo? What's happening here?"

We certainly couldn't ask John Baxter. He came closer now, obviously trying to chase us out. He said, "You got a bomb in your underpants? You think I should pay your doctor bill? You wanna mare each other, you two?"

Azar had heard enough. "Gooseneck," he said. "Indigo. Charge."

## 1560

We leave Santa Inés in three ships. It isn't possible to travel up the Pirahao without one of Daniel de Fo's sun-powered boats, so we must sail to Panama first. We will cross the isthmus at a place called Nombre de Dios and proceed down the western coast of America to Piru, where we'll climb into the cordillera and enter the lowland basin from the west.

The sea is a river that smells like tears and garbage. Our ships are floating houses. For one day all is quiet and serene, but on our first morning at sea, with the low green coastline still visible, Castellana wakes in a evil passion. His eyes are like powder pans. His hair stands on end. When an unescorted Spanish galleon is sighted on the horizon, under the dome of dark clouds, he loses his reason. He cries out that the devil lurks behind the cross. He says that God's malicious design will be realized whether we abet him or not. He orders the men to attack the galleon, their own countrymen, and they obey him. This is their loyalty, which is also a kind of fear. We are one day from Santa Inés and we have already committed an act of treason.

"This is the conquistador's classic mistake," says Daniel de Fo. "They involve themselves in petty crimes right away and they cut off their retreat into civilian life. Then the only solution is to raise the stakes. They have to win their innocence with great deeds and buy it with Indian gold. Is this Castellana's idea? Does he want to bind us all in a fraternity of wrongdoing? I may be giving him too much credit. He is not Cortés."

Sometimes I know that Castellana has no reality of his own. He is only the manifestation of God's contempt for man, as Jesus is the manifestation of his love.

"It's likely that he just needed to purge an excess of choler," says

Daniel de Fo. "The best way to do this is by spilling the blood of one's countrymen."

It's true that Castellana calms down after the battle, nor can he explain why he has done what he's done. He is wild with anxiety about it. He retreats to his cabin with the royal notary, whom he persuades to take his side, and drafts petition after petition. Each one lays out the circumstances of the encounter in more florid language. The galleon attacked first, they were flying a Moorish banner, they were Indians, they were African slaves who'd mutinied and taken the ship. In Spanish the past is written as history, an invention of men, and remains bound to the present forever. In Pirahao it is not proper to speak of anything that does not exist in the memory of a living person.

Every few hours Castellana appears on deck in order to make arcane speeches. Meanwhile the notary comes around with the most recent petition and we all sign it, each according to his ability to do so. For my own signature I draw an obscene picture, but I am ordered to change it. The men spend the hours between these visitations plotting mutiny and darting suspicious glances at one another, but they lack the courage for decisive action. There are those among them who swear that Castellana was floating a hand's breadth above the deck during the recent engagement, and no one will challenge a man like that.

By the time we reach Panama he has gone mad again. His beard is like a shout. His crushed velvet surtunic is soaked with the spittle of command. He is strutting around the deck in full armor, bellowing exhortations, pounding his breastplate, laughing and singing and praising God. He lifts the skirts of his chain-mail undershirt and asks us to kiss them. Kiss my habergeon, he says. One morning he takes off all his clothes and stands weeping in the rain and wind and salt spray. We miss Nombre de Dios and land instead at Cuervo, twenty miles up the beach. Castellana orders the men to sack the town.

"Men cannot prevail over what has been ordained by Heaven," he says.

The men aren't willing to challenge him. They can't desert because they can't expect leniency from the Spanish authorities. It is just as Daniel de Fo says. They are bound by their shared guilt to this madman of a commander.

So they sack Cuervo. They leave it smoking and blackened in the drenching rain. Then we all hurry across the isthmus on stolen mules, in a forest where fish swim through the trees and the lianas sprout blinking watery eyes. We hurry because we need to outrun the news of our crimes. And meanwhile, whenever the weather permits, Castellana drafts and signs documents. This is the great pastime of Christians abroad.

Even in our extremity, especially in our extremity, the vicar general says mass. The men attend to this ritual with greater energy than before because now they believe themselves to be in mortal sin. There is a different mass for each day of the week. On Sundays a mass for Christian kings and princes and for the people. On Mondays a mass for the conversion of the heathen. On Tuesdays a mass for all those who give alms. On Wednesdays a mass for the souls in purgatory. No one knows what day it is.

"What about a mass for Jews cursed with immortality?" says Daniel de Fo, but he only says it to me.

At the South Sea we commandeer some fishing boats and sail down the coast to Piru. Then we debark and begin the long climb up the escarpment of the Andes to the city of Quito. It is an Inka city, and I have heard of these Inka from the Christians. Their stonework is so monumental and precise that the Christians believe it must be the work of the devil. But we soon discover that there is nothing to fear from these people. Quito itself is a city for which there are few words, because the people who built it are now discouraged from speaking their own language. It has begun to fade away. Soon it will exist only in the histories the Christians tell themselves, and it will become a Christian city, and its past will cease to be a true past and will become only the time before Christianity. This obliteration is what I have wanted for Anaquitos, but now I have forgotten how to want anything.

The strain of the climb quiets Castellana's nerves. His only additional crimes are the murder of a mule-driver on the coast and the execution of some fishermen in Piru. He undertakes these crimes while under the influence of an Inka medicine called hanapulpac and he feels he cannot be called to account for them.

We are met in Quito by the Christian governor, Don Hernando Rosa y Blanco, who feigns an intimate knowledge of our expedition and gives us a tremendous feast. It is the first time any of us have had Inkan potatoes, which the Christians call earth truffles. Castellana falls into a dark trance during the meal. He froths at the mouth. Nobody says anything. We are fugitives from justice even if nobody in Quito knows it yet, and we can't delay even for a short time. The next day we depart in a rush, in the rain and cold, and climb once again into the mountains.

In Quito we have enlisted a group of five Muro Indians to help us survive in the forest. The Muro are not known to me and I cannot speak their language. They do not live in cities. They do not build houses. Instead they inhale when the earth itself inhales. They exhale when it exhales. They are interested in time and they have adopted the Christian calendar. For them everything has its season. Now it is May. It is the month to conceive a child. Soon it will be June, the month for drying ants.

For three days we climb. For the first time I see ice. The mountains have lost all their hair. I feel a kind of cold for which Pirahao has no words, and yet I feel it anyway. Daniel de Fo tells stories to keep our spirits up.

"I shipped out one summer with an Irishman called Saint Brendan," he says. "His Christian name was Saint even before he became a saint. Isn't that interesting? In those days the Americas did not exist, but in just this spot there was a drowsy sea monster so large it was like a mountainous island. Its skin was soft and blue and when it sighed, fire erupted from its blowhole. We built cities on its back. I told everyone it was madness to build such ornate palaces and churches when at any moment the creature might wake up and dive beneath the waves, but they told me this is how it is at all times, in all places, and it is a vanity to believe otherwise. We live only at the pleasure of God, who made the world and who will unmake it one day, and our existence on this earth is only provisional. Then the creature did dive and everyone drowned, except for me. I held on to a floating wooden statue of the Virgin. Eventually I was picked up by some Norsemen. They were on their way to the flesh-pots of Vinland. You should have seen Vinland! A land of meat and honey. A land of taverns and intricate puppet shows. But it doesn't exist anymore."

He talks and talks, but at the same time he is listening. Then one morning he is quiet and thoughtful. He tells me that he has discovered an interesting thing. Both Miguel Oreja and Domingos Alvarado have been named *maestro del campo*. Neither knows of the other's appoint-ment. This is a profound mistake on the part of the captain general.

"We can use this to destroy him," he says. He laughs, haha. "We've got him now."

I ask what is to be gained by destroying Castellana, hateful person though he is. He says that we'll never survive in the jungle with a commander like that. He says we'll never be able to do what we want to do. I ask what it is we want to do.

"The point is that whatever it is, we can't do it as long as he's in charge. We can't do nothing either, if that's what we want."

I feel myself growing emptier. My thoughts are scattered behind me on mountain paths. I worry that in becoming both Christian and Pirahao, I have become nothing. But it doesn't matter. A person may do anything and think nothing.

So I do what Daniel de Fo tells me to do. I approach Miguel Oreja, who feels a fascination for me, as all men do. To amuse myself I allow him to gratify his fascination, although this is not part of the plan. This enrages some of the other men. I am the only woman and many of them want to rape me, but I am the translator, a military asset, and I am protected. Now I tell Miguel Oreja that El Dorado is not far below the cordillera and I want to discuss some strategy with him. This is my purpose on the expedition. I know the city and I know how it might be taken. But then I ask him if he is the right man to talk to. Is he not the *maestro del campo*? I tell him I have heard that Domingos Alvarado is the *maestro del campo*.

In the morning Miguel Oreja seeks out Castellana and demands clarification. Castellana will not discuss the matter with him. Then someone brings word of this discussion to Domingos Alvarado, who is furious. An argument begins. Titles are important. Titles determine the share of gold that each man will receive. Thus the expedition begins to unravel, just as Daniel de Fo said it would.

Now Daniel de Fo raises other questions among the men. He has an instinct for mischief and he is not afraid of anything. He has no fear because he can never die.

"Who's the paymaster here?" he says. "I've got a few things I need to buy. I'm going to want my money when we get to El Dorado."

But Castellana has named no paymaster, and before long all the men are arguing and protesting. Who is the paymaster? Who's the captain of horse? Who are the admirals? Castellana cares nothing for any title except the one he holds himself. He grows confused and angry. He begins to hand out titles like they're coconut candy, one to you and one to you. He decides to retain Miguel Oreja as *maestro del campo* and demote Domingos Alvarado, but later he reverses his decision. He shows himself to be fickle and indecisive. He loses his aura of terror. He becomes an administrator. He becomes a mortal man.

Now Daniel de Fo tells me that I must persuade the vicar general to condemn Castellana. He cannot do this himself because he is a converso and the vicar general doesn't trust him. For me it's different. I am an Indian. I am a soul to be saved.

So I seek out the priest and tell him I want to be baptized. I tell him that my soul is in danger as a result of my participation in this enterprise. It is not untrue, although it is what Daniel de Fo tells me to say. It is not untrue and as I listen to myself speaking, I slip in and out of focus. I am a figure in the corner of God's eye, barely seen, barely regarded, and I begin to hope that the vicar general can help me after all.

He is only too happy to baptize me. He doesn't know that I was baptized in Santa Inés. He takes me to a quiet mountain stream, away from the fighting and shouting, and asks me obscure questions. But when he performs the rite, I feel nothing. I am disappointed. I am embarrassed for God. Nevertheless I must play my part, so I recite the Our Father and the Hail Mary and the Anima Christi. I pretend that my recitation is spontaneous, the voice of Heaven speaking through me, even though I've heard these prayers thousands of times. The vicar general chooses to think of this as a miracle. He begins to weep. He tells me of other miracles.

"There's a church," he says, "called Nostra Señora de Gademarche, where there's a painting of Our Lady that runs with olive oil. You can use the oil to cure any sickness, but if you let it run for a year without disturbing it, it turns to flesh and blood. Is this not wonderful?"

I think of an urn full of thumbs and bloody hair. I am not Christian enough to understand why this is not an abomination of the devil.

The vicar general is filthy. His beard has grown long and tangled. His eyes are the color of raw meat. I think of him as he was in Santa Inés, a withdrawn and tidy man, conservative in his outlook, who was scandalized by Miguel Oreja's wild dissertation on the perfection of man. Now I think of Santa Inés itself. I think of the alcalde and I promise myself I will send gold down the river so that the poor man can have his suicide if he still wants it. There is no gold, but I will send it anyway. The idea of suicide is very funny in Pirahao. In Spanish it is one of the most horrible things.

Later I'm sitting with Daniel de Fo on a warm stone in the mountain sunlight. Some of the Muro sit nearby eating dried ants. Daniel de Fo tells us about the East Indies, which are the eyelids of the world. There are baboons like mastiffs, huge and violent, which kill people for sport. There is also a kind of huge bird, the caquesseitan or cassowary. He thinks it must be a relative of the karawa bird, but it's not half so subtle and it cares nothing for music. This creature is covered in black scales, like a lizard. It has pricks on its chin like writing quills. It eats orangutans. It chases them right up into the trees.

"Its meat is so tough that you cook it in a pot with a stone," he says, "and when the stone is ready to eat, the cassowary is too."

This reminds him of the elephant bird of Madagascar, but the elephant bird is not aggressive. It is a mournful creature. It keeps to the sad marshes and lays its eggs in the loneliest places. It does not believe it deserves anything better. You don't need to fear anything from this animal except the contagion of its melancholia.

"And yet," says Daniel de Fo, "what accounts for the differences between these large birds, which are outwardly so similar?"

The next morning I find the vicar general sitting all alone by the fire. He is baking a sweet potato in the coals. I sit close to him, so our legs are touching. I smile. He is a priest and life has given him no defense against such a smile, which in any case is like a thing sent from Heaven. I tell him that surely all of this bloodshed is abhorrent to God. The betrayal of our countrymen. The murder of other Christians. Surely this is ungodly? Surely we will pay for these sins?

"You can never know his will," he says in a quavering voice.

Sometimes I don't understand what anyone says. Sometimes I don't exist. The light shines right through me.

"Did the people of Cuervo deserve to die?" I say. "The men will listen to you. You are the representative of our Holy Mother Church in this kingdom of heathens. You must condemn the captain general Gonzalo de Castellana, strip him of his rank, excommunicate him. If not you, then who else?"

"I don't have that authority."

"Then you will create the authority for yourself, with words, because nothing exists except in words. If a thing can be spoken, it is the truth."

## 2200

---

We left Savannah and now the coast did assume a whole different aspect. Islands and mainland all of it were green with wild trees and it didn't have a city anywhere only a few small towns. It were a kind of rainforest said the captain it were the great Atlantic swamp forest. Oh I could tell you stories of the rainforest said Old Dan I could tell you of the krawa bird plus a clown named Gonzala who were eaten by the dirt.

But I were feeling impatient. I asked Old Dan where is the treasure of Anakitos that will make us rich men. Oh he said it is not so far now it is buried near Saint Augustine. Saint Augustine I said is it a person or a city. It is a city named for a person it used to be called Saint Brendan before it were drowned. Oh I said. Actually that isn't right he said I am confused. What about the treasure I said. We will find it he said I reburied it around there when the seas expanded. You reburied it I said. First I buried it in Fiji he said then I buried it in Greenland that tropic isle and next I moved it to Key West but then finally I moved it to the rainforests of Saint Brendan. You mean Saint Augustine I said. Correct he said. You are sure you can find it I said. I am sure he said however remember that as my helper you must also help me find Anna Gloria. I know that I said but my question is how will I recognize her how could I possibly help. Good question he said. How I said. I don't know he said I don't know how I will recognize her myself I have often been mistaken that is why I need a helper.

One day we anchored off Cumberland Island. Old Dan said it were once owned by Andrea Carnegie King of Scots who had got to be king by selling rat leather. The island were washing away in the sea now but there was some folks living there in the ruins of the palace. We went ashore for water and saw how they lived with their baskets of squids

their cutgrass their sick dogs. It were pretty bad on that island all stran-
gled with fig trees and bugs and old tires it were no longer fit for a king
that were certain. We only stayed a short time but the sight of their
poverty stuck with me for it were my own poverty also. I were a poor
guy in my shorts looking out over the stern as the island fell away. I
thought uh oh Jam uh oh for I worried that all my sadness and anger
would come fluxing back. Then I thought now hang on remember it
don't have to affect you for you are the Independent States of Jam. I told
myself you have seceded from the Union and there is no reason you can't
also secede from unhappiness.

I were thinking of what Old Dan had said of that glorious moment a
hundred years when everyone had a car television air condition the rest
of it. I asked him if you could of took anything from those days what
would you of took. I have heard this question before he said. What would
it be I said. We have all the same things he said it is only that they are
more expensive now. You know what I mean I said just tell me what are
the good things. Well he said for one thing a merino shirt. A merino
shirt I said. Yes he said it were a space-age fabric it hung so good plus it
were microbial probiotic ecksekera. Okay I said that's one thing what
else. Also it grew as a plant he said it were a lamb which grew out of the
ground you harvested the wool. Good I said but what else would you
bring. Well he said it had effective bug spray in those days. I have heard
of this I said but would you really say the best things was bug spray and
merino shirts you are not doing good with this question. I don't know he
said it had other things too it had egoganic foods and it had rivers which
was made not from water but from melted snow and it had rubber microwave drag racing it were simply a general quality of life. Microwave I
said I have heard of that too. You have heard many things he said you
are not so ignorant as you believe. I am I said. You are not he said. I
cannot read and write I said I am a ignorant fucker like those fuckers on
Cumberland Island.

One day Lun-Biao and me were upon the deck we was sweating shading
our eyes very unhappy we was so hot. I were still trying to secede from

unhappiness but it were not so easy. I confided this to Old Dan. Well he said you are not the first to have this trouble for it used to be sadness were considered a disease. What do you mean I said. Sadness were a disease he said. Was it catching said Lun-Biao. I don't know he said but there was pills for it. For sadness I said. Everyone took them he said it were a craze they ate them like ginger candy. Amazing I said did they work. I don't know he said. I would like to try some I said I am once again struggling with sadness. I think it is just being young said Old Dan. But this made it worse for now I thought how Old Dan were so old so shrunken yet even he were happy he were not in my shoes. I am a sad fucker I said. Stop calling yourself a fucker he said. But I am a fucker I said don't you see. You have got to think positive he said. I know I said I am trying. It's the only cure he said how do you think I have been able to stand it all these years all the shocks and traumas. You always think positive I said. Yes I do he said. I am trying I said. Then Lun-Biao said I always think positive I think more positive than anyone. Oh good said Old Dan good for you.

But this were how Old Dan come to feel bad for me and decided he would teach me to read. He kept this promise too what a nice guy amazing. He taught me each day on the boat when it were calm. Together we read Where the Wild Things Are which belonged to the captain. Lovely story said Old Dan and all true I know for I were there. Later we read other books even the Bible it were hard work but he did teach me. The Bible were holy but it were not so easy to follow along. Remember said Old Dan remember that Jesus is the god of love everybody always forgets but you would not forget if you knew him for he were a great dude.

Next it did not rain for two weeks. It were dead calm gray hot still not even the afternoon inshore breeze that were suppose to be never failing. We were just talking drifting going nowhere so that eventually we did come to run out of drinking water. Some of us must go ashore said the captain. Not me I said I am afraid. Yes you said the captain and you he said to Peaches and you he said to Lun-Biao. Joseph would remain aboard with Old Dan for these was the privileges of seniority. It have a river said the captain. He pointed it out to me. I shaded my eyes for though it were cloudy it were very bright. It have a river he said you must row up the river taste the water when it taste sweet fill the drums row back easy as a pie.

It were now Lun-Biao told us I am the grandson of Gingus Can. What I said. Never fear he said I am the grandson of a god. He is joking said the captain aren't you Lun-Biao. Yes sir said Lun-Biao however he winked at me. It is Georgia said the captain to Peaches and me it is the United States there is nothing to fear. I am scared anyway said Peaches. Look he said I will give you the gun careful it have three bullets only it is for protection. It seemed Peaches were more scared than me. Lun-Biao were not scared at all. Scared or not it were time to go ashore and now we lowered the boat.

Mostly this Atlantic forest were just mongrove but when it were higher ground as now it had all kinds of great huge trees. It were the old pineapple state of Georgia maybe but it were a empty fever coast it were enormous trees screaming birds the jungle so thick it were like wild night in there. I saw a flock of fish swimming through the trees I swear it.

Let's go into the jungle said Lun-Biao let's see what it feels like. No said Peaches oh Jesus no. We must row up the river I said. We could see no sign of people except more busted cement rusted cars ecksekera. The whole universe of our old prosperity were swallowed up by leaves and creepers.

Just then we saw something even worse for it had a monster standing on the bank of the river. We all three stared at it. We had no experience of monsters. What is it said Peaches is it a bear. If it is a bear very good I said for bears eat blueberries exclusively. It has got tusks said Lun-Biao it is a pig. Where does it have pigs of this size I said have you ever heard of this. It were a very large monster as large as a horse and maybe larger. It is a pig said Lun-Biao we are going to kill it think of how delicious pork bacon trotters. Oh Jesus said Peaches. First we get the water I said we will just go around the pig. Jesus help us said Peaches oh Jesus do not take us away in the midst of our lives.

We did go around the monster pig we gave him room. He were interested in us he watched us but if he could swim he made no sign. He stood where he was he seemed very curious and intelligent. Up we went until the water were sweet. Then we filled our plastic containers which was very good containers very expensive. But Lun-Biao could not stop talking of killing the monster. We have the gun after all he said. It is only for protection said Peaches. Hunting is a kind of protection said Lun-Biao it protects against hunger. Next thing we know he were out of the rowboat wading ashore. He has never shot this gun said Peaches he is crazy. What can we do I said his granddaddy was Gingus Can. We will wait here in the boat said Peaches. Uh oh I said. I will fear no evil said Peaches for I walk through the valley in the shadow of death. Pray with me he said. Okay I said. For the Lord it is with me he said. Yes I said. Jesus always listening said Peaches.

Lun-Biao were getting close and still the monster pig did not move. We ourselves now got a better look at it for we was drifting past. It were as tall as a horse yes but stronger its muscles were bulging it had tusks also fangs and hooves like a pig. I think it were a giant pig after all. Lun-Biao now fired the gun two shots. This left him only one which he fired into the sand in his fear as the pig charged him. I think it must of got spooked. I don't know nothing of monster pigs but I know what happened. The pig it killed him it tore him apart his arm his head there was only pieces of Lun-Biao.

We rowed back to the ship what else could we do after such horrors. A sad incident said Old Dan but that is the way it crumbles in a sailor's life. One time he said I sailed a eighty-gunner by myself from Jibraltar to Sicily it were when all the crew died of pox or plague or some such. Were you able to think positive about that I said. Yes he said or I tried to for I were glad I weren't dead it is no picnic being dead.

Now I had this thought that even in the empty Atlantic forest it had so much bottles and bags washing down the rivers that it were like all of history washing out to sea. I thought we are losing our history our knowledge our past we just keep losing more and more. It were a unusual thought to come to me at such a time however that were my thought. Then I had another and it were that the treasure of Anakitos did not matter so much if you could of got eaten by a pig any time. Yes said Old Dan for what is the true riches in this vale of tears it is your Anna Gloria every man must find his Anna Gloria that is the real treasure call me a sentimentalist if you want.

---

I passed my youth in a place where men are bought and sold like barrels of biscuit and tubs of herring, and in consequence I formed a strong conviction viz. the importance of money. If money could be thrown into the balance with a man's soul, or so I reasoned, there was no problem that could not be solved but with its application. Even groping death might be averted had one gold enough to pay the devil. I was now stagger'd beneath a montane of debt, for I had lost all I had at cards, and all that Dr. Dan had as well, a fact which he did not begrudge me, but though this problem derived ultimately from an *immoderate desire for money*, still its solution was money and money alone. Where was I to get it?

I had but one recourse, and now I sought out Quaco and asked him had he thought of a plan for stealing Mr. Galsworthy's collection of Spanish coins. Indeed, his reply was so immediate and unequivocal as almost to excite my suspicion, but no matter, for it was that subtlety of mind which had recommended me to him in the first place.

And so, standing beneath the coco palm in the yard, Quaco discovered his plan, and it was so extraordinary that I was persuaded in an instant of its Inevitable Success, and could imagine no other outcome. It was in five parts, as follows:

1 I myself would steal the coins, having watch'd for my opportunity, and picking a night upon which Mr. Galsworthy was in wine, or better yet had fallen down the cellar stares, as he did with such unaccountable regularity.

Then, 2 Having simulat'd illness upon my earlier cue, such that he now could dye without suspicion, Dr. Dan would now dye, tho only half-way, which outcome Quaco could arrange very easily by administering to him a *Zombi Powder*.

And then, **3** Quaco (being now free according to Dr. Dan's will, the Doctor having dyed to all appearances) would fix all the coins to Dr. Dan's skin, and this prior to dressing our friend in that very suit which he had said was fit to be buried in, so that now when he was buried — for buried he must be — the coins would be with-in the coffin, and e'en within his *cloathes*, and no search of the property would turn them up.

After which **4** the coins not being found, & no attempt to search and apprehend the delinquents being successful, & any suspicion devolving to me having now evaporat'd, we would bring Dr. Dan back from the dead, the doctor then hastening under cloud of night to the town of Kings Harbor, there to escape to New Providence and thence to any place on the globe, & I to follow in good time, to collect from him my share of the treasure, with Quaco remaining upon Babylon until the matter of his manumission was concluded, for he was content to leave his own share in trust of Dr. Dan.

And then finally **5** Dr. Dan would sell his own share and employ an agent to secure Anna Gloria's release from her indenture.

It was not only my debts which disposed me to this criminoid venture, but also distressful nights at Babylon itself, in which atmosphere I enjoyed myself less than previously, and was less able to perceive the outlines of that *beautiful idea* — the dream of living as a white man among white men — that had impelled me to leave the Barbados in the first place. For this was a season of frightful turmoil upon the plantation, and my own frequent sotting and gaming attracted little note in the atmosphere of violence and commotion that obtained generally. For ex. one night we had trouble with a clerk, Mr. Bonapple, a decayed kinsman to the proprietor, who one night came home in liquor, his mouth bloodie, as if he had been eating raw flesh. First he undertook to travesty the Bible in doggerel verse, and next he was like a *Madman* in his desire for Ebo Sally, chasing her through the house, & shouting, & all this before the astonish'd eyes of my dear Mrs. Galsworthy and some other women of the island. After his crude behavior, he sat upon the back veranda fanning himself with his forelap, as he had observed Mr. Galsworthy to do, and talking with himself aloud, before at last accepting the invitations of Morpheus. Quaco poysoned him after this, which I thought a very just punishment, and no one was ever the wiser, because Mr. Bonapple was just out from England, unseasoned and timid of disease, and was expected to die of the climate in any case.

Further, while it is true the lives of the slaves had improved now we were growing rats instead of sugar, yet the gentle labor of rat husbandry did nothing to improve the relations of slaves and overseers. These relations were soured by ancient animosities, and not subject to amelioration, with the result that dreadful punishments were yet meted out, though in secret & without the cognizance of our enlightened proprietor. You must not believe the faerie tales of the planters, for no matter how kind-intentioned a master may be, there is not a one among all his slaves does not long to be free as the roes of the forest, instead of what they are, which is whipp'd like dogs with the *dried penous of a bull*. One morning I heard – from a slave, one Vitus, who had been allowed to cut his hair in a Mohican style – a story beside which this business of Mr. Bonapple was but *cakes and gingerbread*, and it was this, that an old woman, Martha, having stolen from the overseer Mr. Prue one chicken, was buried to her neck in the dirt, and painted with molasses, and left for the flies & ants & rats.

And I, dear Reader, even in this atmosphere of *Horror*, even as I schemed with Quaco and felt my time on Little Salt drawing near its ignominious close, I was assailed with the midges of Love, and prosecuted an illegal courtship of Mrs. Galsworthy, the recklessness of which it is today a wonder to contemplate. At first this sensitive woman was not inclined to repeat our drunken game of hunt the slipper, yet I promised it would be more enjoyable for her this time, and I gave her many tenders of my affection, repeating to her ludicrous and diverting tales I had heard from Dr. Dan. I said that I possessed a coat woven from salamander wool, and she could have it if she wished. I told her of mermaids, those beauteous scaly poissardes. I spoke in rhapsodic tones of a monster called the kraken, which ate for one year, & voided itself for one year more, & its excrement was a delicious exhalation that attracted all the fish in the sea. I told her I would make myself rich selling kraken faeces for bait and then buy her an island all her own. She laughed a sweet laugh at all my tales, and one day finally relented, saying enough talk meat me in my chamber when the Lord is fallen down the stares. So I did, and so I did once and twice more, each time this prettie woman growing more fond of me, and I of her if truth be told, so that now I was loath to flee, and knew I should miss her more than all the neats' tongues and Westphalian hams of the planter's life. And yet flee I must, not only from my debt but from this very love, for my fear that Mr. Galsworthy would discover us only increased in proportion with the affection I bore his wife.

I still believ'd that Dr. Dan shared my urgency, though he had not spoken of Anna Gloria for some time, and I felt confirmed in this belief by a peculiar conversation we had at this time. One day I found him sleeping in a hammock, idly pendant beneath the sweet-scented tamarind tree, and when he woke he fixed me with a meaningful look and said, Ah, there you are, I have been waiting.

You have been waiting for me? said I.

There is a Portuguese ship lying at anchor in the lee of the island, all undiscovered I think, and we shall hasten thither and persuade them to carry us away. It is our best method to escape this city.

There is no city here, said I. None that I see.

Is there not? said he, looking about. I mistook this place for another.

I allowed these things were easily mistaken, and we seemed to understand each other, yet now he frowned and said, How came we to escape the Turks, in that case?

Seeing that his mind was turned, and believing him deranged by grief (though he seemed well enough afterward, and laughed at his foolishness), I told him I could wait no longer and I believed we should move forward with Quaco's plan. He seemed less than perfectly eager to do so, suggesting that he had the more difficult part, for this plan required of him his death. Is there not another way? said he. He proposed that we might bring down the whole house in a great conflagration, which would destroy the timber frame and yet spare the metals within. I reminded him it was not a timber-framed house, but coquina, and I felt there were other problems with such a plan, though I could think of no better one myself.

You must be right, said he. In any case it would not do to affront our friend Quaco, for none is more dangerous when affronted than he.

## 2500

After the demise of Anthony Fucking Corvette, I had a vacation of six
months from obligatory political fornications, but the following summer
I was pledged and affianced to the next wealthiest eligible bachelor, a
senator's son named George Washington. He was crazy as peaches, and
very ugly, and so stricken by jitters and worries that he never looked
anyone in the eye and could only burble incoherencies. The first time I
had to do it with him, he was trembling like a camel foal and I felt an
overweening sympathy, although I was also repulsed by his soft thighs
and hands. I had to drink poppy juice until I was too smackered to know
who was doing it with who.

"The president moves you around like a pawn," said Edward
Halloween.

"I don't care anymore."

"You don't care? You don't care?" He shook his delicate eunuch's fists.
"You are not a hooker to be traded around! Time to espouse anarchy!
Time to draw angry faces on the chess pawns of our souls!"

He was garbed in a suit made of yellow feathers. It had a variety of
beak, which was made of heavy paper. It swung up over his head and his
huge black eyes peeped out from underneath. It was poignant to see that
he was so furious on my behalf, but I did not share his feelings. George
Washington was not a vicious chimerical monster, like Anthony Fucking
Corvette, and I intended to resign myself to the dispensations of providence. I was already becoming old, after all. Edward Halloween had
even located two aberrant gray hairs on my head. And I had no faith of
persuading Daniel Defoe to abandon his quest for Anna Gloria, which
had occupied him already for a thousand years. I was only a passing
shadow in the grand narrative of his love story.

Also, and more important, I considered it improvident to fixate on my own misfortunes when the river fell farther every month and our grain reserves dwindled away. I was not starving, nor famishing for want of water, nor forced to live on poppy juice, which stopped you up back and front, and this minimum comfort was all a person could ask for in such times. These months burned away one after another and time brought only increased suffering. The river lands were stressed by salt, and farther inland the banana trees were all dead, and the millet was tiny, and the sorghum became poisonous. Then November came again, and again the skies were clear and bright. It had transitioned from a familiar periodic routine drought to an emergency of agricultural famine, and the city was rife with periodical grain riots, long water queues, and righteous fury. My father had to increase the guards around the strategic dikes and waterworks. His singular fear was that a well-regulated militia would rise up and break the social contract.

"What thrives in a drought?" said Edward Halloween. "Poppies, mama beans, and revolution."

Since we were forbidden from leaving the palace, the calamity was mostly just a distant murmur on the dry wind. In the mornings, when I slipped out to the roof with my hot caffeine, all I could truly see of it was a featureless blue sky without depth or blemish. There should have been mist and rain and roistering clouds, but there was only a feverish sun, which at its low declension cast all the world in deep golden sunset shadows, and the enigma was that it was very beautiful, even though it was the drought, even though it was the end of the world.

My father said the answer was more intensive farming, and he decreed that no land could lie fallow, not even steep hillsides. But how could a more intensive agricultural scheme produce a plenteous crop if we didn't have enough water for the previous level of agriculture? Then he instituted a variety of strategically repressive measures. He arrogated to the government the whole sum of our meager harvest and placed the city on a ration system, as he had already done with sesame oil. He preached austerity in food consumption. He required brigades of children to haul water from the river in buckets. But he also decreed that citizens had to smelt iron in their yards and deliver a certain quota each month, and no one could grasp his intention in this. Then he decreed that it was unlawful to speak of his decrees. All of these decrees were enforced with coercive violence.

"Drought or no drought," he said to his senatorial friends, "we are making a great leap forward into the modern past. We are a western industrial democracy and burgeoning economic superpower, not a pre-capitalist pastoral farming community."

I think he did not understand what was happening, or else his big picture visionary agenda had crowded out the quotidian realities of governance. He had once again ceased reading books, for example, but he started to write one of his own. It was called *A Boys' Guide to Remodernization and Development Economics*. Often it seemed that he had gone around the bend and come back with fireflies in his hair. He slept in the tomb every night.

One day he was illuminated by the sunlight of genius, or so he said, and gathered us all together, including the servants and slaves and vice-secretaries, to announce an original scheme for irrigating the unirrigible lands far from the river. We would use an infrastructure of rubber hoses! He passed around an ancient piece of paper which showed a man spraying water from a coiled tube. This picture was profoundly melancholic, for it depicted a vanished world of consumer choice. The words "XHose Pro Expandable" were legible in fading red ink, but only a low percentage of the gathered crowd knew how to read.

President Roulette stood up on his throne and shouted that we would create hoses that were ten miles long. We would connect them to wind pumps and run them to the arid desiccated devastated farmlands, and our country would once again be fruitful and teem with corn and cassava and even bananas. We would grow the rubber ourselves, in the south, and sell the excess to the MDC.

"We'll gouge them on prices!" he shouted. "They deserve nothing better. They make love to their goats and drape themselves in red cloth."

Now he called upon Daniel Defoe to help him decide where the rubber plantations should go. Together they scrutinized some maps and charts. Then Daniel Defoe said, "Here's the city of El Dorado. Was it always in Arkansas?"

"If the map says so, then that's the truth," said my father.

"I didn't remember it was in Arkansas. I thought it was up the Orinoco. I must be all turned around."

He said that was the place where rubber originated, so that was the proper place for our own trees. It was also good because El Dorado was on the Delta Bay, so the rubber could be floated to the river and then poled all the way up to St. Louis. The only problem was that these lands were said to have reverted to barbarity, but my father had a solution for that. He would decree a special type of colony, which would be called the Extractive Rubber State of El Dorado. He would send an expedition down the river to forcibly nationalize some cropland, and when the trees were planted he would have guards enforce Reunited States law exclusively within the rubber groves. That meant he would only have to project power into one small enclosed area. He said it was a limited liability. It was like filling up a jar of water instead of pouring that same volume of water over a large flat expanse of dirt. Would you rather drink from the jar or lick the earth?

We all knew that this scheme would produce no rubber at all for many years, and probably never, so it would not answer to the current climate of disaster and famine. Even my father knew this, although he simultaneously didn't know it, because even he could not gainsay his own decisions. Therefore we all stood silent as cockroaches in the vast echoing chamber. The only sound was the sound of Christopher Smart licking himself.

Then Edward Halloween decided to exorcise his clownish prerogative of speaking truth to power, like the clowns of ancient drama who alone of all the characters were allowed to utter true statements. From the back of the room, he shouted, "No! Listen! It is like peeing in your water jar instead of peeing all over the place! You have to understand that it's peeing either way!"

No one had ever challenged my father in this way, and now even Christopher Smart was silent, watching and waiting. But my father was inflated with the winds of optimism, and he pressed forward without acknowledging the disruption. He said that it was almost as if the rubber trees, which would be grown from seeds, would themselves function as the seeds of a new economic prosperity. Sovereignty would simply spread outward from the Extractive State and into the surrounding lawless Mississippi jungle territory.

Now we were all dismissed, but Edward Halloween had been galvanized into an unexpected rage. I cannot say why this had angered him so much. It was just one straw too many, perhaps. He rushed to and fro on the outside patio, kicking up the aromatic dust and shouting. He was an outraged figure under the arching high empty pallor of the blue sky. Daniel Defoe and I attempted to pacify him with words and affection, but it was to no avail. I had to mix poppy juice into his wine to mute his treasonous ravings.

"They cut my balls off and dress me in costumes and force me to give silent ear to these idiocies!" he shouted. "My life goes sour like fermenting mangoes. You are all I have, dearest princess Jasmine." And then he pointed at Daniel Defoe with two quivering fingers. "But you! You prop him up in his king's madness. You play into his hands. You advise him! No more. Now is the time for anarchic feminism and sectarian violence. Now we give him no quarter."

"Please drink your poppy juice," I said. "You have to stop talking or they'll pull your guts out by your tongue."

Daniel Defoe agreed with me. He tried to divert our clown's mind with stories. "I will tell you the natural history of mermaids," he said.

"No stories!" shouted Edward Halloween. "I want to talk to Quaco."

"I could tell you about Quaco. I could tell you how he sent me through the earth to be reborn as a rich man. I could tell you how he ruled the city-state of Kish. Would you like that?"

"No!"

Then Daniel Defoe appeared to meditate upon a new strategy. I felt a pang of love for him, and then a concurrent pang of loneliness, and then a pall of ennui.

"You are right to be outraged," he said quietly. "We are prisoners here."

"And what I'm declaring now," said Edward Halloween, "is we should do something about it!"

"Ah, but look around. Time will take care of it for you. There is nothing so ephemeral as a kingdom. But meanwhile you do have to stop talking or they will pull your guts out, like our princess says."

Daniel Defoe was correct that time was taking care of the Reunited States. My father sent a delegation down the river to set up plantations in the Extractive State, for example, but they never achieved their goal. The whole bedraggled cohort came crawling back one day soon afterward. It was the hour of the piggybank, when petitioners came to beg my father for alms or discourse to him on investment opportunities, and the audience room was thronged with hungry dusty people. When my father saw his delegation, he had a seizure of generosity and tossed copper dollars into the crowd, but then the people began rioting amongst themselves and had to be violently subdued by the presidential guard. Then the room was cleared.

A vice-secretary named Green strode forward in the sudden quiet. This room had stain glass and a purple rug dyed with poisonous berries, and the throne was on a raised platform. Green looked all alone out there upon his private acre of poisoned rug, but he manifested a great courage. He said there was unrest and even revolt in the southern countryside.

"They held us prisoner for a little while in Camel Flats," said Green, "where they have elected themselves an interim revolutionary president. They say this is a federation without representation. They let us go so we could come give you the message."

My father required a few moments to understand what Green was telling him.

"They elected their own president?"

"Her name is Rosa de Piedad. We didn't meet her."

"That's the most undemocratic thing I ever heard. How are we supposed to remodernize this place? Are they angry about the smelting?"

Green answered him with grave unsmiling courtesy. "They're hungry."

"It's because of this pattern of disobedience that I've had to institute austerity policies in the first place."

But I could not stand to listen to any more of this. I departed the audience room and went out into the parched garden.

Here in the quiet afternoon, I felt like an occupant of someone else's dream. I joked ruefully with myself that my father should be pleased, for inevitable collapse was the destiny of his revered United States as well. They had succumbed to factional disputes about the extension of slavery into the western territories, including Missouri, and they had succumbed to demographic wizening and the explosion of population, and they had eaten too much candy corn and poisoned the sky. They had even succumbed to droughts, as we were succumbing now.

But I no longer cared about the fall of the United States. Nor did I specially lament the passing of the Reunited States either. Instead I felt mournful that my own life would be reduced into historical footnotes, just as had happened with all the once singular figures of the past. This was the sorrow of history books, which obliterated the details of life and told only the details of politics and war. I had a wish that every history were a sentimental history such as Daniel Defoe was wonted to compose, for it was the sentimental and poetic truth that I longed to know. What did snow smell like? Did gorillas have fingernails? When you lifted from the earth in a spaceship or aeroplane, was it like standing up too fast? Who made my plastic boots? Was it a woman who, like me, felt hemmed in by her milieu, and ate abortion medicine to keep herself free?

I could never know these things. The only glimpse I had of a true past was the glimpse I had in the fictions of Daniel Defoe. All the uncounted myriads of other histories, the true fictive histories of all those vanished people, were lost forever. And also, in any case, Daniel Defoe would leave someday and carry on with his true life, and then I would have nothing at all. Time would stretch out in the sunlight of the ages like Christopher Smart on the ballroom floor, and when the historians of posterior days came to write the history of our time, it would be the same as every other history book. It would be the history of my father's remodernization action committee, his reforms, his unilateral legislative changes. No one would know that for me the sentimental truth was a hard blue window high up on the wall, and date wine, and mornings on the roof under that incommensurate sky, and tense fornications with George Washington, and laughter with Edward Halloween, and an ache and pit of longing for Daniel Defoe, who loved another, and after and above it all, like music from another room, the feeling of life passing by.

## 2016

We had not been able to steal the photograph. It was bolted to the wall. But Azar had taken a picture of it with his phone and we examined it on the walk back.

"Let's be straight about this," he said. "The question is not whether it's a fake. The question is who made the fake."

We were walking down a narrow sandy alleyway on the way back to the ancient mariner's boat. Banana trees and passion fruit vines and ixora and hibiscus and croton. I knew all these plants. I knew this kind of thing. My mind wasn't just a tin can full of irony and fear.

"It's a whole additional aspect of the question," he said. "Who has perpetrated this fiction? Daniel Defoe, a Key West institution, in whose deception unnamed persons are complicit. How much does Daniel Defoe himself know about it?"

"Maybe you would want . . ." I said, fighting for the proper phrase, "maybe you would want to . . ."

"What's the matter with you? You're walking so slow. You're walking like you've been drugged."

"I drugged myself, yeah."

"I thought you were sick."

"I'm on drugs."

"Jeez!" He put his hands on his head and seemed momentarily at a loss for words. "Okay, listen, we should probably have a dramatic confrontation about your pills, and I don't want you to think I'm dismissing this problem, which is a serious problem, but please can we just pause for now and talk about that photo? How does it change things? We've discovered a kind of conspiracy."

"The conspiracy," I said.

"It's very discouraging that you've chosen this moment to drug your-self. Just try to concentrate. What does this new story mean?"

"It's about what people want to believe? What they want an excuse to believe? But that's making it about us. Our faith and our belief."

"But that's true," said Azar. "It's partly about the people who struggle with the meaning of the story."

"I feel strongly that it shouldn't be about us. We're peripheral."

"Maybe we don't have to force it. How do you make a story a story? It's just that I actually want to make the movie. I think there's some-thing here."

I didn't think I counted as a drug addict because I was addicted to a class of drugs that was lawfully prescribed to me, but I often found myself doing things a drug addict might do. For instance, now I was calling my doctor and telling her that the airline had lost my bag. Could she please send a new prescription to the CVS here on Key West?

We were in the ancient mariner's backyard, but nothing was happen-ing. The man himself was asleep in his hammock, wretched and becal-med after his ordeal, and Quaco was studying the *New Yorker.* He would not answer any questions and he still wouldn't consent to be interviewed, so we were on our own for a while longer. Azar seemed wary of me and sat down to look over the footage we'd shot so far. He had some software that made all of this very easy. I was suspicious. Shouldn't it be hard to make a movie? And when had he learned to do all of this? It was evidence of an initiative that I assumed neither of us possessed.

I took another green pill. I had what must have looked like an enor-mous number of pills, green and blue and white all together in an outsized Tylenol bottle, but the axiomatic truth of the drug person's life is that for every number $x$, where $x$ is the number of pills, there exists another number, $y$, which is the correct and sufficient number of pills, such that $y$ is always greater than $x$. There is never a time when it's not advisable to seek more pills. There's no arguing with math.

So I went out to the CVS to retrieve a fresh bottle. The flamboyant trees were blooming. The ocean was a distant ribbon of blue at the end of the street. There were many bums, ten or more, in the parking lot. They shouted slogans at me as I went by.

"Obey your thirst!" shouted one.

"Swerve," shouted another, "to avoid stopped emergency vehicles!" He ran beside me for a moment, cheering and pumping his fists. "No trucks in the left lane! Enhanced penalty zone!"

There was a long line at the pharmacy counter. The man in front of me was wearing a T-shirt that read *You'll Be the First on My List When I Snap*, but his mood was buoyant. He grinned from the vast frothy depth of his beard. There was tinfoil poking out from beneath his hat. I was calm and none of this bothered me. He wanted to talk about methamphetamine.

"What'll they, snort it?" he said.

"Sometimes."

"Abuse anythang these days. Gasoline. Kerosene."

"Kerosene?"

He was picking up a prescription for his mother, but he didn't have any documentation. He had to call her up and ask her some questions.

"Ma!" he shouted. "Ma! Remember give Carlos his heartworm chew!" He nodded. The pharmacist waited patiently, with a guarded expression. "Yeah yeah yeah," the man said. He rolled his eyes and gave me a conspiratorial look. "Yeah yeah good. Ma! What's your driver's license number?" He nodded for a while longer and then he covered the phone and whispered to the pharmacist, "She's letting Pansy use her license. Pansy's my sister in case you get any ideas."

At the other register, a slow-moving black woman was being denied the posted discounts on a bottle of Coke and some Band-Aids. She kept retreating to check the prices on these items. Her own T-shirt said *Gator Dad* and she had compression socks and big clunky black shoes. She never got her Coke, and instead of Band-Aids she settled on a travel-size tube of Crest. I wanted to buy her whatever she wanted, but I didn't have the courage to offer. She needed history to have happened differently. She needed Quaco to poison someone for her.

Later I stood outside in the warm wind and tried to reorient myself. It was good to think about those less privileged than myself. It was not good to think exclusively of pain and suffering and hardship. In this as in all things it was good to strike a balance. I took another green pill. The sun had come out again and there were small white clouds dashing across the sky. Climate change would sweep all of this away. I was exhilarated by the largeness and strangeness of this thought.

While I was standing there looking at my shadow and trying to remember who I was and what I cared about, I saw Lena coming toward me. I smiled, but it didn't feel natural or persuasive. She walked right by and then stopped and turned around.

"I got addicted to these green anxiety pills," I said. I held up my CVS bag. "The blues and whites are good too but the greens are the best. It's the pills themselves that make me admit it."

She stared at me for a moment and I worried that she might walk away and pretend she'd never seen me before. Then she said, "I've taken a lot of pills myself. At other times. Not these days."

"I was in the CVS with all the saddest people, but I was one of them."

"Aha. A tough thing to figure out."

"But I had this insight. Maybe all of this—" And here I gestured at the people, the CVS, the palm trees. "Maybe all of this is part of someone else's story. Maybe I'm playing a bit part. Maybe I'm a minor character."

She considered this. Then she said, "It would take the pressure off."

"Wouldn't it?"

"It would be nice to know that the main problem doesn't involve you. Are you okay?"

"I was doing pretty good earlier but now I'm a little the worse for wear."

"Do you want to go to the beach?" she said.

"How about some coffee?"

"I have to meet Bee at the beach. I also have a craving for a Moon Pie. Or any of those squishy chemical desserts. Gas station desserts."

"We could have some Moon Pies. Why not? We'd just be two minor characters eating Moon Pies. One scene. Half a scene. The main characters would mention that we were off somewhere. They wouldn't know where. They wouldn't know we were eating Moon Pies."

"That's a good insight. For a minor character, I mean. But I guess we're not allowed to have Moon Pies."

We went inside again and I bought a towel and a bathing suit so I didn't have to go back to the boat. She was right that we were not allowed to have Moon Pies. We were not allowed because of high-fructose corn syrup, disposable packaging, globalization, etc.

"This is good," she said. "Now we're two minor characters walking to the beach. Somewhere out there are more important characters having conflicts, and in the course of their dialogue maybe the two of us are said to be at the beach and that's the end of it. Nothing more is said about us. We're free."

"We're free. But I should admit that I didn't come up with this myself. It was this guy I met on the street. A con man. He says he's the main character."

"Even better," said Lena. "The main character delivers a bit of wisdom that sends us pinging off in all directions." She paused. "I'm talking like you. Your ridiculous way of talking is contagious."

Bee was already there when we arrived. Lena pulled out her sun hat and hunched up underneath it, as before, and Bee lay on her back like she'd been dropped out of the sky. I sat on my towel holding my CVS bag in both hands and squinting into the distance. I wasn't wearing sunglasses because I thought they made me look like a creep. Everyone else on the beach had sunglasses. Even the little kids had sunglasses. The glare was unbearable.

"We took your advice and visited John Baxter," I said. "Do you think it was him who doctored the photo?"

"Yes," said Lena.

Bee said, "I don't think so. That guy is an idiot."

"Has Daniel Defoe told you about Anna Gloria?" said Lena.

"He mentioned her but he didn't really go into it."

"Anna Gloria is the woman he's been after all this time. It's unrequited love that keeps him alive. He meets her in different ages of the world. Fate drives them apart. You know how the story goes. She's literally the woman of his dreams."

They went swimming. I went swimming. We all lay in the sun for a while longer. There was nothing to say. I watched Lena walk down to the water. Hips, breasts, shoulders, red hair. I tried not to think indecent thoughts about her. Each moment I had a stronger and more joyful sense of my peripheral role, and I knew that if we were to fall in love, there could be nothing indecent about it. Nothing complex or troubling. It would have to be a charming subplot.

I must have slept, or else I succumbed to a sleeplike trance. When I came around I saw Azar squatting next to me, signaling obscurely and mouthing unintelligible phrases. Suddenly Bee opened her eyes and sat up. Azar was only a foot away. He grinned. She screamed.

"It's just Azar," I said. "Don't worry."

"Don't worry about Azar," said Azar. "Why should you worry about Azar? Just wander away in a drug stupor and don't even think about him. Just go to the beach, for instance."

"Sorry I screamed," Bee said.

"Sorry I wandered away," I said. "It was a last-minute change of plans. Didn't I send a text?"

"I just want to feel I'm part of the organization and planning process. It doesn't matter. I filmed Quaco chanting and clapping for a while. The ancient mariner is still sleeping."

I explained that Quaco had poisoned Daniel Defoe.

"Is he going to be okay?" said Lena.

"Quaco says so. They're looking for buried treasure."

"They're always looking for buried treasure."

"When I was small," said Bee, "he would tell me stories about the island of Maldive."

"Maldive," Azar said. "Interesting. The thing for us is when is he telling the truth and when isn't he? We want to believe whatever it's possible to believe, if possible. We are done with cynicism and irony."

"Irony," said Bee.

"Irony," said Azar. "Correct. You want to know what irony is?"

Bee said nothing. She seemed irritated.

"I'll tell you what it is," he said. "It's when you wear a Minnie Mouse T-shirt, something you'd never wear, and then someone looks at you and thinks, What an idiot, but actually they're the idiot because they don't realize that you'd never wear something like that."

"Even though you're wearing it," said Bee.

"Even though you're wearing it, yeah. You're wearing it but it's not something you'd wear. That's what makes the irony."

"That's the dumbest thing I've ever heard."

"You can see why we're done with it."

"As for me," I said, "I'm just trying not to be so gloomy."

"You guys are nuts," said Bee. She turned to Lena. "Aren't they nuts?"

She'd had enough. She got up and went for a swim. I thought everything was going well, but now Lena was angry.

"I don't like you guys making fun of Bee. You don't know anything about her. So what if she doesn't know where the Maldives are?"

Azar was instantly contrite. "Did it seem like we were making fun of her?"

"I don't know. Never mind. Just don't think she's an idiot because she doesn't know it's Maldives plural."

Azar looked down at his hands. "I had no idea," he said. "I had no idea. I'll make it good."

"It's fine. It doesn't matter. I overreacted."

But Azar wouldn't listen. He peeled off his shirt, took his wallet and phone out of his shorts, and ran down to the water. In a moment he and Bee were laughing.

"He really took that to heart," said Lena.

"He did."

"I overreacted. I feel bad."

"You were looking out for your friend. As recovering cynics, we appreciate any kind of genuine sentiment."

"Is that a joke?"

"It's no joke. It's just the way I talk. It's ridiculous, like you say. Years from now I'll look back and think, Oh Christ, what an idiot. But it doesn't help to know that. It doesn't make any difference."

She pulled her dress over her knees and lifted the brim of her hat to look at me.

"Are you okay?" she said. "Your eyes are pretty red."

"It's the salt. And I need some sunglasses. I'm out of my zone here."

She fished around in the Victoria's Secret bag, but there were no extra pairs of sunglasses. She asked if I wanted a drink.

"It has a terrible effect on me," I said.

"What's the matter, anyway? What are you so worked up about?"

"It's the Maldives, for instance. They'll be underwater. And we won't do so much better here at home. Goodbye Key West. And the Great Plains will turn to desert. Nebraskans will need to learn how to drink camel milk."

"This is what, cynicism?"

"Gloom."

"But don't you see? You're worried about the future. You're not despairing of there *being* a future."

"There's this other thing too. It's that I'm excited about it. I'm excited that we might live to see the end of the world."

She thought about this. We heard Bee laughing. The sun was high and hot and even the seagulls were subdued. She said, "Who isn't?"

When we got back, the ancient mariner was awake and partially coherent. He had drawn a treasure map on the wall with a piece of charcoal. Azar thought he could take a picture with his phone and then generate a small printout at the copy store around the corner.

"I've seen men in the East with one giant foot," said the ancient mariner, "which they used to shade themselves from the sun. I've seen the great cities of the Orinoco, which vanished without a trace."

"Okay," said Azar, getting the video camera out of its case. "Just hang on."

"I've seen the enormous mokèlé-mbèmbé in the jungles of the Congo, and I've seen the banana-toothed terror-bird of Madagascar, which science teaches us to call *Tyrannosaurus rex*. On a riverbank in the province of El Dorado I saw three women whose faces were set right into their torsos, below their shoulders and just above their breasts. I was a pirate in the Caribbean. I've been up every dark feverish river on earth. I crossed to the other side of death and came back again. In Tierra del Fuego, beneath the blue glaciers, Magellan had me whipped until the sky was green. I've been everywhere and it was all as hot and buggy and beautiful as you can imagine. It was cold like the dark side of the moon. The sea was like a pane of glass and the waves were as high as the cathedral at Ulm. The sun was hot enough to kill a man right where he stood on the deck at noon and the sun had no more heat in it than a paper plate. The sun never set and it never rose. The sea was never the same. It was always the same."

His eyes were bright. He was waving his arms. We followed him out into the yard. Another Key West sunset, smooth and pink and soft.

"The thought you have today at noon is the same thought you had in a dugout on the Pirahao River in the year 1558. You can have the same identical life-changing revelation year after year."

"I believe it," said Azar.

I did too, but I was having trouble keeping my eyes open. Drugs and sunshine and soft tropic air. I was thinking about Lena.

"Every time, you think life will never be same," said the ancient mariner, "and you're right. It never is."

# 1560

Supporters of Miguel Oreja murder Domingos Alvarado in the night, and the next morning the vicar general denounces Castellana. Then Castellana gets him pinned over a moldering tree trunk and cuts his arm off, screaming that whoever excommunicates him also excommunicates God.

But the men respect the vicar general. They feel a superstitious regard for him. When he speaks out against Castellana he is not only confirming their own suspicions about their commander, he is also absolving them. He is setting Castellana apart. And when Castellana cuts his arm off, Miguel Oreja orders the men to place the captain general in irons. A number of them wrestle him to the ground and bind his arms. Maybe they intend to take him prisoner, but in the confusion a poniard finds its way into Castellana's belly. More than one poniard. He lies bleeding in the dust and the smell of his distress attracts small black ants, which begin to devour him.

"I know it's not a pleasant spectacle," says Daniel de Fo, speaking loudly so I can hear him over Castellana's screams, "but you have to have a strong stomach if you're going to be a mutineer." He is silent for a moment. Then he says, "I'm a little surprised that my plan worked so well."

So now Castellana is gone. We waste no time thinking about it. We have shed a great burden and even I feel better, although by now I have ceased to exist, and I feel nothing.

We descend through the clouds and into the forest, where there are mushrooms as big as houses, more monkeys than leaves, no up and no down and no heaven or hell. Instead of trees there is only one tree, as large as the world, with innumerable trunks, with leaves and fruits of every possible variety. The forest does not exist in Spanish, language of cows and wheat and war. It does not exist in Pirahao, language of city streets. Only the Muro can see the forest because only the Muro have words for it, and suddenly these five men are much more considerable than they were in the mountains. They walk one in front of the other, making no sound, their hands crossed on their chests. They show us what roots to eat. They hunt and fish. Their reasons for helping us are their own. They could escape very easily. They burn their hair into a rounded fringe.

Daniel de Fo speaks to the Muro and together they decide our route. The rest of us are lost. In this state of helplessness a surprising thing happens. Miguel Oreja, who has taken charge of the expedition by universal acclamation and by the bloody suppression of alternative claimants, grows mild and cheerful. He claims to perceive in all of this the hand of a benevolent God. He makes speeches in which he says that in El Dorado we will found a new church, free of the corruptions of the apostle Paul. He says that God will be served and honored there more than in any other place on earth. He rejoices to think that we are the agents by whom God is pleased to bring the Indians to an understanding of the Faith.

"Truly they must be a godly people," he says, "if they are anything like our beautiful Maria."

We will not conquer the city at all, he says, shaking his fists in the underwater gloom of the forest. Instead we will simply reduce it to civility by introducing private property, wages, horses, industry, the use of money, and Spanish goods. We will teach the people to wear shoes, to speak as we speak, to cook meat in the right way, to walk properly, to cut their hair.

"Indians in a state of nature are just like children," he says, "easy to persuade, and under the influence of a hot and humid temperament that inhibits them from making rational choices and exercising free will."

Everything he says is wrong, and everything he says is the truth, and I can't tell the difference in any language, but now I understand something about the distinction between the Christians and the Pirahao. It is true that none of us can see the forest, but for me it is a void and for the

Christians it is populated by the familiar ghosts and devils they carry with them wherever they go. This is why the Christians can cross the ocean so easily. This is why they can live in cities and in the forest and in the mountains. This is why they never flicker in and out of existence, as I do. Christianity is the world of things that don't exist, and nothing can harm it, and nothing can intrude upon it, and it is everywhere all the time, and they are always at home in it. That is how I come to understand that I am not a Christian, and never have been. After I realize this, I begin to exist again, if only a small amount.

This is also why they can disagree so profoundly among themselves. Each of them lives in a world apart, and each has his own relationship to the ghosts and spirits and gods. Now we have an illustration of this, because not all of them agree with Miguel Oreja. There is a one-eyed man named Avellaneda who says that the violence with which we've been living on our expedition, and all the violence of the religious wars in Europe, and the destruction of Tenochtitlan and Tahuantinsuyu, is in truth the violence of Armageddon. If we can look forward to a period of harmony in El Dorado, it's only because our arrival there will be marked by the return of no less a person than Jesus himself. He will rejoice at the conversion of the Indians, he will reign in love for a thousand years, but at the same time he will ring in the horror and majesty of judgment day. At this time the great majority of us will be damned forever.

"Do you think it's strange," says Daniel de Fo, "that a thousand years does not seem so long to me? To me it's like saying 'all afternoon' or 'a whole week.'"

These theological differences are irreconcilable, but at least there is no more violence. Avellaneda and a few other men simply depart one morning with cordial wishes for our happiness and success. Avellaneda makes the argument that because no one knows where El Dorado is, it cannot be said that, in striking off on his own and traveling in an entirely different direction, he is not also, as surely as we are, going to El Dorado.

Daniel de Fo and I stay with Oreja because the Muro stay with Oreja and they are our only hope of remaining alive. We do whatever they tell us. When the Muro say that August is the month for ridding oneself of parasites, we eat the leaves they gather and in the morning we eliminate a menagerie of diverse creatures. We feel stronger afterward. And this is also how I learn that Daniel de Fo is a Jew after all. If he were a Christian, he could not take the cure, because for the Christians Indian medicine is a terrible poison that sends them directly to hell.

"But what is a Jew?" I ask him. "In what world do the Jews live?"

"Good questions," he says, but he doesn't answer them.

Soon Oreja has gone mad, as every captain general must, but it is the madness of love. He gives speeches each night on the subject of the Indians of El Dorado. He says that God has told him everything. He says the Indians already have a rudimentary knowledge of Christianity. He says they know that God has given us a heaven and a day of rest. He says that even though they worship the lightning, there is no witchcraft. He says there is no evil of any kind in El Dorado.

"And there are no whores!" he says. The men look disappointed, but Oreja is beaming. "The women are not given liquor and they are always pure until marriage! Isn't it true, Maria?"

"It's true," I say. And it may be. El Dorado is a Christian city that I have never visited.

He asks me to share some Indian prayers. I invent one that will please him. "O Lord," I say, "where are you? In the sky? On earth? In the inferno? Where are you?"

"This prayer demonstrates an aspiration to be Christian," he says.

This is the central problem for the Christians in America. If God is infinitely powerful, then how could there be so many people with no knowledge of him? Oreja imagines that they have simply lost this knowledge in the long journey from Jerusalem to the New World. But it is a problem that bothers him more and more as we travel deeper into the forest, because now we begin to see wild Indians. They are naked, bewildered people. They speak languages that neither I nor the Muro have ever heard. They make their arrows in an unfamiliar way and they are as far from a knowledge of Christianity as a rock is from singing the tapir song. The Muro say we must leave them alone. This is not the season for making friends. But Oreja feels he must comply with the letter of Spanish law and make an attempt to bring these people into the faith, so he orders the reading of the Requerimiento. This is a Christian story that describes the origins of the world, the nature of the Spanish monarchy, the existence of God, the existence of his representative on earth, who is called the Pope, and all manner of other things. Its purpose, says Daniel de Fo, is to establish a legal basis for conquest.

"It works like this," he says. "We claim the lands and territories for the monarchy, which makes the Indians Spanish subjects. Then, if they refuse to convert, they're said to be in rebellion and they can be attacked. This is just simple jurisprudence and legal maneuvering. Of course it's not the same thing as justice."

The royal notary is gone, so Daniel de Fo reads the Requerimiento himself. He reads it in Spanish. It must be read in Spanish because only in Spanish do these things exist. He reads the story each time we see wild Indians, and they do not understand what he tells them. Then Oreja decides that I should translate the story into Pirahao. Some of the men believe this is a heresy because it suggests that God does not have the power to make the story comprehensible to the Indians regardless of the language in which it's read. Oreja argues that I myself am the agent through whom God will make it comprehensible. It doesn't matter because it is not possible to speak a translation, nor do the Indians understand Pirahao. In place of a translation, I tell stories of my own.

"I am the mother of bees," I say. "I am the mother of bats. Look at my army of dead men. They have stomachs in their heads and brains in their bellies."

Daniel de Fo is the only one who understands what I'm saying. He thinks it is a fair translation. Oreja asks the Muro to translate it into their own language as well, but they refuse.

We make slow progress through the forest. The mosquitoes don't bite me because I only exist for a few moments at a time. They don't bite

Daniel de Fo because his blood is thin and sour, like vinegar. They bite the Christians and the Christians speak of heaven, where there are no mosquitoes. Meanwhile the Muro hunt and fish. They find roots. They milk the trees. The mosquitoes bite them but they don't care. September is the month in which it is proper to die, but we try to stay alive.

I have forgotten my desire for vengeance. I have left it in the mountains. Now I understand that it doesn't matter whether Anaquitos is destroyed or not, because as soon as the Christians arrive it will be known to their gods and it will become a Christian city. It will become El Dorado. What can be done? The Christians are only the groping fingers of their gods.

Oreja laughs and raves and pulls at his hair. He is dissatisfied with the Requerimiento and offers explanatory appendices. He asks me to explain how wonderful everything will be in El Dorado. It will be a place of concord and harmony. There will be bread every day, and wine, and meat. He pauses after each wild sentence so that I can translate. He does not understand that Pirahao means nothing to these people.

"October is the season in which it is evil to sleep under the moon," I say. "The white men are ghosts. Daniel de Fo is looking for his wife. Who will help him?"

We reach the confluence of two enormous rivers and camp there for a month in order to build a small flotilla of brigantines. Now we will travel by boat. The Muro say they will have to leave us because for them it is not the season for traveling on the water. They tell us to continue down the river until we reach a place where there are high cliffs, flattened on top by the feathered forehead of their own god, Xagigai, to whom they now address the prayer of homecoming. They say we will reach the city in twenty days. Oreja tries to compel them to stay but they slip their chains and vanish into the forest.

We eat sweet potatoes that we find in abandoned Indian villages. Daniel de Fo and I eat the white worms that live in palm stumps in the gardens, but the Christians don't know how to eat them.

We know the city is nearby because the villages are closer and closer together. There are wide clearings. There are large rounded buildings with thatched roofs like those I remember from my childhood. We know the city is close because we see people wearing the simple clothing of the Pirahao, a strip of cotton cloth hanging from the waist and no ornament but a necklace of palm nuts. These people are not Pirahao but they live within the dominion of the city.

Suddenly I recognize a hill, a bend in the river, a rock. Suddenly I am not able to speak. It is not a failure of language but a failure of the spirit. I have brought the Christians to this place, which is the only place, the last place, and it vanishes before us like corn before a knife. Daniel de Fo must translate the Requerimiento for me, which he does in the same spirit.

"I am coming home from death," he says. He speaks Pirahao very well, though I am supposed to be the only translator. "I am just appearing around the bend. Come with us. You will enjoy a bigness of honey in the rivers of the sky."

And at last we receive an answer. An old man in a canoe tells us, "I do not remember how to eat honey."

And Daniel de Fo says, "Hello, little father."

And these two old men have a conversation. They discuss fish and rain. The Indian does not fear us. He is a Pirahao and has never had to fear anything. He tells us that a terrible thing has happened in the city and then he laughs. I laugh also. A laugh that emerges from the empty air of the river.

The city is a short distance downriver and we know now that we will reach it within three days. Oreja stands in the bow with a beatific smile. He proclaims his love for all the people we see. Daniel de Fo translates.

"Where is Anna Gloria?" he says. "In the sky? On earth? In the world beneath the world?" He shouts at everyone we see. "She is a pretty woman. She has hair like the Xagai River."

# 2200

_____

It were dead wind platforms all up the coast one mile off shore in a long line. Each night we come close inshore for we didn't want to get ourselves smashed to pieces. We bobbed in the sea we was at ease we was sailors. Have some corn whiskey said the captain passing it to Old Dan. Not me he said. Not me said Peaches I am a abstinent. Joseph and me and the captain we drank corn whiskey passing it back and forth. As I drank I longed for women again like always it were tiresome. However I also thought some day I will meet my Anna Gloria. This were a new type of thought for me. Usually I only thought oh I am sad oh I want riches oh I have got a reseca.

One day I said to Old Dan I don't know what kind of treasure to hope for anymore I don't know if I want the treasure of Anakitos or my own Anna Gloria which is the true riches as you say. You want both said Old Dan. Maybe I said. You are young he said you want the whole world. Oh no I said I really just want small things my desires fit in a little green bag. Haha he said. It's true I said sometimes I just want a cool place to sit not even air condition just a shady tree and no bugs. Well said Old Dan there are many kinds of treasure and a shady tree is one kind. Yes I said and reading is a treasure too it is probably as good as streamy media. That's the spirit he said think positive. Who needs streamy media I said. Yes he said who needs it I never even understood what it was.

Each time we come to a new place I compared it with Boston. How the air smelled how the sky looked the plants the weeds ecksekera. I asked Old Dan if the place you grow up always did get in the way of your imagination. Oh sure he said. Then I asked him where he grew up. A man never forgets where he grew up he said. I said where was it then. He scratched his head. He said Lisbon I think yeah I am pretty sure it was

Lisbon or else it was a town in La Mancha. Suddenly Peaches said how old are you. 750 said Old Dan. You are joking said Peaches. I am not said Old Dan. It is amazing I said you have seen everything nothing surprises you. No said Old Dan it is not true everything surprises me for I keep forgetting I have seen it already. Wait said Peaches you are 750 years old. Yes said Old Dan. Are you a demon said Peaches. A demon said Old Dan laughing I am not a demon. Are you a vampire said Peaches. I am not said Old Dan vampires are not hardy I think they have gone the way of extinction like everything. Are you Satan said Peaches. Now there is a possibility said Old Dan laughing again. Are you Satan said Peaches now very loud. Maybe I am said Old Dan. You are a creature of Satan at least cried Peaches you are a creature of darkness damn you damn you.

The captain now turned to me he said Peaches must be neutralized. What would you like me to do sir I said. He has got religious madness said the captain. Would you like me to restrain him I said. No said the captain we will wait.

Next it begin to blow and gust after all these days of calm. We crossed into Florida running before the wind however the wind were not steady. It had a calm again and then suddenly a great storm come up. You could see the hills and mountains of cloud glowing like they was luminated with electronic light. They was like the hills where the rich people lived. Then the sea come up very suddenly whereafter our yacht rolled up like a carpet. The masts was broken the hull split and we was all tossed overboard. Call me Jonah shouted Old Dan. However we was close to shore we was tossed upon the shore alive all of us except Joseph who was drown sad to say.

This were another terrible vicissitude which followed close on the vicissitude of Lun-Biao but I guess I were getting use to it. Maybe I were tougher now at least by a little bit. Old Dan of course were not troubled. He stood up he tightened his belt he said ah Florida this were my home smell the air. Joseph is drown I said. Oh he said. Then he saw the captain and Peaches who was both lying down stunned coughing. Well he said one bonus is that the treasure of Anakitos is somewhere pretty close we won't have to make a special trip. Okay I said are you sure. No he said I am never sure of my treasure. It's okay I said. Maybe we can also find Quaco he said. Quaco I said. It were not his true name said Old Dan it were only his slave name you should not tell your true name it is why I call myself Daniel Defoe. Aha I said. We was having a conversation you see. We was on the shore the yacht rolled up and Joseph drown and at our backs the great dark forest mile after mile yet Old Dan were standing with his hands behind his back talking like he were a old man in a city park. This is my twenty-ninth shipwreck he said I am Robertson Crusoe I am Crusoe at large. He were just thinking positive like always.

Old Dan made a fire in the rusted skull of a truck and we talked while the captain and Peaches recovered. He told me about a device it used to have which were a computer that told you the probability of everything. It were a supercomputer he said. You pointed it at a man in a chair and it said he had got a ninety-eight percent chance of nothing happening a one percent chance of falling asleep a half percent chance of falling out of his chair. Okay I said. But listen said Old Dan eventually they made this instrument so sensitive it could show how this man had also got a tiny percent chance of growing wings a chance of being raptured straight up to heaven a chance of the house falling down. Okay I said. You could mathematically demonstrate that everything were possible he said. Could you tell the future I said could you tell that the world was going to be halfway destroyed. It was only accurate to several hours he said but once we did see there were a chance an asterisk would strike the earth. Interesting I said. For example he said it could also tell you the probability of shipwrecks. I could tell you too I said for the probability of shipwrecks is one hundred percent.

In the morning I climbed a tree to see where we was. Don't bother said Old Dan I already know we are near Jacksonville and Saint Augustine you see I were stationed here long ago. Okay said the captain then I must go to Saint Augustine for it is there I am charged to meet my passengers. That's okay said Old Dan but Jam and I must look for buried treasure. Forget about that I said I have got a change of heart let us find Anna Gloria instead. My Anna Gloria or your Anna Gloria he said. Yours first I said or both together if possible. Well he said I don't know where she is this might not be the time to find her. Where did you see her last I said. I saw her in Miami he said but she will be elsewhere now for Miami were drowned. Are you sure I said did you see it drown. Yes he said I were living on a garbage mound in the bay after Key West were swamped. A garbage mound I said. Yes he said it were a imperfect domestic arrangement. You will find her I said don't worry you will find her in all this enormous world.

Peaches were sitting upon the sand with dead eyes crying. He had been crying all this time but he now begun screaming. Quiet please said Old Dan. Quiet said the captain. But Peaches did not stop. We started wondering how we would make him stop. He has got Jesus in him we must get Jesus out said the captain. Old Dan said we simply had to poison him. Poison him I said. Not to kill him said Old Dan only to make him quiet. Very good said the captain. We was all talking loud now to be heard above Peaches screaming. Very good he said how do we poison him. Old Dan stood shading his eyes looking into the dark forest. I will show you he said.

So Old Dan and me creeped into the forest to look for some herbs vines shrubs to poison Peaches with. I were his helper after all. The captain he stayed on the shore with Peaches poor guy who now it seems had truly got a psychosis he had gone coconuts. We crept through the mongrove which were everywhere and up to a higher place where the forest were thick again with trees plus lots of garbage trash broken plastic the ruins of houses. I looked at these vestiges all faded and smashed. It were the ruins of a whole civilization. The world is ending after all I said. Oh yes said Old Dan it always does. But then I said to myself think positive think positive don't think of Cumberland Island. I were not scared for I had already endured shipwrecks pigs a cruel reseca plus the discomfort of eating so much fresh coconut. Also I were not scared of the pigs anyway for I knew the pig only ate Lun-Biao because he tried to kill it.

Up ahead Old Dan were moving very carefully very quietly. There is not such good bioversity here he said but we will find something. He picked a leaf he smelled it he crumbled it he said now this leaf will be good for mosquito bites try it. I rubbed it on my arm whereafter my arm went dead. Wow I said. Yes he said you could bite a chunk out of your arm you would not feel it. But what are we looking for I said. We are looking for anything will knock Peaches on his ass he said. He needs to walk I said he has got to be tame like a dog that's all. Aha said Old Dan yes we must not forget we must not knock him too far on his ass good thinking. Then he seen a small green plant shiny with white berries. This will get him he said he will never know what happened it will be days before he come to himself. But listen I said we must not poison him too bad he will need to walk. Yes said Old Dan good thinking I forgot you are right.

But there was many poison plants in this rainforest and I had little hope of not poisoning poor Peaches out of his mind. Each time we saw one Old Dan said aha this will turn him on his head aha this will blow his soul inside out. Later he begun laughing he said I will tell you a secret which is that I don't know much about plants I am just guessing.

As we was walking we did discover an amazing thing it were a kitten. It were small gray with yellow eyes tiny paws a tiny voice it were so perfect I couldn't stand it. Can we take him with us I said. Of course we can said Old Dan. You are not just saying so I said. Of course not he said kittens are good to have around. What should we name him I said bending down looking at the tiny kitten face what are the good names for cats. The best name for a cat is Christopher Smart said Old Dan that is the name of the most famous cat in literature. Okay I said. Good said Old Dan. Great I said. Now you have a helper too said Old Dan the kitten is your helper as you are mine.

When we come down to the shore Peaches were sleeping if that is the word for the captain had knocked him out with driftwood. He got violent said the captain it were nothing to be done. No matter said Old Dan. He had some leaves with him now. He said they was very mild leaves but he were not even touching them with his own hand he were carrying them wrapped in bark. It have something here that will make Peaches our slave he said. Will it scare the Jesus out of him said the captain for I cannot tolerate more talk of Jesus he were screaming this whole time Jesus this Jesus that. Yes said Old Dan you could say so but maybe it will fill his brain with other gods. Fine said the captain so long as it is fresh gods. Not fresh said Old Dan in fact very old have you ever heard of Namwa spirit of the forest. I don't care said the captain just get the Jesus out of this guy.

Now the captain saw Christopher Smart who were sitting on my shoulder very alert and happy. Who is this he said. It is Christopher the kitten I said. The captain looked closely at the kitten. Then he said good to meet you Christopher.

Next we gave Peaches the leaves we shook him awake we made him chew them. After he had ate it were not long for soon he were seeing stars vomiting saying he were the mother of bees and I were the gentleman in the moon. I am surprised this worked said Old Dan. But it did work said the captain and now we will walk to Saint Augustine can you walk Peaches. Of course he can walk said Old Dan. Peaches can you walk I said. He can walk said Old Dan watch it is like talking to a dog. Peaches he commanded Peaches walk. To our surprise Peaches did start walking though not so good or fast.

Old Dan now said a shocking thing. He said I were thinking maybe we should ot just ate Peaches for he is named after a food. You are joking said the captain. He is joking I said haha. Oh sure said Old Dan I am joking or else who knows maybe I am just not civilize like you fellows. Civilize said the captain civilize what do you mean you are the last coal of civilization. True said Old Dan well then again civilization it were not very civilize.

## 1750

Mr. Galsworthy had been selling his ratt leather to a man in London, who was said to make from it the most beautiful kid gloves in all Europe. In the space of just a few months, those very months in which I had gambled away all I had and arrived at my present indebtedness, he had greatly augmented his wealth, & had grown concomitantly less gracious in his treatment of the slaves, or else more negligent in respect of their maltreatment by the overseers, who drove them harder now the profitability of ratt leather was established. It would seem Mr. Galsworthy's dalliance with philosophy was not so great an affair of the heart that it could dissolve his marriage to the *Golden Goddess*, Wealth.

I looked upon this as evidence of his villainy, for I wanted to justify the necessity of robbing him. I also wanted to believe he regarded me now with less indulgence than he had done, so that it should be easier to do him this nasty turn, yet I could turn up no evidence it were so. It was inarguably the case that he had been kind to me, nor, for all my fears, had he yet given me reason to think he entertained any suspicion I was not who I said I was.

But it mattered little, for our course was plotted, and all being left in readiness it was my concern only to pick the day. Soon the night came when there were strange guests upon the place, & grate bowls of punch to be drunk, & the occasion so proper and good it was madness to delay. I was very much *griped in my stomach*, but I impute my gripes to cassava beer, and not to apprehension.

Dr. Dan did now complain of a head-ache, and accordingly took to his bed, there to *dye*, as Quaco would arrange it, the next morning. However, a very troubling thing happened now, which was that after Quaco gave him the *Zombi Powder*, and I sought to console him by saying he would soon have his Anna Gloria by his side, he told us he had been mistaken after all.

In what have you been mistaken? said I.

It is not Anna Gloria, he said. It is another woman. Did I not say so? I went to Melanie plantation again and learnt my mistake.

I stared at him, Reader, and meanwhile felt the whole fabric begin to unravel. Yet seeing my distress, he quickly amended his own statement, saying that even if it were not his Anna Gloria, he had a certain friendliness for this woman at Melanie plantation and would happily carry out the plan to free her. Nor did he wish to disappoint Quaco and myself. Nor, I should say, was there anything to be done, for Quaco had given him the powder and he was even now slipping into his false death.

So I put this discovery from my mind and went to the great house to eat a feast once more. There I spoak to a Mr. Corvette, a fellow not seven hands high yet said to be vice-secretary of the International Trumpet players guild, a notable attainment for one of his stature. He was harrowed by the pangs of an Embittering Passion, having heard in town that day just off the shippe from England a man playing the trumpet.

> Despite the severe penal mandates issued previously, said he not only watchmen, care-takers, jugglers, comedians and gamblers are sounding the trumpet, as is only tolerat'd of them on towers, in comedies & juggling games, & on gambling stands, but now also many peasant musicians have commenc'd to do so anywhere and everywhere it pleases them, not excepting feasts, weddings, and baptisms.

Appearing to sympathize with him in his distress I clapt him on the back, and pour'd him more punch, yet I had taken against this man who would unfairly legislate the playing of trumpets (which playing I thought should be free for all to whom it gave joy). When he further said that trumpet playing should be entirely forbid to Jews and Negroes, my anger was roused and I had an idea that I might cast suspicion upon him. Ask our host, said I to Corvette, if he would show you his collection of Spanish coins. And so Mr. Corvette did, if only to be polite, saying to me in confidence he cared nothing for such things, and so Mr. Galsworthy gave him a long look, wondering if he was a robber.

I now drank claret, brandie, and other things with Mr. Galsworthy & Mr. Corvette & other guests whose names I do not recall. These spirits cured me of my gripes. Then, when I judg'd Mr. Galsworthy past the point of memory, I swore off intoxicating liquors and asked the lovelie Quamina that she bring me a cup of coffee. I will not say my heart was light, for indeed I thought often that Mr. Galsworthy had done me no foul turn at all, not one, and indeed had tolerated me, though I was incompetent at my assigned job, for many months. When Mr. Corvette asked what it was I did upon the place, Mr. Galsworthy laughed, & asked me, Yes, what do you do? acknowledging in this way I did nothing, yet giving no sign of displeasure. Later he said I was a kind of clown here to dance and sing, though when Mr. Corvette asked to see proof of my acquirements in dancing, Mr. Galsworthy passed on to another subject, for he knew that I was the very smallest bit lame in my left foot, and could not dance but in private, for exercise (as I do now each morning). Instead he began to speak with passion upon ratt leather, his eternal theme, which he held to be the font and wellspring of a new kind of nation that he would himself bring forth, and call himself not king but *First Minister*, a nation upon which the light of culture would shine, and one in which slaves would live almost as men did, for the character of a nation must be judged by nothing more or less than the condition of its slaves.

So he talked. He was a person of whim and humor, perhaps, but he was a slave-master, and his fortune was got in a most inhuman way. I had a green idea of government, Dear Reader, but I knew that no true philosophical republic could ever ripen in a climate where slavery thrives, even if today my countrymen in South Carolina would sing you a different song.

Two hours rough toaping took my employer to the pantry, where he accost'd the slave girls Mimber and Betsy, saying he had concealed in his trousers a pillar of Herakles and did they not want to see. These girls meanwhile sang hymns, for they knew that nothing keeps the devil away like singing hymns, & directly he repented of his concupiscence and begged their forgiveness. I followed him and thus was witness to his nightly fall down the stairs (preceded, as he hung totteringly upon the very edge of that topmost step, by a waving of the arms and a cry for help), his attraction to that place being mysterious. The boy Samson clapt and laughed, and I patted his woolly head, afterward going down the stairs to assure myself poor Mr. Galsworthy was not dead, which he was not, & also to slip the key from about his neck.

The house slaves being occupy'd with serving, and the ladies all removed to speak of such things as pleased them in the safety of the withdrawing room, I now crept up the back stares & with the greatest expedition possible unlocked the cabinet & placed the gold and silver in as many pillow slips as I could find, tying them up with string and drop-ping them from the window, where Quaco stood waiting. This being done, I locked the cabinet and listen'd a moment, but heard only the sounds of revelry, as before, the clock having struck that particular hour at which quarrels and havock ride triumph through the house.

I replaced the key after that, and went down to bed, but I slept not a wink and in the morning was startled by Samson beating upon the door to tell me Dr. Dan was now dead, as he had seen himself with his own eyes. Mr. Galsworthy was in a state of terrible grief over this loss, having apparently come to love his physician very much, and Mrs. Galsworthy too was up-set, so that it grieved me I could not assure her all was well.

In such a climate the burial must take place immediately upon confir-mation of death, and therefore Dr. Bankcroft was summon'd from Green Gardens not far away, and pronounc'd Dr. Dan *dead on sight*, and went away directly so he might return home in time for dinner, leaving only Quaco to wash and dress the body. This he now did, affixing such coins as would fit to Dr. Dan's skin (the doctor lying now upon the table with his stomach swole, and his lips blue, circumstances by which I was badly affrighted), and fixing the rest to the floor of the coffin such that none could be seen after we had lifted our friend inside. I grew fearful as we nailed shut the coffin lid, yet Quaco did assure me there was no cause for apprehension. All of this being done we executed the rites of sepulture with all appropriate solemnity, Mr. Galsworthy weeping meanwhile though I had ne'er seen him give concern to any death that had occurr'd.

My next task was to ensure the discoverie of the theft, it being necessary to bring this crime into the air, & allow accusations and volleys of interrogatories to fly freely, so that all suspicion might have time to dissipate like a foul odor before such time as it would be necessary to rouse Dr. Dan from his false death. This gave us a period of not more than three days, or so Quaco judg'd, from the instant the *Zombi Powder* had been rubb'd beneath the doctor's hare.

Reader, in my youth I did many rash and incautious things, yet perhaps none were so rash and incautious as the following, which I did without reason. It might have been the great Erratum of my worldly existence, except that it was not. It proved the happiest of all my rash choices, which is why I am inclined to wonder if it were not some ancient spirit of love or fate that drove me to that appalling recourse.

What I did was this, namely that I met Mrs. Galsworthy in the kitchen garden and discovered the whole thing to her. I told her of our plan, and confess'd, & begged her to keep silent. I told her of my debts (of which she had known) and of my unseasonable youth (though she was not but one year older than I), which disposed me to bad actions, and I told her I did not know why I risked it all in confessing to her. Then I asked her could she do me the great favor of my life, and cause Mr. Galsworthy to discover his coins were missing, for if she did so it would be a great favor to Dr. Dan. I now dared to take her hand, and in a voice mild as goose-milk, with hardly a thought for what I said, I told her I loved her. Only when I pronounced it did I know to a certainty it was the truth.

# 2500

In the year 2370, during another epochal drought, my great-grandfather had triumphed in a water war against the MDC, but now, when the MDC began to divert so much water that the river was only a pestilential trickle by the time it reached St. Louis, my father cowered from such conflicts. Instead, as the months totted away and drought chewed apart the peripheries of the city, he simply enacted one fruitless reform after another. He founded a bank. He declared himself the godfather of everyone in the country. He printed national currency on cheap husk paper because he thought it would be a psychological inducement to prosperity if people could hold large piles of money in their hands. Later he tried to extend the grope of the governmental hand by establishing new agencies, for example a Department of Motor Vehicles, which was truncated to DMV. The name was just euphemistic. As Daniel Defoe explained, a DMV was a place to hang out and tell stories. It was a place for poor, sick people to congregate. It had nothing to do with motor vehicles.

Concomitantly with these reforms, he enacted a propaganda campaign to exalt the pillars of the Roulette dictatorship. He wanted to start a cult of personality, which would galvanize the public spirit and persuade everyone to take up the task of remodernization with renewed comradely zeal. We were amazed at the resiliency of his self-belief, which flowered and flourished even though we lived now within a penumbra of doom. It was almost wondrous to behold. First he had inspirational woodcuts of himself printed and distributed to all of our famished citizens. He thought it would be harder to do unlawful actions or foment revolution if the benevolent gaze of the patriarch was always in sight. Then he sent vice-secretaries into the city to disseminate glorious rumors about him. Edward Halloween was charged with writing the rumors.

"The president contrives fresh torments for me," he said. "He lies awake thinking, 'How will I outrage my clown tomorrow?'"

But he could think of ten rumors a minute. He spouted them off in fluent paragraphs. "The president single-handedly beat the MDC at volleyballs. The president can stand on his head for three hours without losing consciousness. The president is able to expel dog malaria from any sufferer by the force of his voice alone. Knives melt before they touch him. He has a videoscopic mind with which he can see everything that happens in the Reunited States."

Meanwhile, my father bustled around the palace, a hive of industry and craziness, muttering to himself things like, "Light bowls. Toothpaste. Radiant consolidation. A DMV on every corner." I watched him and it was like looking at him through the wrong end of a telescope. It was like watching an ant struggling in a jar of water.

And all throughout this time, while I was sitting with poor George Washington or eating my cornmeal porridge, the citizens of the Reunited States perished of famine. They fled north and perished heat-struck in the wilds. They drowned trying to swim to the MDC because there was no buoyancy left in their spirits. Then Nevada fever broke out again and they died of this malady also.

But my father saw empty shops, empty fields, empty carts, empty piers, empty streets, and he said to his vice-secretaries, "It would seem that Nevada fever creates jobs as well, doesn't it?"

One night I submitted a bribe of copper dollars and corncakes to the guards tasked with keeping us confined in the palace. They were so hungry that they forgot their duty at once, and now, after a full year of supervision in the presidential compound, I walked down into the city once again. I wanted to harvest some intelligence and see the disaster with my own eyes. I brought Edward Halloween and Daniel Defoe with me, and we compelled Mina the dwarf to accompany us in the expectation that she could introduce us to authentic people and not simply the drunken night-life characters we had known long ago in Fat Tuesday's. She was one of the palace hookers, but before this comfortable appointment she had been a creature of the street. She mandated that we cover ourselves in the unimpeachable disguise of soot and grime.

We went down into City of the Sun, a shanty neighborhood of uneven streets and trash houses. Here our impression was of a wasted locale abandoned by gods and men, where even the fabric of the universe seemed dusty and frayed. The hibiscus bushes were all picked clean and denuded from people employing the sticks to clean their teeth. The banana plants were gone, and the people had cut down most of the trees, even though it was illegal, and the camels were vanished as surely as all our yesterdays. There were ubiquitous signs about my father, however. They said, "For Best Results, Support Your President!!" and "He Is Hereditary Lifetime President for a Reason!"

We consumed millet beer at a corner tavern, but there was no riotous gaiety, as in previous eras. It was just people getting fuckered up by necessity, because for them the millet beer was their only nourishment. We discovered by inquiry and interrogation that it came as a charity provision from the MDC. My father must have been ignorant of this international aid mission, because he would never have permitted it.

Edward Halloween accosted a pair of silent old men and said in his mocking clown's voice, "Why so downhearted? Don't you know the president loves you?"

One of them said, "The president can wither crops by speaking the name of the farmer backwards."

The other said, "The president is a spirit from the mists of the Mississippi."

"These things are true," said Edward Halloween.

Now the first man was roused in a fog of millet beer and anger and he said, "May he sleep on the doorsteps of the city! May he drink what flows along the alleys!"

It was a traditional curse, and Edward Halloween took it up himself in a solemn melancholic voice: "May there be signs of vomit on his clothes."

Next we went to Mina's sister's house. This woman was called Pilaf, and her husband had the noteworthy ethnic name of Instant George. Mina told them that Edward Halloween and I were both whores from the palace and that Daniel Defoe was the supervisor of the honey harvest and guardian of the fruit. She wanted to be supremely careful with our anonymity, so she had insisted that I was not allowed to speak. My accent would give us away. But Edward Halloween could speak freely because his own accent in Mississippi Spanish was devoid of refinements, and Daniel Defoe merely sounded like a foreigner, which he was.

It seems that these people earned their income from selling jungle products in the market, but I expect that Mina sent them food and money also, for they were more prosperous than their neighbors. For example, they were excessively proud to show us their chicken, which had as yet gone uneaten. They kept it in their house so it would eat the scorpions. The other chief fact was that they were devotees of the illegal cult of Jesus and Mary, and this was why they slept in two stages, from sunset to midnight and from two until dawn. During the two-hour break, they watched for the coming of Jesus.

"Tell us about the palace," said Instant George. "Is it true that the president is building a marble boat, and that's where all the wealth goes?"

"It's true," said Daniel Defoe.

Instant George said this was an insult to all those who suffered from hunger and thirst, and he acclaimed the deeds of Carlos Pedigree, revolutionary crusader for liberty, who was said to have effected the recent explosion of a senatorial house.

This inspired Daniel Defoe to tell one of this stories. He said, "I knew a revolutionary named Thomason Jeffers. He built a radio from a dog's ear bone. I've been meaning to tell you about this. Using this instrument he broadcast his Unilateral Declaration of Independence, which made New England independent from the tyranny of the British Queen. Did I ever tell you about New England? The coffee plantations of Pennsylvania. The marshmallow plants of Cape Coral. The aspirin trees of Massachusetts."

"Let's talk about this later," said Edward Halloween.

Then we had some sweet potato wine, which was fermenting in a crock by the window. This was another sign of their prosperity and they were terrifically proud to share it with us. Edward Halloween accepted it eagerly, and even Daniel Defoe drank a tiny measure, just a spoonful, after which he was dizzy and fuckered up, but I was bashful about taking from their meager stores. Surely they could not spare this nutriment. I was also thinking of Thomas Jefferson, who was a real person, a historical revolutionary terrorist from the time of the jihad against Great Britian. I had read something about him, though as a matter of principle I now preferred Daniel Defoe's lyrical revisions. The interesting circumstance was that my own distant Roulette ancestors, who were buried in the family tomb and whose stories were told on Independence Day, could be considered revolutionary terrorists themselves, on the order of Carlos Pedigree and Thomas Jefferson. They had freed us from the yoke of our colonial rulers in Minnesota. But now my family was at the other end of the yardstick, beating the revolutionaries from the door. It seems that history comes in circles.

"Are you able to find food?" Edward Halloween was saying. "Don't you dream of a glorious revolution? Doesn't it outrage you to know the president eats cornbread and shamo? He even has wheatcake!"

Pilaf explained how their life was hard, but life for poor people was always the same and that was their lot in life. She said that it was a great blessing that Mina was born a dwarf, since this anomaly had enabled her to rise up in the world, but for the ordinary multitudes there was no way to get out of City of the Sun.

The high creaking sadness of their bedeviled existence came home to me in a rush. Here was their life, I thought. They were ensconced in this crowded enclosure with a chicken to eat the scorpions and sweet potato wine as their only indulgence. Soon, one fatally beautiful drought morning, they would consume the chicken and the scorpions would multiply in geometric profusion and drive them into the street.

Suddenly I was seized by a longing and I said to Daniel Defoe, without reason or warning, "Marry me, won't you? What does anything matter?"

I spoke this proposal in Modern English, so our hosts would not grasp the meaning, and Instant George said, "Sorry we apologizes. We doesn't speak it." But meanwhile Daniel Defoe only laughed and said, "If only I could, my friend. If only." Then he sang a bar of music and placed a warm hand on my leg. I saw he was increasingly fuckered up from his wine, so I shimmied close to him. He said, "I'll sing you a song off Mr. Jeffers's magical radio. I'll sing you the greatest hits of sea chanteys."

"Look at this proper palace gentleman," said Instant George, who hadn't understood any of this. "He knows we're all going to starve. He wants to get it while the getting's good."

I had contracted a dislike for this person, though I exhorted myself to generosity because he was just a slim and dirty fellow in a shirt made from a sugar bag, and furthermore he was doomed. I gave him a sad smile and thereafter I was quiet, as prescribed, like a stone listening to the wind, and all this time I held Daniel Defoe's hand.

Edward Halloween did not notice these intimacies because he had made himself drunk in the evening's protracted course. On the way back to the palace he outlined his own philosophical troubles and he was impervious to the thoughts and speeches of others. He said he was having a crisis. He said he wanted to choose whether he was a man or a woman and then cleave to his choice. It was hard to be neither or both, for that meant he was always only himself, which was an insuperable burden for anyone, and most especially for a poet. It did indeed seem like a problem, although he later forgot about it.

When we were safely returned to the arcades and pergolas of our palace, Edward Halloween vanished and I was alone with Daniel Defoe. I wanted to ask him to come up with me to my rooms, but then I thought it would demean his oath to Anna Gloria, which I honored. I was feeling melancholic to an extreme.

"Time keeps passing," I said. "Life passes by whether I pay attention to it or not, and then it turns into history and it's like a desert mummy and no one knows what it was truly like."

He was quiet and stared off across the dark wasteland of our dehydrated garden.

I said, "What is it like to see the world swallow up so much time?"

"To me it seemed like the sixteenth century lasted forever, but the seventeenth century was like a feast day, which is hot and clamorous and rapidly concluded, and then the eighteenth century was like a turn around the garden before dinner. The nineteenth century was a cup of cutgrass tea. Everything since then has been wind under the door."

"Is it really modern medicine that keeps you alive? You seem almost to be retrogressing and becoming younger. What is the secret formula?"

"It's no secret. Take nutmeg for insomnia and Ceylon cinnamon for tonsillitis. Try to eat some fat from a camel's hunch. Eat roc's liver, if you can get it. Eat as many vaccines as you can find. It must be that the thought of Anna Gloria keeps me animated as well. But now, my princess, I have to say good night."

So I walked with him to the yawning dark mouth of the camel pen, and he kissed my hand and issued inside. Out in the dry crisp darkness with all the stars above watching me in my loneliness, I had only Christopher Smart to talk to, for this cat now emerged from the shadows. I petted him and he vibrated with purring sounds.

## 2016

The next morning we were down at the marina, where the ancient mariner knew a man who'd let us use his boat. It was a small fishing trawler that could be steered from the covered pilothouse or from up above, in what was called the tuna tower. Azar had made a printout of the treasure map.

"I'll explain how to provision an expedition of this kind," said the ancient mariner. "First we need cassava bread, which keeps better than any other bread in the heat and the damp. Cassava beer would be even better. Then we need some salt pork or ham. We also need a few horses, if we can get them. In Mexico I had a horse named Little Richard. What a horse! The thing about a horse is it makes the fighting safer, because usually the Indians will simply surrender rather than face such a terrifying beast. They trick themselves into believing that man and horse are one creature, like a centaur."

"It's just a day trip, isn't it?" said Azar.

"Now, as for drinking water, we have one thermos of water, but we also have these bottles of low-calorie water drink."

He'd purchased a case of something called "FreshWater." The package identified it as an "all natural artisanal functional beverage." It was just scented water in plastic bottles. He had raspberry, strawberry-basil, tarragon-blueberry, and plain.

"Plain?" I said.

"Water-flavored."

"You like this stuff?"

"I love it. Quaco does too."

"I do not," said Quaco.

"You do."

Quaco thought about this. "I like the strawberry-basil," he said.

The ancient mariner had mostly recovered from last night's ordeal, but he wasn't yet so steady on his pins and just after we cast off he seemed to slip into a trance. After a few minutes of silence, he said, "Have I been making any sense?"

"You haven't been saying anything," said Azar.

"But if I had been, would I have been making any sense?"

I wasn't doing much better. I'd slept like a tailor's dummy in my hot sweaty tent, but because of the green pills I hadn't been able to wake all the way up again. I had three cups of po but it was no good. Squinting red eyes, matted hair, dead man's cheeks. If I sat still for too long my mind seemed to shut off, like a Prius.

We motored slowly out of the marina and headed north, into a maze of mangrove islands. They weren't real islands. They were just groves or stands of mangrove trees growing out of the water, and there was no soil and no rocky foundation. Apparently they often shifted their positions or blew away entirely, and no map could represent their locations, certainly not one drawn on the wall in a fit of delirium. We were looking, however, for a true island, a dome of coral rock covered in dirt and trees and a small Calusa shell mound. I did not trust the ancient mariner to find it, but I trusted Quaco, with what possible justification who can say. He was standing in the bow, scanning the horizon, keyboard swinging around his neck, bracelets of human teeth, but even so, even so, he had an air of real competence.

Meanwhile, Azar and the ancient mariner were having a cheery conversation in the stern. Azar was filming this, hardworking documentarian that he'd become. My own role in the project seemed to have diminished, which was fine with me.

"Here's another thing I've been thinking about," the ancient mariner said. "Have you seen that there are cacao beans for sale in the supermarket?"

"They're an Aztec superfood," said Azar.

"Of course they are! Now think about this. You can buy some, maybe a hundred beans let's say, for ten dollars. Correct?"

"Correct."

"But in Mexico you can purchase a beautiful embroidered cloak for a hundred cacao beans. So think about it. You can sell the embroidered cloak here for a lot of money, maybe a hundred dollars. Do you understand what I'm saying?"

"You can exploit this disparity."

"Ten dollars for a hundred cacao beans. A hundred cacao beans for a cloak. Sell the cloak for a hundred dollars. Buy ten bags of cacao beans, for a total of a thousand beans. Buy ten cloaks. Sell the ten cloaks for a thousand dollars. Buy ten thousand cacao beans with that same thousand dollars. Exchange the beans for a hundred cloaks. Sell the cloaks for ten thousand dollars. And so on."

"Only two more cycles and you're a millionaire."

"What is it?" I said. "Cloaks?"

"Cloaks."

"It's the cloak and bean scam," said Azar.

"You're talking about the economy of old Mexico," said Quaco, unexpectedly the voice of reason, "which you yourself helped to destroy."

The ancient mariner reflected on this and then shook his head dismissively. "You'd need some initial money for the transportation costs, flights to and from Mexico, etc., but after a few rounds the scam would pay for itself. Maybe this is how I'll use my share of the treasure."

Deep in the bay, after about an hour, we saw three middle-aged men fishing from a little boat. I was thinking that they looked very peaceful, but the ancient mariner grew tense.

"Give me your shirt," he said.

"My shirt?"

"Am I supposed to use Azar's? Azar's is white! I suppose you *want* to surrender?"

My shirt was red. I gave it to him.

"Actually don't give it to me. Just get up in the crow's nest and start waving it."

While I was doing this, the ancient mariner began a chilling recitation: "On the part of the King," he said, "Don Fernando, and of Doña Juana the mad, his daughter, Queen of Castille and León, subduers of the barbarous nations, we their servants notify and make known to you, as best we can, that the Lord our God, Living and Eternal, created the Heaven and the Earth, and one man and one woman, of whom you and we, all the men of the world, were and are descendants. But on account of the multitude which has sprung from this man and woman in the five thousand years since the world was created, it was necessary that some men should go one way and some another, and that they should be divided into many kingdoms and provinces, for in one alone they could not be sustained."

He was speaking too quietly for the fishermen to hear, and after a while he seemed to lose track of his text and fell silent.

"I don't remember the rest."

"It's okay," said Azar. "I think you said your piece."

"You have to say the whole thing or it's not legal."

"We'll all sign something. We'll tell them you said it in full."

"I remember this," I said. "I know about this. This is the Spanish Requerimiento. Why does he know this?"

"Never mind," said the ancient mariner. "It never mattered anyway. It's more of a trick than a law."

In a little while we got close enough to the other boat that we could say good morning. They said good morning too and one of them asked us if we were catching anything.

The ancient mariner said, "Anyone who wants to join our crew can do so without fear, but anyone who resists will be killed."

They all laughed in a pleasant way and then one of them said, "A pirate, huh?"

Now the ancient mariner slipped into the clear water, no more than eight feet deep in this part of the bay, and swam with surprising grace over to their boat. They helped him in and congratulated him on his excellent swimming. The ancient mariner thanked them and then picked up a metal bucket and bashed one of them in the head. It was not a tremendously forceful blow, but the man's face went blank and he sat down and put his head in his hands. His friends thought this was very funny and slapped him on the back.

"Uh oh!" said one.

The other said to us, "My own granpa was taken that way too."

"Your grandfather turned into a pirate?" said Azar.

The wounded man had his head between his knees. He said, "Ouch."

The one with the pirate grandfather, a large man with a red face and a Boston Celtics T-shirt, said, "He's fine. Ain't you, Stan?" But Stan didn't say anything more. "Stan! Stanislas! He's fine. Don't worry about Stan."

The ancient mariner was stuffing lures and things into his pockets, and now he snapped the whole tackle box closed and heaved it into the water. The fishermen retrieved it and recovered their other things too, but they let him keep a bright yellow lure. I was still up in the tuna tower with my shirt off, but Quaco had gotten behind the wheel or whatever it's called and maneuvered our boat a little closer to theirs.

"You boys had better get him back into the boat," said the man in the Celtics shirt. Then, seeing Quaco for the first time, he said, "Whoa! Nice keyboard there, my man!"

In a little while we were motoring away again. The ancient mariner seemed to feel that his act of piracy was a great success, and we indulged him. We complimented him on his skill and on the beauty of the lure his victims had let him keep. But when we got well clear of the other boat, he revealed that he'd also stolen a dry bag, which contained a watch and about a hundred dollars in cash.

"I just took the other stuff as a diversion," he said.

This warranted some discussion, but no one said anything. I looked out over the water. Mangrove islands, wading birds, deep blue channels, even a manatee in the sea grass. It was a very beautiful place. I tried to imagine that I was looking at part of the Chesapeake Bay five hundred years in the future.

"But you haven't talked much about piracy," I said. "We didn't know you were a pirate."

"I'll tell you about piracy. The average life span of a pirate was about two years. For two years you drank and stole things, but you knew you'd be caught. There was a sickening feeling about it. There was this carnival-at-the-end-of-the-world feeling. Tears and wildness, that was piracy, because every night was the last night and in the morning you were going to hang."

"Why did anybody do it?"

"Why does anybody do anything? It was less bad than being a sailor on a merchant ship. On pirate ships you had big crews and everyone pitched in. Also these were kids, most of them. They didn't understand they could die. They knew they were going to die but they didn't understand it."

"You didn't die."

"I spent some time in Newgate, though, until I was able to convince someone that I was just a merchant sailor who'd been forced into piracy, which did often happen. I was an old man, and what were they going to say? No one wanted to admit they had anything to fear from such an old man. I have often used my age to my advantage. I get no end of profit from it."

"Maybe I should've been a pirate," I said. "I've always had this feeling that I'm not meant for a quiet life. I'm biding my time now but I have this idea that I'm meant for immortality and destruction."

"All young men have that feeling," said the ancient mariner. "All young people, probably. Even me. Even in my long-ago days as a young person. Although in my case it proved to be true."


We'd been out there for more than two hours when Quaco looked up at the sun—I should say he looked directly into the sun—and said, "What o'clock is it?"

"Eleven o'clock," Azar said.

Quaco consulted the map.

"There's the island," he said, and there it was, higher than the islands around it, maybe eight feet above the bay, ringed with mangroves but with some real forest on it also.

Azar said, "It'll be good to do some digging. Stretch out a little."

We dropped our anchor and waded ashore. The island was bigger than I'd realized. There were at least two acres of old-growth tropical forest, gumbo limbo trees and mahogany and sea grape, an enormous fig tree, tall silver palms. The leaf litter was crisp underfoot. The wild coffee was flowering. I saw a blue snail.

"And this is lignum vitae," said the ancient mariner. "You can cure the clap with lignum vitae wood. Quaco taught me that, didn't you, Quaco?"

We had given no thought to the possibility that we would find any treasure. We were drifting along, so to speak, taking things as they came. But we'd hardly started digging when the ancient mariner told us to hang on. He stepped forward and lifted a small figurine out of the sand. It was a woman with the head of a cat.

"This isn't right," he said. "This is the wrong treasure." He slapped his thigh in frustration and sat down in the sand. "Forget it, boys. I'm sorry. It's a bust."

We were staring at this mysterious artifact, which was significantly weathered but still artful and stylish.

"It looks pretty authentic," said Azar. "And it was right here where you said it would be."

Quaco was digging around. He found a corroded metal box with a broken latch. Inside there was a worn amulet of some kind, a flattened grimacing face, and another figurine. An animal like an ostrich.

"What is this?" he said.

"I think it must be the stuff from El Dorado. That's a karawa bird."

"From El Dorado?" said Azar. He was peering through the view-finder on the camera, trying to ask leading questions, but he was out of his depth.

"El Dorado," said the ancient mariner. "Sure."

"Where are the coins?" said Quaco.

"I don't know. I'm sorry."

"It doesn't matter. I never cared about the coins."

"I'm sorry anyway. You trusted me with them."

"I'm not clear on the main point," said Azar.

No one was listening to him. Quaco was sifting through the sand. This was all more than I could assimilate. My mind shuddered to a halt.

Quaco said, "Don't feel so bad. You can sell these things to a museum."

"Oh sure," said the ancient mariner. "I guess."

Then he seemed to perk up again.

"Do you remember the kid who helped us steal the coins?"

"No."

"I remember him a little. I want to say he was a Turk."

"He wasn't a Turk."

They stood together, squinting into the past. Azar and I had nothing to contribute. We were speechless.

"But I didn't steal these things, though," he told us.

"It doesn't matter now," said Quaco.

"It matters to me. This particular treasure I didn't steal. It was given to me by a goddess."

## 1560

---

When we arrive in Anaquitos, we do not find houses roofed in gold. We do not find bread made from crushed pearls. We do not find a king who covers himself in gold dust and takes a ceremonial bath each morning. We do not find white Indians. We do not find Indians with some intimation of Christian theology. We do not find the city I remember.

We abandon our brigantines on the beach upriver and walk down the white highway. We meet no resistance. There are no gates. We see the great earthen mounds, which were once as smooth as a bald man's head, and they are dotted with trees. We see the canals and streams that watered the manioc fields, and others that carried away the sewage, and they are not flowing at all. The fish ponds are dry. In the dazzling white plazas the macha trees have died and the fig trees have gone wild and pulled up the paving stones. The air is thick with flies. There are filthy people drunk at midday but many of the streets are empty and many of the houses are falling down. The market women have nothing to sell. They regard us with revulsion but without fear.

I see all of this, a city in decay, but the Pirahao do not, because for the Pirahao it is not proper to compare what exists now to what existed at an earlier time. The Christians do not see it either because they are not here, because for them Anaquitos does not exist at all. The Christians see a beautiful white city instead. They see El Dorado. They see heaven on earth.

"It's like a dream from the tale of Amadis," says Miguel Oreja.

Here is the city where I was born. I do not think about it. I can't stop thinking about it. The city will not be destroyed and it will be destroyed and it has already been destroyed, and I have no home in the world.

We march into the city and nothing happens. We stand in the white plaza looking around and waiting. The air is the color of inaga fruit. There are iguanas here and I wonder if the people have forgotten how to eat them, or if there are now so few people that those who remain cannot eat the iguanas faster than they hatch. For a long time no one speaks to us, and then a madman comes. His speech is unintelligible and his hair is matted with monkey blood. The Christians think he is a priest. I tell them there are no priests in Anaquitos. There are no rituals. There are no gods. I try to make them understand how this world is different from their world, but I know that for them there is only one world.

Here is the city where I was born, and here are the people with whom I once belonged, but I have forgotten how to see them. I can see parts of them, but I can't see them whole. An old woman is a strip of cotton cloth and a yellow incisor. A hungry boy is an eyebrow and a shoulder blade. I do not think of my childhood, although I think of it continuously. I do not think of the pet monkey in the basket and the tapir stew and the pieces of old pottery I dug up in the courtyard. I do not think of my father or of the days he spent teaching me to make black earth for the garden. I do not think of these things because it is not proper to think of the deep past. The deep past is not here anymore. The person to whom those things happened was called Xiako and she is not here anymore. I am Maria. I am not a Pirahao and I am not a Christian. I am nothing. I don't think of this and I think of nothing else and I am stupid like the monkey when we made him drunk with rotting fruit.

There is no time for these things. There is no time to see the city or to wonder at its disintegration, because now we must undertake the business of politics. We must convert the Indians. We must read the Requerimiento. Miguel Oreja bounces on his toes and sings. His beard is a long bawdy sailor's song.

I try to explain that there is no government to usurp, no king to negotiate with, no judges or mayors with whom we must come to terms. This city does not function in the way Christian cities function, and now it seems it does not function at all. But the Christians cannot understand this and because they cannot understand this I take them to see the Xipaohoani.

These are the oldest men in each family and they meet in the house of darkness at every change of the moon, but they have no power. They make suggestions and they are ignored. They are just old men. I take the Christians to see them because there is no one else for them to see.

Miguel Oreja is very pleased. He tells me that the Xipaohoani are the city's governing body. He feels certain that once I explain the precepts of Christianity to them, we will immediately and spontaneously create a new Christian polity, the Kingdom of El Dorado, in which we will all live as brothers and sisters in Christ.

So I explain Christianity. I say, "In the upper sky there is a man. He makes the world. He has a wife but no man has eaten her. She is called Maria. He nails his son to a tree. This happens so long ago it is forgotten."

"Maria," says one of the old men. He tilts his head in my direction. I have already introduced myself as Maria. They think I am telling a story about myself.

"Yes," I say.

To himself he says, "She is Maria. Her husband makes the world."

All of this is meaningless. It is a joke. In Pirahao, a story is true only as long as someone in the story is still alive. Afterward, when there are no witnesses left, the story is never told again. A golden crucifix is an idol that represents the execution of a god in a time beyond memory. How can the Pirahao understand this? Even if they could understand it, it would be improper. Only the Christians make idols. To the Pirahao it is meaningless to revere an object.

But the Xipaohoani do not laugh, as I expect them to. They don't laugh because they know the Christians are a people to be feared, strange and disgusting as they are. And this is when I learn what has happened to the city. The old men tell me that when the starving and wounded Christians came here for the first time, their presence coincided with the eruption of a plague. The Pirahao physicians, who can cure everything, could not cure it, and it was this plague that reduced the city to its present condition. Now the Pirahao have come to understand that the Christians are themselves the plague. I ask what they will do about it but they don't understand my question. There is nothing to do. I ask them if they think the plague will come again. The plague is already here, they say, pointing to the Christians.

For the Pirahao, the only truth is what happens. For the Christians, the truth is what doesn't happen, the truth is everywhere, the truth is unknowable. I know that there can be no understanding between them, but there is no way to say this that is true in both languages.

I leave Miguel Oreja with the old men, to whom he tries to speak Spanish. I walk through the city looking for Daniel de Fo. I see the houses arranged neatly around each circular plaza, but their roofs are falling in. I tell myself I am Maria. I am not Xiako. Xiako is not here anymore and her anguish doesn't exist.

Daniel de Fo is buying xaxa from a woman in the market. Rat meat and manioc. He takes a few bites and pronounces it the best thing he has ever eaten.

"If I live a thousand years, I'll never have a meal so good," he says.

He doesn't finish it. He is in the sun but he isn't sweating.

"There's no treasure. I realize this now, but you must have known it all along. You tricked me!"

"Everything was different. I apologize."

"I forgive you. But how will I get back to Spain now? How will I find Anna Gloria?"

"You have to find the world in which she exists. The language in which her name can be spoken. Otherwise you won't know her even if you're looking right at her."

"That isn't very helpful," he says. Then he laughs and shakes his head. "What if she's left Spain by now? She could be in Zanzibar, or Achem, or Goa. Every night I dream of camels and dust. What does it mean? It is the city of Aden?"

When the sun sets, there is a dance in the central plaza. I wonder if the Pirahao will murder the Christians as a way of controlling the spread of the disease, but they do nothing. They dance. They are a bare leg, a necklace of palm nuts, a wrinkled breast, a strong jaw. There are prostitutes and they are nothing but their painted black teeth. At first the Christians will not dance because they say the music is idolatrous, but then they make themselves drunk with cashew wine. The Pirahao value drunkenness but I have trouble understanding why.

Soon everyone is drunk and laughing. There is a feast. There are electric eels, brazil nuts, piranha, otter, caiman, paási fruit. I eat baahóísi, the wild pig of the forest, and think of the alcalde of Santa Inés. There is nothing funny in the world but I'm the only one who isn't laughing. I am the only one who can find no truth in any of this. The Christians are laughing and singing and Miguel Oreja is praising God and shoveling xaxa into his mouth. He is living in the kingdom of heaven and it is as good as he thought it would be. Even Daniel de Fo is happy, already thinking of Zanzibar, already looking forward to his reunion in the East Indies.

And this is how it is for weeks, laughter and cashew wine, xaxa and dancing. Miguel Oreja grows too fat to wear his armor. The vicar general is given a medicine that makes his arm grow back. This is the conquest, which succeeds and fails at the same time, and leaves everyone babbling absurdities, their lips greasy, their cheeks stuffed with rat meat.

All I see is a doomed people, black teeth, a strip of cotton, the forest picking apart the houses at the edge of the city. The truth is what happens. The world is only what it is. The world is filling up with numbers and gods, and soon the Pirahao won't be able to live in it anymore. That is the truth. That is what happens.

# 2200

We was just walking now mile after mile. I were tired but the shoreline were interesting the air the smells the cries of birds. Also I had my helper Christopher the kitten who sat on my head. I were surprised to realize one day how I were not longing for corn whiskey. It is because corn whiskey made a hole in me could only be filled with more corn whiskey but if I didn't drink it then it didn't make no holes in me. It seems the cure for this problem of corn whiskey is to be shipwrecked. Amazing. I were not gloomy no more it were like magic. I said to myself I am a adventurer I am the happy helper of Dan Keyshote Knight of the Feverish Courtingplace.

We was on our way to Saint Augustine which Old Dan called Saint Brendan. We was going to dig up the treasure of Anakitos which were buried just outside the city. However I had now got a superstition about the treasure I were not sure about it. I had a great belief in treasure you see I believed it could change everything yet now everything were already changed. I were feeling pretty good at least for now and I did not want everything to change again. Nothing will change said Old Dan. It will I said. No he said you must trust me I have gained and lost many treasures nothing has changed. It has I said for example the world ended. Oh he said yes that's true. Well I said. I still think you are going to want that treasure he said.

The captain were quiet as we walked for he were exerting himself he were very tired. Peaches however had great powers of stamina he never stopped even when we rested he just kept circling us stumbling his eyes rattling in his face like peas in a can. He were not himself yet even after hours of walking. Oh said Old Dan oh no haha it will be days yet for poor Peaches he should of thought of that before he went crazy.

Meanwhile Old Dan told us stories about Florida. Long ago he said this

were such a wonderful place everyone came from everywhere to escape
the cold and snow. I did not doubt him for I had seen snow once myself. I
were a boy very young but I remembered how it were so cold you knew
you could die of it. It killed many trees many plants three hours it snowed
but the next day were hot. Old Dan said just imagine that times a hundred
for in the deep winter all Boston was covered in snow up to the tops of the
greatest buildings. The people traveled from place to place in tunnels
beneath the snow he said and they ate seal walrus orca but they was so
strong so fat that the cold never hurt them they was like walrus themselves. They was rich I said that is why they was fat. Yes said Old Dan and
also from eating chemicals for they loved their chemicals as you would
too. Chemicals I said. They was delicious he said. I believe it I said. Also
one other thing he said which was that they had so much electronic light
they had lost the faculty of seeing in the dark.

I asked Old Dan would they tell me about when Florida had secede
for I had seceded myself after all and I were interested in secession.
Which time said Old Dan for it seceded many times. This most recent
time I said. It were nothing to tell said Old Dan the United States it let
them go. Was you living in Florida when this happened I said. Yes he
said however I did not know it happened. There was no wars about it I
said. No he said it were not worth the trouble there was bigger troubles
it were Hurricane Devaun it were the robot war with China it were all
number of other disasters manmade or sent by God or both. What did
you say I said do you believe in God. Of course he said in God in Buddha
in Zagigai in Namwa spirit of the forest too. What about Peaches I said.
I believe in Peaches he said. I mean Peaches does believe in God I said
but you poisoned him for it. No said Old Dan Peaches he just repeats the
name of Jesus that is because he is mad. Now we looked at Peaches he
were mad yes for he were chewing his hand bloody.

Old Dan knew this country pretty well but he said it were all changed
for there was no more piney woods. It is now become the great Atlantic
swamp forest said the captain. Okay said Old Dan that must be what is
different. It were certainly a swamp for there was just green trees water

mushy grass and only one kind of bird which was blue and yellow parrots. Also there was millions of bugs they bit us and bit us our faces were all swole. Even Christopher the kitten was bit though not as bad for his fur protected him.

Sometimes there was old buildings grown over in vines. Other times we seen foundations down in the muddy water for the sea it had come up and swallowed the beaches plus the outlying islands plus the beachfront properties. I looked at the foundations they was all covered in slime. Imagine the people living there long ago I thought imagine if you could say to them in two hundred years here is what your house would be just a crust of cement plus slime. Here is your garden you could say just swamp and muck. It were a amazing thought how everything changes but then I also thought how Old Dan said it changes back again. Even more amazing it all goes in circles.

Old Dan and me was going to break away soon and go in search of the treasure. The captain he didn't believe in the treasure but even if he had believed he were obliged to go to Saint Augustine. He were going to take Peaches for we didn't know what to do with him. We thought maybe the captain could give him to a church. These plans was frustrated however when we stopped at a knob of dry land to eat berries and the captain revealed that he had got a parasite in his foot. Oh I said what parasite. Nematode he said. You have got it in your foot I said. It buried its self in my foot yes he said. Are you sure said Old Dan. Would I lie about this said the captain. Very well said Old Dan we must go into the forest we will find hwaraca to cure it. The captain looked at Peaches to see the effect of Old Dan's medicine. I will simply dig it out he said. He had got his knife still for it were hung to his belt and he now begun cutting into his foot. Uh oh said Old Dan bad news my man it will not heal in this heat and damp. Dammit said the captain I know what I am doing dammit old man suddenly he were very angry.

Old Dan were right however for in the morning his foot were swelled up two times it were like a squash with toes. It is the nematode makes it swell said the captain not the digging and cutting. You can't walk said

Old Dan what will we do. I can walk said the captain. You can't said Old Dan. I can said the captain. It were very clear he could not. He could not even stand up.

We did not like to abandon the captain so we waited on our knob of land to see if his foot would get better. Instead of getting better it swole up even more. Now it were a melon with toes. Why are the toes not swollen I asked. No one could tell me. We had got some shade but the mosquitoes was so bad I cannot even say how bad. Plus there was other flies fleas chiggers and bees that did sting us in our armpits. All this time Peaches were slowly coming to himself for now he said where am I. You are in Florida said Old Dan. Oh said Peaches whereafter he said once more where am I. This time we ignored him. It were hard to think positive about all these things but I tried.

Next it were two men and a lady come past in their canoe. They was true Florida types said Old Dan later. We asked how far to Saint Augustine or was there a town closer for the captain needed help. I am fine said the captain waving his hand. His face were very pale plus it were covered in mosquito bites. Aint five mile to Saint Augustine said the lady who was brown and wrinkly like a leather bag where someone had drawn a face. I can fuckin walk said the captain. What are you all doing out here said Old Dan. What does it look like granpa said one of the men the tall one. I don't know is why I ask said Old Dan. We is not out here for pleasure said the man we are huntin gator. He pulled back a sheet so we could see. It had a gator there at least three feet long so dark scaly with a pink mouth fearsome teeth. Old Dan said oh it is just a baby. Baby said the man very loud very angry it is huge lookit this thing. It used to have gators thirty feet long said Old Dan they was like two boats end to end. Okay granpa said the old man now he were laughing. Okay said Old Dan.

We had some food with these three we shared yucka bread. They had some caju wine also but I said no I don't want any wine no thank you whereafter I felt very proud. I were suddenly in high spirits again despite our setbacks. But the captain he did have some caju wine and then he were fucked up laughing vomiting poor guy. Then Old Dan thought he would try them on Anna Gloria. I am looking for a woman he said you might know her as Anna Gloria. Anna Gloria said the lady. She was working in the library he said or so I remember. Don't know her said the fat man.

Suddenly the captain begun shouting. Hey he shouted. What we said. We are getting away from the point with all this eating and drinking and talking he said the point is I can walk just fine where is Saint Augustine. Aint five mile said the lady again who were a expert on where Saint Augustine were. Oh fantastic said the captain my ordeal it is at a end.

The fat man were looking at Peaches. This fellow is not well neither he said. No I said Peaches is not well that is a fact. I will buy him from you said the man. No I said he is not for sale. Now hang on said Old Dan let us hear him out maybe we could sell him after all. You had better take this chance the man said you will have trouble selling him I promise. No I said we are not selling him end of discussion. Very well I were just asking said the man did you say his name were Peaches. Yes I said Peaches like more than one Peach. Interesting he said once I knew a man called Oats are you sure you will not sell this fellow Peaches. I am sure I said.

Soon these three left saying enjoy Florida for it is the best country it is the land of freedom liberty no carbon tax. After this the captain begun shivering even though it were so hot. We stayed through the next day we ate swamp insects and then Old Dan skum some slime off the water which me and Peaches also ate. Isn't it delicious said Old Dan though he did not eat any himself. Food of the Meshica he said. Delicious I said for I did not want to hurt his feelings. It were the worst thing I ever ate.

Next day I said okay what is our plan. Well said Old Dan the captain he may die. What I said. Yes he may die do you remember you asked what I would take with me from the past now I have a new answer I would take antibiotic. It have antibiotic in Boston I said it doesn't work. It used to work that is my point said Old Dan it were magic. Is antibiotic like probiotic I said. Similar he said yes however you apply the antibiotic to kill the probiotic if it gets in the wrong place for you see the captain he has got a probiotic in his foot. It is bad to have a probiotic in your foot I said and good to have one in your stomach. Yes he said you've got it exactly. But what will we do I said we have not got any antibiotic. I don't know said Old Dan. Maybe there is a antibiotic leaf in the forest I said you mentioned hwaraca. I am looking he said I haven't seen any. You don't know another leaf I said. No he said I should have listened to Quaco when he tried to teach me damn it damn it.

The captain now begun to go mad as Peaches. In our journey to come it were a saying with us mad as Peaches. Don't eat that berry said Old Dan laughing you will go mad as Peaches haha. That were later however. For now the captain were going mad. He said fuckin trees and fuckin bugs and I can fuckin walk don't touch me. Christopher the kitten avoided him carefully. He were a nice man until he gone mad as Peaches we did not hold it against him we knew it were only the nematode had got into his brain.

Next day I were doing good and Peaches were better and Old Dan were the same as always but now the captain were dead. It were the nematode or the swole up foot that had got him in the end. I were very much saddened by this death for I had felt I knew the captain. Also the specter of death renewed my interest in treasure just as Lun-Biao's death had suppressed it. It were a enigma how the same thing caused the opposite feelings. It were because human thoughts is just random like marbles rattling around.

Fine I said okay let us go find the treasure of Anakitos it seems we will need riches after all. Well said Old Dan now my conscience is pricking me about Peaches. Oh I said I forgot. We have got to deliver him to Saint Augustine said Old Dan. We looked at Peaches. He grinned. He were a impediment but we was going to take care of him for we had seen enough suffering.

I had bad feelings about Saint Augustine and I were correct sad to say for no sooner did we arrive when I begun drinking corn whiskey. I don't know why I done this it were almost a kind of accident. All my positive thinking was gone to waste after that. In the first taste I got a feeling of chaos immortality death violence the falling away into sweat crime ecksekera. The more I drank the more it mattered to me about the treasure. Now I wanted it so bad and I thought again of air condition like I use to. It seems that corn whiskey makes a hole can also be filled with air condition.

At least I did learn something of why Florida had secede. This were told to me by a man called Hwan. It were a question of dikes dams walls he said. It were a proposal to wall out the sea as in New York Boston Savannah except here it were a wall around the whole state. The government would not agree to this whereafter Florida simply left the Union stating it would not pay taxes to such a government. Next all Florida pitched in they built a wall it were the great wall of Florida. It were only twenty miles long however. The water come in north and south and up from the ground what a mess what a mess and the water still rising. Wow I said to Hwan what were they thinking. They was trying to save themselves he said. Oh I said. But it just keeps going said Hwan for we have now heard that Minnesota is seceded too they have got a king.

All was darkness after that. In the morning I were sad as I always was after such a night but I hydrated with coconut juice and thought positive as much as I could. I pardoned myself as it was my right to do for I were king of the Independent States of Jam.

Peaches were meanwhile beaten up in the street for Old Dan had filled his head with thoughts of Namwa spirit of the forest. He were carrying on saying Namwa this Namwa that and they beat him for it as they should. He were a crazy fucker. We brought him to the church to have him exorcised and then at last it were time for us to go find the treasure of Anakitos. But I were trying to renounce treasure I said. Well said Old Dan you can always renounce it after we find it.

Mrs. Galsworthy did not betray me, and instead she did as I asked, and made Mr. Galsworthy aware that some thing was amiss with his coin collection. Soon he had forgotten the loss of his physician for the greater loss of his treasure, and up and down he went, raving & tearing at his cloathes, & also, it grieves me to report, tormenting the slaves that they should tell him what had happened. Far from accusing me he now lookt upon me as the only one he could trust, and it was then he made a shocking assertion, for he said at this time I can only trust Green, I can only trust Green though he be a *Son of Africa*. Passing on thereafter to another aspect of his grievance, he made no more of this terrific discovery, as if it were of no consequence.

So, dear Reader, he had found me out after all, or known it all along, & never cared a particle for it. Is there not a great moral to be picked handsomely from this? Yet I know not what it is.

I was in such a position as required great self-possession and courage, but I felt the buttons and stays of self had come all unfastened. I had lost all of Dr. Dan's money at cards, and all of my own as well. Then Dr. Dan had confessed he was mistaken about Anna Gloria. Now I had learnt Mr. Galsworthy had always known my secret, yet I had abus'd him by stealing from him, and betraying him with his wife. And though I knew all these things, and saw myself in a new and frightful light, what could I do? I was criminated, and there was nothing for it but to continue with Quaco's plan, knowing now that there was more concealed in the glassy depths of the human heart than ever I had suspect'd.

I had as a final stroke placed some small number of coins in Mr. Corvette's room, which room Mr. Galsworthy now caused to be searched, finding also that Mr. Corvette was hastening his preparations for departure. The slave Herodotus discover'd the coins along with some china and silver that Mr. Corvette had stolen upon his own option, & thus was any investigation diverted. This outcome at least spared the slaves further molestation, and even earned them a fat pink hog, which my employer gave them in apology, and also so that they could feast themselves in honor of Dr. Dan. No doubt it made a welcome change from rat meat.

I ne'er saw Mr. Corvette but one time more, and this as he was taken away to town, there to be lock'd away. Now and then I see him in my mind's eye, pusillanimously venting his griefs, and talking of trumpet playing, & I lament the part I played in his misfortune, though one could see he was a man especially marked for misfortune.

I did not visit Quaco at this time, not wanting to excite suspicion. I did not speak with Mrs. Galsworthy either, for I was ashamed, and felt that even though she had not betrayed me, she must think I was a fool. Instead I wrote her a letter telling her all I felt for her, and explaining once more why I had done what I had done, or rather saying that I had no reason. Even as I wrote I felt I were writing for myself, and said so, and begged her forgive me for it, saying I had never done anything but that I did it for myself. I became lost in a wilderness of epistolary and philosophical conceits, and my tender missive swelled to a varicose proportion. Finally, with a despairing wish that we should meet again in another life, I left off writing and went down to the white coral beach.

Thus I was occupied for the next day, which I also passed with Samson and his young friends, who were enjoying their holiday, and with the groom Fred, whom I had got to know well. He was no darker than me, and perhaps lighter, and I wondered if everyone knew my secret.

But soon the evening of the third day was upon us, and as Dr. Dan had been dead now for a considerable interval, Quaco judg'd it was right to dig him up again and restore him to life, which morbid task we now undertook. There were two ways in which this resurrection could be effect'd, said Quaco, the first being what he had planned, that he would raise him and leave it be, and the second being that we would raise him and yet also enslave his sprit, and make him a *Zombi*, forever bound to do Quaco's bidding. I allow'd it was good to have slaves, yet perhaps this time we might preserve the doctor's liberty, for he had put himself at risk for us. He agreed, though he lamented it was a shame to lose an opportunity of making a Zombi.

Quaco now paused and look'd at the moon and said an interesting thing, namely that in executing his great design he was curing himself, as it were, of slavery. In all the time I knew him, this was the only instant I had any window into his heart.

Our next concern was to dig up the coffin, which we removed to an arbor Quaco had construct'd, & laying the coffin upon the earth we now prised open the lid. Here was Dr. Dan quite awake, for as he said later he had woken up some minutes or hours before, and had nearly stifled, there being hardly enough air in that coffin to sustain a dead person, and certainly not enough for a living one. Waking up in that darkness, said he, was the most terrible thing that had happened to him, and he had been seiz'd by panic, not wanting to dye a second time.

He was yet unable to move so much as the least of his toes, and there was this problem too, that we had driven the end of a nail into his cheek when closing the coffin lid. I regretted this very much, for I felt I had so much else to regret without I should also drive nails into my friends' faces.

Now Quaco produs'd a packet of bonano leaf, which contained his special medicine, and he spread it upon the doctor's gums with two fingers, working this electuary into his mouth with great vigor. Then we lifted him out and stood him up, and Quaco began chanting, & calling down such demons and sprits as he requir'd, & even then to my surprise beating the doctor with a sisal whip. Later Dr. Dan spoke of this moment – recalling the night breeze, & the tossing crowns of the palm trees, & the bite of the whip – & saying this was when he perceived how lovelie it was to be alive again, after being dead.

We had made a narrow trench beneath the arbor and now we layed our friend within, for he still could not move of his own accord. We cover'd him with a sheet, and Quaco placed beside him the skulls of small jungle creatures, and a bonano sucker, and all manner of other things improvised in the moment viz. a stone, a calabash, and a broken candle. Then he broke a water jar over the doctor's head, and crushed wax into his hare, and kicked dirt and sang, and spoke the Lord's Prayer. Lastly he passed a dove over Dr. Dan, which he did in order to absorb the death sprit. It was not well with the dove after this, true enough, and only today do I wonder from where had he produced that dove? (There was more to Quaco than ever I knew, and today I have the sensation that I was but an actor in a story that was properly his own.)

Now Dr. Dan was cured, for when Quaco urg'd him to stand, so he did, a man returned from that undiscovered country, death.

We must now, Quaco said, remove all the coins and set you on your way. Dr. Dan nodd'd. What are these coins you speak of? said he. When he perceived they were Spanish coins he began telling a story, namely that he had once been a sailor on the Flying Dutchman, that lost cruiser from which no one can free himself without he persuades some passing ship to carry a letter for him, and so Dr. Dan had done, by placing his letter in a sack and filling the sack with Spanish coins. We could not make him understand the importance of haste. He returned again and again to this story of the Flying Dutchman, and meanwhile we picked coins off his skin, & removed them from the coffin, & set all to rights again in the grave yard.

Now Dr. Dan said he must be going, for he would be late to an appointment he had made with a fellow to buy some Flanders laces, which he could get at an advantage, & also his shippe would not wait for ever, the Captain General Chris Colombo being an impatient man, and eager to return to Spain and claim his riches, & further, said he, as if the foregoing were not enough, he had also to do one thing more, which was to buy some fish from a young woman he had seen, and this tho he needed no fish, and abhorr'd it if the truth be told. It was only that he wanted very much to speak to this woman, and if he did not, he would regret it all his life.

Now we three friends, met for the last time in a grave yard, were parted at last. Dr. Dan and I took the long road to town, for I knew I must escort him to Kings Harbor, & in any event I desired to escape as well, for I thought I had made a mess of this, my first essay into the world, and required to start again in a new place. I gave Quaco my letter for Mrs. Galsworthy (of whom, however, I shall have one thing more to say) and then we bid him fare-well, I myself knowing I would never see him again until the morning which wakes us to eternal doom.

## 2500

---

One night George Washington and his father, the eminent Senator Washington, came to the palace and partook with us of the evening meal. They brought actors with them, or maybe they were eunuchs, or maybe they were sexual workers. George Washington spoke for many minutes about lizards, and meanwhile his father gazed about with the green face of failure. He had lost his poppy crop to a disease, and his best river lands were rimed with salt, and the MDC had stolen his water. But he vowed that he was going to make an atonement in order to appease the universal forces of providence. He was no longer going to bathe, for example. He would eat twelve date kernels a day and he would eat bread made from sesame husks and ashes. He wasn't going to form any friendships with women or children or poor people. These were traditional abstentions, although I knew my father abhorred them as the superstitions of a primitive mind.

In the midst of the senator's speech, sounds of hurrying footsteps came to us from the hallway, and also a great tumult of banging doors. Then two vice-secretaries of intelligence came running into the room and spoke desperate whispered phrases to my father. Soon the air was chocked full with rumors. It was the MDC sneak-attacking us. It was terrorists from the desert. It was the long-ago overlords of Minnesota. But no, it was only the anticipated shattering of our own social contract. A troupe of the presidential guard had been killed to a man by rioters, and then the rioters had begun to sow flames and mayhem throughout the city.

My father placed his knife and fork on his plate and proceeded across the room and into an office. He comported himself, for all his confusions and his impoverished grasp of realities, in an extremely presidential fashion. But now that we were here, poised at the tipping point, he hardly seemed to exist. He was only another despot in the long march of historical despots, each one so much like all the others, each one the open door through which the angels of chaos came humming on bent wings. I had the strong conviction that history had dreamed of him before he dreamed of himself. And what did that make me? I was a dream engendered by a dream.

My own safety was considered paramount, for I was the essential hope of dynastic continuity, and Daniel Defoe had contrived an escape plan on this basis. Across the street, in the storehouse where our contingency tunnel opened up, there was a wagon and camels and provisions and jars of water. Vice-secretaries would issue from the front gates in their implausible disguises, and the terrorists would mistake them for me, and meanwhile I would steal away unseen in the company of Edward Halloween and Daniel Defoe. It was important, argued Daniel Defoe, that our escape party be minutely inconspicuous. We were supposed to rendezvous with my father in the north, at a place called Winfield.

So now, without a sigh or a waver, we left the room and descended into the tunnel. Christopher Smart walked along behind us, although he looked many times over his shoulder because he didn't want us to think he was following us. He wanted it to look like he only happened to be going in the same direction. It was all an unceremonious and almost unremarked occurrence, and you would never have known that the last hope of the Roulette dynasty had just walked out the back door.

And I never said farewell and good luck to my father, nor in all that confusion of voices and torches and clanking weaponry did I think of doing so, which speaks volumes to the real tenor of our relationship. Instead I thought, Goodbye, George Washington.

We did not go north. We went south. At an unknown moment in the depth of the night, we passed the final ruins at the far southern periphery of St. Louis, and when morning came blushing into the sky, it dawned upon the sweet whistling quiet of an uninhabited world. Here in this suburb, the few abandoned cane huts were creaking away like locusts in the deep shadows. The trees were leafless petitioners who waited now for the spark that would set them spinning away from the earth in flame and ash. I fancied the land was probably choked with salt. It was a vista of final things and final reckonings.

Edward Halloween gazed about and said, "It is funny to me that my first idea is to wonder where I will get my hair barbered in this waste-land. I have softened in the palace."

"I'll barber it myself," said Daniel Defoe. "I was once court barber to the king of Coca-Cola. You'll see now that I am truly in my aliment. If I am a failure in policy and government, I am God's own traveler. I could travel forever."

I squeezed my eyes shut and felt the pitch and roll of the wagon on this old road, which was little more than memories of yet older and older roads. While I pretended to sleep, Daniel Defoe asked if Edward Halloween had ever had occasion to visit Arkansas, but he said no. He had grown up in country poverty outside St. Louis. He had never seen anything.

"Then I will tell you about Arkansas. The capital was a city called Manoa and the governor lived in a mud hut with a beautiful Indian woman named Maria. Is that right? I don't know much about Arkansas. Have I ever told you about Texas? It was a contested Mexican province right across the border from Arkansas, and there was constant strife between the illegal American immigrants and the native Mexicans. The Americans were eight feet tall and they were so fat that they couldn't make love to one another, so they died out in the end and the immigration problem was solved. The Mexicans were only three feet tall, but they were much more cunning and hardworking. It was just another strange border story."

Without opening my eyes, I said, "I know this story. The American immigrants had grown fat from drinking oil, which they pumped out of the ground and carried around in their hats. At the end, when they were dying of this addiction, they had another problem, which is that their cities kept exploding. There was a place called Houston, but it blew up."

"That's correct," said Daniel Defoe. And it was, at least partly. The explosion of Houston was a famous event.

"Right," said Edward Halloween. "And there was a city called Akkad, which was raptured up to heaven. And a city called Venice, which was just underwater tubes and chambers. I can play this game too." But then, with his finger raised in a mocking gesture, he started to laugh, for he had spoken himself into the spirit of it all. "But an underwater city is natural, because humans were originally aquatic animals. We are the primordial creature from which all others evolved, as is evidenced by our not having claws or teeth or hair. Our heads previously served us as floats, which is why they're large and round, like river buoys. They kept us afloat in ancient seas."

"But that's true also," said Daniel Defoe. "All of this is true. And you think you're only joking."

For many days we climbed over the rough lands of the plateau, which was a vast reach of loneliness and crags and rocky mounts that walled off our city from the barbarous jungle regions of the south. Ancient chemicals had rendered it uncultivable and no soul stirred in this drought-struck realm of ripped cloth and traumatized earth and thorn trees and salt palms. I lay in the wagon and felt the palace ennui bleach away like the stripes on Edward Halloween's cotton gown. The night was peopled by thousands of myriads of stars, and the days by broken concrete and colored plastic and the other deserted vestiges of man. We slept packed together in the wagon like sardinia and we ate salted shamo and dried fruits and miracle leaf powder. I repeated to myself, Goodbye, George Washington, like these were the words of a prayer. I also philosophized in detached moments upon the fate of my father, President Roulette of the Reunited States, whom even then I seemed to know as you know the incoherent people in dreams, who look like themselves but are known by the dream consciousness to be someone else.

Then, after ceaseless travels, when the groats for the camels were all exhausted and we ourselves had drunk away the warm and repellent dregs of our water jars, we began to slide down into the slot of the Mississippi, and soon we perceived spreading vegetation once more, and we rejoiced in the tang and savor of living dirt. The rubble of old days, so visible upon the plateau, was here overcovered with bushes and sediments, and the world seemed new. At a dark pool the camels drank themselves bloated and sloshing, like wine bags, and we all rested together, and Christopher Smart devoured a lizard, although he disdained the tail.

There were people in the valley of the Mississippi, but even though my father held nominal suzerainty over them, they were subject only in the schemes of theory. They had made themselves free, as Green the vice-secretary had intimated, but it was less the violent fracture of revolution than the parting of two canoes in the river. It seems that our dominions had shrunk and withered naturally, like fruits on a parched vine. It must have been long ago, during the reign of my hated grandfather, that they achieved their peak of ripeness. So we had no fear of these valley people, who had no way of knowing who we were, and we said, "Hello, friends. How's it swinging?"

I could appreciate that Daniel Defoe had begun to think of his Anna Gloria now that he was once again set at liberty. I could appreciate as well that Edward Halloween was discombobulated by our great change of state, for he had now ceased to be a clown and regressed to the poverty of his origins. As for me, however, I seemed to see it all through a long vista of time. Nothing was surprising to me. The collapse of the Reunited States was like a play I had seen before. I knew how it would proceed. A new king would rise in St. Louis from the cadre of revolutionary leaders, just as my ancestors had risen in their own days, and in time a fresh revolution would come spinning up out of the city to depose him, and then a new king would rise once again, and a fresh revolution, and on and on it would go. Once more and once again, a new Jasmine St. Roulette would slip from the city in the company of a decommissioned clown and an old cat and the man she loved. It would happen forever and always until the syllables of time died away on an empty earth. It was beautiful to think of this. It was a way of thinking that I would not be lost to history after all.

Night after night and day after hot day, the air grew heavier, as it had been heavy once in the old St. Louis of my juvenescence, and the hills began to redound with green fecundity, and vines and creepers, and trees that came ratcheting out of the ground. We perceived small green birds and rotund clouds, which threw splendid shadows on the earth. There were reaches of sickness too, where only one kind of tree thrived and the forest floor was empty of undergrowth, but these poisoned places gave way again to robust growth. In the course of time we had to sell our camels and wagon, which were impractical in the trackless wilderness. We sold them to a one-eyed man named Aveyaneda, who abided alone in the husk of an aeroplane.

The next day we reached the town of Babylon, which Daniel Defoe had vaunted and advertised as our preliminary destination. There were pigs in wallows, and naked people stricken with dog malaria, and the houses lacked walls. It was a poor place indeed for a princess in flight, and this suited me right down into the muddy ground.

And then, to our greatest surprise, Daniel Defoe held up a hand and peered with good humor into a fist of cassava and melon plants, and he said, "Hello, Quaco. There you are. You were hiding from me."

So this was how we came to meet Quaco again, whom we had met before in another world and another time and another context. He was sitting upon a log braiding old plastic fibers to manufacture a rope, and he said with modest inflections, "Oh hello." Then he saw Christopher Smart and said, "Hello, Christopher."

I had some questions for this dark enigma of a sorcerer. I wanted to ask had he really poisoned Anthony Fucking Corvette, and if so, why should such a person as him have felt sympathies for such a person as me? But I quailed in my heart from this brazen inquiry, nor did it matter now, so instead I asked was it true, as Daniel Defoe said, that he had killed the passenger pigeons.

He nodded.

"Tell them the story," said Daniel Defoe.

"I destroyed the pigeons to starve the white man out of America."

"Was it effectual?"

"Many people starved, yes."

"Tell them how you contrived a magic to change the weather," said Daniel Defoe.

"I wanted to make it too hot to grow wheat, because I didn't think the white people would be able to subsist on cassava alone."

"I enjoy cassava," I said.

"But you, dear princess, are not white," said Daniel Defoe.

"Of course I'm white."

"You're toffee-colored. You're beautiful. It stands to raisins you would like cassava."

"Changes in the weather precipitated economic calamities as well," said Quaco. "You will appreciate that I wanted to destroy the material basis of their prosperity."

During the meantime, Edward Halloween was crumpled into himself on a log. I had trouble guessing what he was thinking. There were small children watching us from the bushes and he clapped and shouted and endeavored to put the scare in them.

"Will anyone recognize us?" he said. "Will anyone come to steal us back to the city?"

"These people don't know anything," said Quaco.

"How can we be sure?"

"Quaco will make a magic to wipe their minds clean," said Daniel Defoe. "Won't you, Quaco?"

Quaco sighed. He would do this, yes, but he gave the impression it was tedious for him.


We stayed here in Babylon to recruit our strength. We ate bee maggots and mashed pounded plantain, which Quaco denominated by the term fufu. We anointed ourselves with tarbush resin to keep off the stinging insects and we drew our zest from cassava beer in squash gourds, inaga fruits, avocado, mango, and miniature red breakfast bananas. There was a seasonal rainfall disruption here as well, much lamented by the people of Babylon, but it was not grievous and one soft morning a shower of rain fell. It was all the rain we had seen in two years. I walked around with my legs black with mud, all the way up to the regions that men exalt, and I was happy. It was as Daniel Defoe sometimes said: Comfort was an artifact of the mind's creation. The only genuine comfort was positive thinking.

The truth is we had no fear of capture and torment at the hands of terrorists and revolutionaries. We had passed unnoticed from the realm of the Reunited States, and my father was just an indefinite and unspecified force. The people of Babylon knew no law but the ancient law of human concordance. They ate squirrels and trembled for the fear of superstitions. They believed that leeches were the dead man's revenge against the living and they believed you could be carried to heaven on a bolt of lightning. They believed Jesus and Mary were always watching them. They believed you were required to hunt meat in this life in order to provide yourself with food in the next.

It was an easy primeval life and I might have been happy here, except that Daniel Defoe would not leave off speculating about Anna Gloria. It was a thorn in my mind. He thought she might have been a goddess he knew in the jungle, and he became certain and convinced that she was waiting for him in El Dorado, Arkansas. He said we had to go there and meet her. And this is why I confided my heart once again in Quaco, who had heeded my griefs once before. I asked him had he ever seen this Anna Gloria? Was she real, or was she only allegorical?

"That depends," he said. "What is the difference?"

I waited for a breath and a heartbeat, but he said no more.

"No riddles," I begged him. "I have walked out the back door of my kingdom. I have eaten bee maggots. I feel cold with dog malaria. I only want to know the truth."

His eyes seemed to soften a microscopic amount. He pointed to a puddle at his feet and said, "Look here. What do you see?"

I could envision only my own face waggling in the muck. Then I saw Edward Halloween peep over my shoulder. We were both slimmed away from our weeks of dried shamo and travel.

"That's her," said Edward Halloween, grinning and champing on a banana. He pointed a filthy finger at the puddle. "She's you."

I blinked at my watery visage and suddenly the truth came home to make its roost. "Color me with crayons," I said. "I should have known."

Leave it to Edward Halloween: genius, eunuch, clown, poet. "It's her," he said again, and Quaco smiled.

## 2016

_____

When we got back to Key West, the ancient mariner said he intended to start packing. It was time to go, he said. Time to leave the island. Time to resume his endless fruitless search for Anna Gloria. There was no time to lose.

"Where are my keys?" he said. He patted his pockets and then spotted them on the table. They were enormous, two pounds apiece, three inches long, like keys in a museum exhibit about ancient keys. They were green with oxidation.

"Are you going to tell us what this stuff is?" I said, handling one of the figurines we'd dug up.

"It's probably just ancient junk."

But I couldn't concentrate on the problem of the treasure. Like John Baxter's photograph, it was a mystery with which I felt unable to engage. I could not stop thinking about my green pills, my blue pills, my white pills. It was a genteel way of being a drug addict, but that didn't matter.

"You're so old and you're in such good spirits," I asked him. "What's the secret?"

The ancient mariner said, "Take cinnamon for tonsillitis and remember that you can drink seawater in small quantities if you're extremely dehydrated. When a poison wind like the simoom starts to blow, just go inside and splash water on your face."

"That's not what I mean. I just mean how do you stand it, year after year?"

"All you young people," he said, laughing and fitting one of his keys into an old trunk. "You dudes have got to learn to be less hard on yourselves."

"I've gotta not be a shithead."

"This is what I mean."

"But how do you learn?"

"You get older."

He opened the trunk and pulled out a weathered art object, a wooden panel with an image of Mary and a skinny, hideous baby Jesus.

"I could sell this thing for about a trillion dollars," he said.

He looked around the interior of his boat. There were some silver spoons, an old leather-bound copy of *David Copperfield*, a ginger root that had started to sprout. There was a low wooden table and two orange plastic school chairs. A hammock. There was nothing he seemed to care very much about.

"Are you going right away?" said Azar.

"Soon."

"Will you miss Key West?"

"I expect I'll be back someday."

"Not if it's underwater."

But he wasn't listening. "I'll go to the East Indies. I've always wanted to go back to Goa. For some reason I've always been fixated on the East Indies. It's like I have some unfinished business out there."

"It might be dangerous out there now."

"Do you think I lived this long by getting myself killed all the time? I know how to survive."

Quaco said he wasn't going to leave until the water was at his door. It was surprising to hear him say he had a door.

"By then it'll be too late, though," I said.

"Too late for what?"

"Too late in general. Climate change will destroy everything. It will destroy the material foundation of our prosperity."

Quaco grinned. There was an energy in the air. I hadn't seen him smile before.

"The material foundation of *your* prosperity," he said.

Eventually, the ancient mariner went to sleep and Quaco wandered away. We were too worked up to go to sleep ourselves, so I called Lena and asked if she and Bee wanted to meet us somewhere. Bee was working, she said, but she would come herself. She hoped it was okay if she brought her brother along. He was going to rehab in the morning and she had to look after him until then. She had to make sure he didn't get away. She permitted herself this candor because I'd been so straightforward about my green pills.

We went to a place called the Blue Macaw. We waited for Lena and watched a basketball game. We didn't know what to say.

"Was the treasure hunt a success or a failure?" Azar said.

"I think it was both."

"What is that stuff? What's happening here? What if this man is five hundred and sixty years old?"

"I don't know. Somehow it's hard to think about."

He ate some peanuts and frowned and looked around. "Here we are," he said, "in the United States of America."

"But we can't lose focus on account of that."

"It's almost like a letdown. Is that crazy? I was really hoping they'd find those coins."

There were tourists buzzing all around us. There was a man smoking a cigarette and breathing oxygen through a tube. There were strangler figs and old mahogany trees. There were palm trees clattering in the breeze, like always. We were tourists ourselves. We were in the United States of America, and the world was getting hotter and hotter and more and more crowded.

"Can you carbon-date a person?" said Azar.

"You can't carbon-date a living thing."

"I guess that would be the cynic's way out anyway." He ate some more peanuts. "I meant to tell you, I remembered a thing from Kierkegaard about irony and sincerity."

"You're going to quote Kierkegaard? That doesn't seem fair."

"I can't quote it, but the gist of it is that irony and sincerity aren't incompatible. He's kind of down on pure sincerity, as I remember."

We were quiet again for a little while.

"I think what I'm struggling with is the everydayness of it," I said. "You know what I mean? The everydayness of the ancient mariner. But this is how these things go. Think about cell phones, for instance."

"I think about them all the time."

"A cell phone is a piece of glowing glass in which you can see all the information in the world. It should be a magical thing, but instead I hate my cell phone."

"Yes. Because it's a part of life. It's not magic."

"It's a part of life and it's implicated in life's troubles. It's a portal through which bad news might come. The only magical things are the things that don't exist."

"The ancient mariner exists," said Azar, "so it becomes impossible to say that some aspect of him is magical. Nothing that exists can be magic. Cell phones are magic right up until the moment you can buy one in a store."

This was why we could not persist in being amazed by the things we'd seen. John Baxter's photograph, the treasure map on the wall, the treasure itself. Life was still just life. Peanuts and warm air and a pill hangover. And it occurred to me that even if the ancient mariner were as old as he said he was, even if he really had done such miraculous things, still his life would have been just like this, just like our lives, cluttered with the trash of daily experience. Even on all those big historic expeditions, his main concerns would have been how cold his hands were and what he was going to eat when his watch rotated below. He'd worry about a dream he'd had and he'd tell himself he had to patch his pants. There would be no magic in any of it. The magic was what he invented, and it didn't matter if he was seventy or seven hundred.

"What's magical about the ancient mariner are his lies," I said.

And for a moment, I thought that I almost understood something. I could almost say what it was. But then Lena arrived and interrupted my train of thought, and that was important too, another kind of lesson. Real life was all about interruptions.

"This is my brother," she said, jerking her thumb at the tall, handsome man bouncing on his heels behind her. "This is Ben."

Ben grinned. I'd imagined a furtive creeping person with wild eyes. Instead he was impressive and substantial. Immediately I had the sense that he was a major character.

"Don't miss the haunted pub crawl!" he said. "Meet me at the south end of Duval at ten tomorrow night! Only way to meet the ghosts of old Key West! Brochures available on every corner!"

Lena hung her head and rubbed her eyes. Ben laughed. He said, "I feel like a million Confederate bucks. How do ya'll feel?"

"So, Ben," said Azar. "What do you do?"

"As I was saying, tour guide. We're all tour guides. Destitution or tour guide are the only options for long-term Key West residents."

He had all the important characteristics. Forceful gestures, a winning smile, a tragic flaw.

"Sorry about this," said Lena. "We should've stayed home. I don't know what I was thinking bringing him to a bar. It's been a long day."

"Us too," said Azar.

"Not like my day."

"It's rehab in the morning," Ben explained.

Azar nodded briskly, as if rehab were a subject on which he was a great expert. I worried that he was going to mention my own drug problem, but instead he asked, "What are you going for?"

"No reason."

"Those painkiller patches," said Lena. "Alcohol. Things you can smoke. Who the hell knows? Craziness."

"Et fucking cetera," said Ben.

I tried to explain what the ancient mariner had said about pirates. That they lived on borrowed time. That eventually, one morning, there was an accounting.

"On what morning is there not an accounting?" said Ben.

Lena started to cry, but she stopped as quickly as she'd started. Azar was looking at me and I knew he was thinking that for me too there would be an accounting one day.

"So let's all just have a drink and try to forget about this," Ben said. "Like pirates."

Azar shook his head. "Not on our watch, my man."

And then I thought again about the ancient mariner. More particularly I thought how incredible it was that we weren't talking about him. We weren't talking about Quaco either. We weren't talking about the buried treasure, whatever it was.

Now Ben was delivering a speech about LeBron James. Azar was laughing. The man with the cigarette and the oxygen tank was laughing too.

Lena said, "Shit. I shouldn't have come. I just wanted to say hi."

"I'm glad you came," I said.

"It's embarrassing."

"Once I overdosed on headache medication that I'd stolen from my aunt. It was two days before Christmas and my little cousin found me stumbling around the kitchen. Everyone else was out shopping or something. My cousin was only nine."

"That's not so much embarrassing as really horrible."

"Well," I said, looking at Ben, "I'm sure this is really more horrible for you than it is embarrassing."

"It's just hard to think it's me and my own brother in this situation. It's a thing you hear about or see on TV. It's very surprising to have to live it. He was a nice kid. Everyone liked him."

"Everyone likes him now."

"There's nothing to like. He's no one. Talk about cynicism. He's a nihilist drug addict."

But everybody did like him. I liked him. Now he was talking about facial hair. He said, "A beard occurs incidentally, over time, like the Grand Canyon. A mustache is a contrived object, like Michelangelo's David." It sounded like something Azar or I might have said, but it sounded better when Ben said it.

Lena was going to take him to a rehab in Boca Raton. She was planning to leave at three in the morning so she could be there when the office opened. There was no one else to take him and she was worried he wouldn't agree to go. I said that he was being very agreeable so far, but I said it just to say it. I knew very well that it wouldn't last. I knew how these things worked. I myself felt very sharp, but just yesterday I'd taken so many green pills that I couldn't remember going to sleep.

"I'm just wandering around with him," she said. "I can't go to sleep because he'll run off, so it's just more of this for the next few hours."

I didn't know what to say. I said, "Would it cheer you up to know that Isaac Newton calculated that the world will end in 2060?"

"Yes."

"He also thought Jesus had come down to earth to operate the levers of gravity."

## 1560

---

We are an army of dead men and one Pirahao girl named Maria, which is not a Pirahao name. We tell stories about a man named God, who lives in the sky. We tell stories about his son, Hiso, whose sorrow is that he must live in the sky with his father, who hates him just as he hates everything in the world. But Hiso loves the world as much as his father hates it, and he especially loves his mother, who is called Maria, just as I am. We tell these stories and the Pirahao listen carefully and they understand that they are stories about me. Why else would we be telling them? I am Maria, mother of Hiso.

This is how I become a god. It happens because I have no home in the world, because no language is my true language, because I am lost in the spaces between what can be said and thought.

"You deserve some congratulations," says Daniel de Fo. "It is not an easy trick to become a god. Once I was the god of Amahamagupta, but it was only a very small island and my only power was to make coconuts grow. I think they'd have grown anyway. It is better to be the god of America."

There can be no god of Anaquitos because there are no gods in Anaquitos, but Anaquitos is not here anymore. I am the god of El Dorado. The Pirahao accept this. Every Pirahao changes her name many times over the course of her life. It is no trouble to change the name of the city.

But they have never known a god before, and Daniel de Fo must explain how they should behave. He tells them to bring me gifts. Gold. Pearls. But they do not have gold or pearls. He tells them to pray to me, but they have no prayers. He tries to explain how a god differs from a person.

"A god is like a person disappearing around a bend in a river. A god is what doesn't exist. A god is what isn't here anymore."

They accept that they must try to change the way they think. They accept that I am a creature of a different kind, from a different place, who must be treated in a different way. The danger of the Christians is obvious to them.

By now Miguel Oreja is very angry at me. He tells me that he knew I was a witch all along. He has seen me speaking with vultures. He has seen me eating iguana eggs. He has heard me speak the languages of dreams. I explain that there are no dreams, there are only the things we do when we're asleep, but he takes this to mean that I'm abroad in the night casting spells. He has grown fat with xaxa meat and miserable with the indifference of the Pirahao, who say they embrace Christianity but give no sign of their faith. He says I have bewitched him. He says he will destroy the city after all. I tell him he should hurry or it will destroy itself.

Just as Daniel de Fo must teach the Pirahao to worship me, so he must teach me to behave like a god. There are customs and manners, just as there are for people.

"What are the characteristics of a god?" he says in Spanish. "They never apologize."

"There are no apologies in Pirahao."

"They love nice clothes," he says. "They are forgetful. They never die."

"You're describing yourself."

He laughs, haha, but then he says, "Gods don't make jokes. Try to remember."

I have cut the bottom of my dress off, so it only reaches my navel, and I wear a strip of cotton below, and this is the costume of the god of El Dorado. It drives the Christians mad. There is no beauty like the beauty of a god.

But they are mad already. They wander aimlessly through the city. They are the disease, but the disease is not the plague. The disease is the future. The disease is time. The disease is a way of thinking. It doesn't kill anyone yet, but it kills things. It begins to kill the world.

The hills fall away in the rain and trees consume the mounds at the edges of the city. A person does not need to be a god to see what's happening.

And in the end the Pirahao cannot learn to see what the Christians see. They try very hard but they have lived in this place where there is no way to mark time, and the only colors are the colors of things, and it is not proper to mourn longer than a change of the moon. I am the god of this place, but I am no more real to them than time is real. I am the thing that vanishes around the bend in the river.

So they live as they always have. They live for the day in which they live. Instead of saying goodnight, they say I'm going. They talk all the time. They talk to no one. They talk about things they're doing and thinking. I will have some fish today. I will walk in the sun. Xohoi is bringing me a toucan. When they go to void themselves in the river, they shout with joy and enthusiasm. I am an anaconda. I am a jaguar. The plague has left the city many times larger than it should be. The city is full of people who aren't here anymore. Everyone has lost the person she loves most. It isn't proper to speak of this. Those who remain stand in the river and say I am an anaconda, I am a jaguar.

And then it is time for Daniel de Fo to leave. He must search for Anna Gloria. It is a search that will never end, because she is herself a god, she is what does not exist, and the language in which her true name can be spoken has not yet been spoken by anyone.

I make him a present of clay figurines, amulets, carved bone. These are not Pirahao objects. They are things taken in tribute long before and then forgotten. There is no gold for the alcalde of Santa Inés, poor man.

"I want to say goodbye but I know I'll see you again," he says.

"Say I'm going. Don't say goodbye."

"I'll see you in Vinland. On Saint Brendan's island. I'll see you in Zanzibar." He laughs, haha. "We'll go to El Dorado together. You'll have your vengeance and I'll have my woman. We have all the time in the world, but let's hope it doesn't take that long."

And he does leave. And then whores murder three of the Christians.

And then the Christians leave and the rest of them are murdered in the forest by the Omagua. But this is only what happens.

It is not easier to be a god than it is to be an Indian, a Pirahao, a slave, a whore, a Christian, but it's easier to be a god than it is to be nothing. For now, and there is only now, for now I am a god and that is what happens. That is the truth.

## 2200

---

Now Old Dan were telling me about El Dorado. It were a great city of course like all cities in the past. In fact Anakitos were only a suburb of this great place or so he recalled. They had cashew beer plus fast food plus movies televisions streamy media rollercoasters. It were there he saw Anna Gloria once but he didn't realize it were her until much too late.

We was now at last digging for our treasure on a little slope of rising ground outside Saint Augustine. It were funny to me I had objected to digging up this treasure. How could I of thought I did not want treasure.

Old Dan also told me of old Spanish Florida and Saint Brendan before its name were changed to Saint Augustine. He told me that in Castiyo San Marcos they had got a tide-operated latrine. He told me he were a dentist then. Later he were not Spanish at all but British. It were hard to keep track.

We dug one hole and another but we did not find the treasure. We sweated and sweated. My beard itches I said does your beard itch. Of course said Old Dan for it is about a million degrees out here. I wondered if Christopher the kitten was itching. Maybe he was but he were also playing at killing a lizard.

I asked Old Dan how old he was really and what was his secret. Are you a vampire I asked remember it is not Peaches asking you. I am no vampire he said you would not mistake a man for a vampire they have long teeth plus white faces. What is your secret of eternal life then I said. I don't know he said it is just that I have not died. You said probiotic I reminded him. It is not that he said. Have you age very slowly I said or were you young for many years then suddenly old. Interesting he said interesting question. What is the answer I said. The answer he said well I don't remember. I don't believe you I said. It is true he said when you get old you won't remember how it happened neither. I will not live to be old I said nobody does no more. You will he said you will shrink you will grow white hair all the trimmings of age you will be so much happier you won't be a sad young man anymore. I am not sad no more anyway I said I think I am cured. Wow he said that's good. Yes I said. But what about Anna Gloria I said. She also is very old he said though not as old as me she is fifty years younger I think. You like them young I said. Oh haha said Old Dan yes I like them young give me a young lady 700 years old.

Next we paused we were quiet for a time we were thinking. But where is she I said. I don't know he said. How do you know she is called Anna Gloria I said. Good question he said.

Then he looked around he examined the trees he looked down at his feet. Here it is he said the treasure is right here. Oh sure I said oh sure haha. I no longer believed we would find it but who cares I were happy anyway I were king of the Independent States of Jam. It is here he said again. I dug a little bit laughing saying it is all just looking for a grain of sand on the beach isn't it. No he said it is here stand back. He stooped down groaning saying my back my back and then he scrabbled around in the sand and pulled out a plastic box. Oh I said. Inside was some plastic bags and inside these bags was gold coins. Wow I said amazing incredible wow wow it is treasure. But Old Dan was not so impressed. He looked underneath the bags of coins he scrabbled around in the dirt some more. Interesting he said do you know something this isn't it. What I said. This isn't the treasure of Anakitos he said. Yes it is I said it is gold coins what could be a more iconic treasure. He were frowning he were very disappointed. I think I see what happened he said. Old Dan I said you are not getting it this is treasure this is gold coins we are rich. He did not hear me. I think I see what happened he said for this is the treasure which I robbed off that Turk and his friend which was bigshot movie producers.

It didn't have no way to explain things to him. We was rich now we could have anything. Don't you get it I said. I get it he said I am just thinking. We can do anything I said what will we do. Yes he said. Cheer up I said. Sorry he said yes it is treasure I see that now. What will we do I said. I don't know he said I guess we could be pirates. Haha I said. I am not joking he said I were a pirate once I were just like Saint Francis Drake. Okay I said. I might just be a pirate again he said what's the difference. You are unhappy I said. It is just one treasure after another he said and never the one I want. I didn't say nothing but of course I knew he were talking about Anna Gloria.

Next we walked back to Saint Augustine. He cheered up on the way whereafter he said let us have a lavish meal to celebrate our findings. We went to a restaurant I ate some iguana meat with sauce and bread and Old Dan he sniffed flowers for his nutrients he were like a bug. After my iguana I crunched fruit drops. We had the treasure with us under the table just a old box no one would of guessed what it was. Christopher the kitten was guarding it and eating egg. Meanwhile I had a great joy in my spirit but it was not what you think. It was because now that we had the treasure and we could do whatever we wanted I knew I just wanted to do all the same things. I wanted to find more treasures. I wanted to help Old Dan find Anna Gloria and also I wanted to find my own Anna Gloria if I could. This discovery were another kind of treasure in addition to the fabulous wealth of the gold coins.

Saint Augustine were built up back from the water but it had a old part which were drowned. After we had ate we went down there to the water lapping at the broken stone crushed cement dead buildings dead cars plus lizards in the ruins. They should clean this place up I said no sense in leaving all this garbage here they should secede from the ruins of old times. We was quiet for a while now the sun setting at our backs. I saw that the mangos was radiant in the trees. But even though I had got a change of attitude I still wanted to know what had happened. How did the world get so fucked I said why didn't they stop it people are smart why didn't they think of something. Oh well said Old Dan haha they just did not manage to do it in time they couldn't turn it around. But they tried to fix it I said. Oh yes he said but I remember a fellow once who told me it were all just ecknomicks it were too expensive to save the world it were cheaper to destroy it. That doesn't sound right I said that's crazy. Well he said anyway later they did try to fix it with the carbon tax tide power sustainable divestment ecksekera. But it didn't work I said. No he said. Oh well I said breathing the sea smell it doesn't matter now. No he said that's the one truth of everything it is that someday soon it doesn't matter.

While we was standing there we met Hwan once more who had told me about the great wall of Florida. He were joined by his brothers they was all going out to sleep on their boat. His brothers was Hose and Gabriel. Hose I said that is your name. Hose he said. Hose I said. Hose he said. Hose said Old Dan. All around we all said Hose including Hose himself who were just repeating his own name. Finally when this comedy were done they said they was shipping out for Savannah next day and would we join them. Maybe I said. Maybe said Old Dan. It were not a sincere offer I don't think. Then they three walked out on the rubble pier to get in their canoe which would take them out past the bar where their boat was anchored.

Old Dan and Christopher and I we all watched them some time longer. I had got a chunk of pineapple and I were chewing it up with the juice running down my chest. We could do anything. We could rent rooms at the grand motel or buy fine linens or air condition or anything. We had treasure. It did not have to change us but it could if we wanted it to.

Then I said to Old Dan we will find her we will find Anna Gloria. Oh sure he said. I mean it I said we will find her you have got to think positive. Now you're the one telling me he said the helper has become a helper. We will find her I said it is logical to think so for we found those improbable coins after all. I hope you're right he said for if the truth be told I am lonely. We will find her I said and in the meantime we can be pirates we can rob Hwan Hose Gabriel we can steal their boat. Haha said Old Dan. It were a joke but we could do it too for we could do whatever we wanted. It were a amazing thought. It had been true all along but I never did understand it until now.

It had a soft pretty sunset out behind us over the swamp. It had pink waves in the bay. Quietly and privately I now decreed how from this moment it were illegal not to watch the sunset in the Independent States of Jam. That were the first law I made as king. Then I decreed it were illegal not to eat pineapple if it were available. Amazing how I had never tasted pineapple until this trip. I had never known there was such a superior fruit. And it were also amazing how I had never thought before of seceding from all the things that made me angry and sad. It had so many amazing things out here. Who cares about trash ruins whatever. My life were just beginning even though it were the end of the world.

## 1750

Dr. Dan grew stronger with each step, and by morning he said he felt a new man, and young once more. In Kings Harbor, thronged that day with market women selling plantain and mawbee and a farrago of other vendibles, we hired an open boat and traveled to the island of Great Heron Cay, where a pyrate or smuggler or some such agreed to carry us to Boston. Dr. Dan said those New Englanders would care nothing for our looks and dirty cloathes, so long as our money was good.

But our adventures were not yet at an end, dear Reader. No sooner had we set out upon the Bahama channel than our ship was blown westerward by an adverse gale and wreck'd upon a Florida beach. Dr. Dan and I were, so far as we knew, the sole survivors, for sailors as a rule do not know how to swim, yet we did recover one of our trunks (in which we had placed one half of the coins), or Dr. Dan did, salvaging it by the miraculous artifice of floating upon a spar, and fishing it inshore with a small anchor.

So we were cast up like Crusoe upon this cape, which formed the very extremity, indeed what a vulgar man might call the penous, of America. I learned it was not the first time Dr. Dan had been wrecked in that place, and in the lingering confusion of his false death he mistook the year, or the centurie, talking all this while about things which had long since passed away. When I had managed to call a halt to this wild disquisition he apologized, saying that imagination and memory were all confounded one with the other, and assuring me that he knew where he was, for it was the year 1870 or near enough, was it not? And not wanting to add to his embarrassment I said this was near enough indeed, for no greater accuracy was requir'd, not by one such as me, certainly, nor here upon this lonelie island. I then asked him to tell me the story of his first

Florida shipwreck, for we had no thing in such abundance as we had time, except if it be sea shells, of which we had a great number.

It was many years ago, said he,

upon some islands off the southerly part of this cape. They were covered in bones, in consideration of which I named one Cayo Hueso, and not far from there I buried the treasure of El Dorado, from which I had lately come. It was El Dorado in the Popish tong but in the Indian it was Memphis, I believe, or Achem, or Paniau, or Akkad, who can say after so many years. Have I not already spoken to you of this city? I do not remember, yet I remember very well the look and indeed the scent of that city in the deep forest, the scent of lemon and coriander, and of mint, unless I am thinking of another place, and not Achem at all, or Paniau.

I wanted to tell him what a fool I was, and receive a kind of absolution from him if he would give it, yet I said nothing. Instead I asked him was it there in that city where he had known the queen of America.

It was, said he,

Maria Yako was her name, unless I am thinking of two queens, one called Maria and the other Yako. In truth I don't know, but whoever she was, she was very beautiful, for she looked as if she had ridden down from Heaven upon the white horse. In fact the conquest of Paniau, or El Dorado, was undertaken for the love and lewd desires that all men had for her, and not for riches at all. I thought for some time she was Anna Gloria after all, but I think I was mistaken, as I was mistaken this time also. She was only herself, just as you are, and me.

Thinking upon these times, and recalling his life among the Spaynards, those Popish villains, Dr. Dan now became frightened, suddenly recalling that we were ourselves in Spanish territorie, and that it would go ill with us were a Spanish ship to happen by. Now he began to scrabble about in the sand, saying we must bury our remaining gold, for we could not run the risk of losing this half of the treasure as well. I did not argue with him, saying only give me my own share so I am fixed, & then helping him to bury the rest, for in his scrabbling and digging he was most ineffectual.

When a shippe did at last come, which happened only after a period of *one week* — which week was a restful time after our struggles, though we had none but sea snail to eat — it was a British vessel out of New Providence. They gave us rum and salt beef and biscuit, and a better feast I never had, but in the morning we woke to find the ship under way, carrying us farther each moment from those buried coins. Thus Dr. Dan announced he would leave the shippe and travel south again to retrieve them. I did not like to hear this, for I was frightened to go north alone. I offered to let him keep my own share, and in truth I begged him, but he would not do it. He left the ship at Charles Town, and I proceeded to Boston, where I was to make a new life for myself, and live faithfully as a mulatto, which is what I am, for I had learned at least this one Thing, namely that it was easier to be what I was, than what I was not.

I was most affected by my parting from Dr. Dan, and I ne'er knew what was come of him, nor whether he found the coins again, except that one way or the other, two years after these events, he did hire an agent to spring the false Anna Gloria from her indenture. How should I have come to know this? I will tell it now, for it is an easy thing to tell.

As I put a period to this chapter and this story, the smells of a rasp-berrie cake drift thro the house to my study, which gives upon the garden, all in flower now it is the summer season, and who is it you ask that waits to dine with me tonight, but Mrs. Galsworthy herself, or I should say the former Mrs. Galsworthy, now Mrs. Green (for Green I still am). She is my bride, my own Anna Gloria, and the balm and repose of my life. Quaco delivered my letter, and she wrote me one herself, with the result that when Mr. Galsworthy went to his reward some short time later, she came to Boston and sought me out. Thus after our trials and amazing surprises we have braided up our lives together, which ending, says our Son the scholar, makes my story a comedy despite its dark tones.

---

One morning we bade our farewells to Quaco and walked south out of Babylon toward El Dorado, Arkansas, where Daniel Defoe thought he would realize the aetherial dream of his reunion with Anna Gloria. Meanwhile I knew that Anna Gloria was there beside him on the paths and byways, but for now, in an unwanted timidity of spirit, and also in my feeling for the sensitivities of the heart, I could not conceive how to reveal this to him. One day I attempted indirect revelation by asking what he himself saw in the oracular puddles of the forest.

"There's us," he said, "and there's some worms and water bears. Probably nematodes in there as well. All manner of invisible plankton. The world of the microcosmos is actually bigger than ours. It is the paradox of perspective."

After this I held on to my tongue and we penetrated southward. Initially we stayed away from the river, in case there was anyone looking for us. Whenever we saw jungle people, which was not very often, Daniel Defoe cried out to them in a language called Pirahao, which he said was the language of El Dorado, but it turned out to be a purely historical language and there were none who understood it. Most of the time we just marched along in our own contemplations. We slept in palm thatch contrivances of Daniel Defoe's personal design, and I chewed upon lemongrass, and Christopher Smart was happy as a clam in milk, apparently accustomed to forest travel. Edward Halloween wore a look of stricken vexation because now, as we walked, he was composing a novel about St. Louis. To me it seemed right and proper that history should be spun away like this and condensed to a poetic echo in a eunuch's mind. I also appreciated that he did not goad me about revealing myself to Daniel Defoe, although at times he was rattled up with the expectation of it.

The vestiges of imperial grandeur lay all around us. They were covered over by the forest or else, in places where chemicals rendered the landscape poisonous, they bared themselves in crests of cement and ejected bits of plastic. Truly it was a incitement to meditation. One night I lay in our shelter while outside, by the fire, Edward Halloween was trying to make Daniel Defoe tell him how it happened that the international technological human world had fallen into collapse.

"Oh," said Daniel Defoe, "well, you see, it waned away back into the riot of nature from which it came. I saw both the coming and the going."

"But how did it wane away?" said Edward Halloween. "Why did it happen?"

"I can explain by the rivet hypothesis. If you melt all your rivets by flying too close to the sun, your spaceship will fall out of the sky. Do you understand?"

Edward Halloween said that he did not understand.

"Or think of it this way. There used to be a creature called the barnacle goose, which reproduced in two different ways. First, it could be produced from a scum that developed on fir timber tossing in the waves. The baby bird hung from the timber until it was coated with feathers, at which time it flew away. But it could also be produced when the droppings of a mature goose fell into the water from a high cliff. The droppings became barnacles, and the new geese hatched out of these barnacles in the spring and burst through the waves. Now, consider this effect: If you have climate warming, the water becomes corrosive, as everyone knows. This melts the barnacles before they can turn into geese, and it melts the feathers on the baby birds that grow on driftwood. You might not see the connection between warm water and the destruction of geese, but this anecdote shows how everything was connected. That is what I mean by rivets. All the rivets melt, but only when the final rivet melts does the spaceship fall out of the sky."

I stretched out on my reed mat, which was placed for comfort on a soft tinder of leaves, and his voice sang on into the booming brightness of the night. I had a great feeling for these tangled connections, which were the real substance of the world, and Edward Halloween appeared to feel the same way. He said, "That is a beautiful story. That is the true apocalyptic poetry."

When we had passed even from the nominal dominions of the Reunited States, we crept our way closer to the inhabited country of the riverbanks, a bustling but unincorporated territory, and here Daniel Defoe traded a bag of nuts and a hunting knife for a canoe. It was made from one hemisphere of a tree, burned and hollowed out by eager hands. Our velocity was much quicker after this.

I promised myself I would tell Daniel Defoe the truth when we arrived in the vicinity of El Dorado, but one day, judging by the inquiries we made of river people, we did arrive there, and I quailed from telling him. We walked inland upon the slender neck of the path and he began to hunt for this old fabled town, but even though Edward Halloween continually gave me encouragements, and even though he prophesied to Daniel Defoe that Anna Gloria would manifest herself very soon, I could not find a way to tell him.

Daniel Defoe was meanwhile excited to show us El Dorado, which he remembered with fondness and longing. "But if we see the goddess or queen," he said, "I'll do the talking. She is not so scary when you get to know her."

"In Babylon you said this goddess was Anna Gloria herself," I said.

Edward Halloween gave me a significant look, but I ignored him. Daniel Defoe said, "Did I? I don't think so."

In any case, we could not find any town. We might have been traipsing through El Dorado but simultaneously we were also lost in the untenanted wilderness, for El Dorado wasn't in El Dorado anymore.

"Where is it?" said Daniel Defoe. "Where are the earthworks and the round white houses and all the places to get rat meat? But this is the main feature of El Dorado. It is hard to find."

Eventually we induced him to leave this place, which he did in a mood of great disappointment, and I didn't tell him then, not even then. Instead we went down to the Delta Bay to look for a barge, for now Daniel Defoe had seen enough of these lands. He wanted to pole away upon the pillowy swells of the sea.

"But you have to tell him," said Edward Halloween. "This man is deranged by longing and his dream is before him plain as day. You have to tell him as a mercy."

"My tongue is tied. You have to distract my mind. Tell me a chapter of your new novel. What is it a novel of?"

"It is a story of doomed cities. St. Louis and Akkad and New York and El Dorado. But listen, my friend, it is also a story about an ageless sojourner and a president's daughter. Better that you tell it to yourself." And now he smiled. "Better that you tell it to him."

"Yes," I said. "That is what I should do."

"That is what you should do."

He gave me his thumbs-up, but I perceived that he was thoughtful. I said, "Is there a clown in your story also?"

"There is. And then he is not a clown any longer, and what is he?"

"He is only himself."

"Yes. But I don't understand what happens to him then. Does he cross the river into the other country and become a millennial wanderer himself? Does he return to Babylon, where a sorcerer teaches him to speak to gods? What is the ending of this story?"

I could not think of an ending. No ending existed. But Edward Halloween was not saddened or melancholic and all he did now was heft a nice laugh into the green trees and kiss me on the hand. I felt a great love for my dearest oldest friend, and I found that I could almost have cried with emotion if I had been that kind of person, which I am not.

"Or maybe the story does not tell what he becomes," he said. "It is enough that the clown has ceased to be a clown."

That afternoon I walked with Daniel Defoe and Christopher Smart across the scree of uneven ruined ground to the Delta Bay itself, which was not a bay like I'd visioned in my dreams of oceans but instead a jellyfish wallow full of palm islands and cutgrass. It went on and on interminably and it was shallow enough to slop across on foot. But the magical thing was that it was full of very many birds, two hundred at least, or three hundred.

"Interesting," said Daniel Defoe. "The wading birds are coming back. This raises the question of where they've been."

He told me that once, many years before, so many years he could hardly count so high any longer, he endured a shipwreck upon an island in the south of the Delta Bay, where the water ran deep and blue. This island was constructed from the bones and shells of sea creatures. He was marooned with a young man named Jam, who was a filmmaker, and together they excavated some gold ingots he had buried after an utterly different shipwreck, centuries previous, in the very same place.

"Do you know what a filmmaker is?" he said.

I did, or at least, as with so many things that used to exist, I knew and I did not know. But I said nothing. I was watching for my chance.

"We dug up the treasure and I was going to use it to buy Anna Gloria out of everlasting bondage and servitude. She was enslaved on a caffeine plantation in the island of Brasil. The problem was that I couldn't go back to Brasil right away because I was a wanted man in those regions. I was the pirate Blackeye. Jam was rescued one day but I had to stay behind, to wait for my piratical statute of limitations. Then one day I took a nap and I slept for fifty years. When I woke up I had learned to speak to the parakeets, who had many interesting things to say, but I knew I'd slept too long. I knew Anna Gloria would have given up on me by then."

Thus he talked and talked and it may be he was anxious, feeling that an event of true moment would soon crowd upon him. He said he had gone back to Spain eventually, where at last they had forgotten he was a Jew, and there he lived in a town in La Mancha.

I swallowed a big breath and turned to him with a gentle look, and I said, "But now let me tell you a story."

"The storytellee is become the storyteller. Very good."

"It's a story about an eternal millennial wanderer."

"Aha!" he said.

"A long time ago, in a time beyond memory, he was taken by slave traders and sold to a king. This king lived at the edge of the desert in the ruined city of St. Louis, a city of camels and scorched weeds, and there he worshipped the vanished gods of America."

"I know this story."

"You do not. Listen. Then the rain ceased to fall. The sorghum became poisonous. Thomason Jeffers perpetrated a revolution. Our protagonist watched these disasters from the stables in the royal compound, where his only associates were a clown and a cat and a princess. All this while he dreamed of slipping away and going in search of Anna Gloria, his fiancée, whom he had met in a dream. It was not until much later, in the loneliness of the southern wilds, upon the shores of a fetid estuarial region, that he realized his mistake: The princess of St. Louis was Anna Gloria herself, the object of his eternal search."

Then I was quiet. He too was quiet, with an expression I had never before seen upon his face. The air was cool and the birds were standing with their necks cocked and straining. Christopher Smart watched them with the greatest attention imaginable. It was the season of short days and there was only a gentle wind of solar particles coming from the low sun. Now that I'd said what I had to say, I felt calm.

"I like this story," he said.

"I hoped you would."

Then he started to laugh. "You let me tell all my stories, and for this whole time you knew the ending!"

"Oh no, my friend. It's only recently that I thought of it."

He shook his head. He laughed again. He caught me up in his sinewy arms and sighed into my bosoms. "I'm as perceptive as an eggshell. I'm always the last one to figure it out."

## 2016

The ancient mariner was leaving Key West, as he had left so many other places at so many other times, or so he said. He was overwhelmingly cheerful about the prospect of travel. He said that he did not like to remain in one place, and he couldn't understand why he'd stayed here so long. Azar, however, was planning to go with him. He intended to finish the documentary, to learn something, to prolong this moment with the ancient mariner, whoever he was. I was amazed. Azar had made a real resolution, like an adult.

Quaco reappeared around noon and Azar filmed him while he chanted and burned some leaves in the kitchen shed. The ancient mariner talked about all the places he'd been and all the places he still had to go. He talked about Anna Gloria. He waved his arms and threw stuff into his trunk.

But I thought only about Lena. I was trying to attend as well as I could to this bizarre scene, which seemed in some empirical way like the most interesting thing that would ever happen to me, but I thought only about Lena and in the late afternoon I left them to their chanting and packing and filmmaking and went to see her at her house. This was a kind of resolution as well.

She had taken Ben to rehab, as promised. Now she was sitting on the porch in a state of emotional dissolution. It was a tiny white bungalow with peeling Bahama-blue trim. There was a tire on the porch and a deflated basketball and an old cooler with no lid. There were areca palms in the yard and a huge mound of bougainvillea where the fence had been. It reminded me of the future. It was a tropical ruin. She lived there with her brother and her dad, but her dad had gone somewhere, Idaho or Iowa, and now her brother was gone too.

"Don't tell me," she said. "You love the house. You love that it's *small*. A tropical bungalow and all of that."

"Yes."

"But try growing up here with those guys. It's a shitty house."

"It's not. It's a tropical bungalow. I love that it's small."

"Very funny. The truth is you can only be happy here if you know there's somewhere better in your future. Only if you *choose* to live like this."

We sat watching an old lady push her clothes to the Laundromat in a green shopping cart. It wasn't the right shade of green, but it reminded me of my pills anyway.

"I didn't really understand about your brother," I said. "I took so many pills the other day. I kept talking about it. I didn't mean to make light of it."

"It's okay."

"But it isn't. It's a bad problem. I've gotten myself into a bad spot."

"Yes," she said. "You're fucked." But she said it sweetly. She patted my arm.

"Maybe one day I'll have a great revelation and I'll be saved."

"You said it."

"I mean maybe one day I'll snap out of it."

"I hear you. It could happen."

And it could. It was possible. It was possible to envision a scenario in which I was okay, in which I did not take pills or sweat with fear, in which I did some mild kind of work and loved this lovely woman. It was a stretch but I could imagine it.

Lena had a bottle of vodka under her chair. She took a little sip and her eyes watered. She drank like someone who didn't drink.

"It's not good to drink vodka after you take your brother to rehab," she said, "but the other way of looking at it is, when are you more justified?"

The bougainvillea was just as good as everyone said it was. The sky was clear and the day was hot. Somehow I knew that the areca palms produced a psychoactive nut, but just because I knew it didn't make it true. Lena had a little more vodka and made a terrible face.

"Give me a green pill instead."

I only had one with me, but I gave it to her. She swallowed it dry and she winced and I knew she wasn't used to taking pills either.

"I didn't want you to see this place," she said. "I didn't want you to meet my brother. I didn't want you to know anything about me."

"But you brought Ben to meet me."

"Yes." She paused to consider this. "Because I wanted you to see that I kind of get what you're going through."

"It's fine, anyway. Don't worry."

"But everything's all fucked up! You're fucked up. I'm fucked up."

"It's true."

"And you'll leave in a few days."

I hadn't been thinking about this. In fact, I had nowhere to go. I had no plans. I had no return ticket.

"Where will I go?" I said.

"You'll go home. Haven't you got a home? I'm just the stunningly beautiful girl you meet on vacation."

"That's not the story! Remember the lesson of Tom Rath. Our story is very simple. It's a subplot. It's a story told again and again, so many times that it doesn't need to be told at all. It only needs to be gestured at while the main plot moves forward. In our story, there's no room for class tensions. There's no room for worrying about what comes next. We just fall in love, that's our story. In the foreground the grand narrative is being told, conquests and wars and politics and whatever else, but we don't have to worry about it."

"We don't have to worry about it," she said.

"No."

"That's good. I like it. Think of those main characters out there, sweating and arguing."

"And we're here on this nice porch. There's a whole alarming future in which to do all kinds of worrying, but we don't have to worry about that."

## ACKNOWLEDGMENTS

The books that stick in my mind are: *The Once and Future World: Nature As It Was, As It Is, As It Could Be* by J.B. MacKinnon; *Tristes Tropiques* by Claude Lévi-Strauss; *The Emperor: Downfall of an Autocrat* and *Shah of Shahs* by Ryszard Kapuściński; *Passage of Darkness: The Ethnobiology of the Haitian Zombie* by Wade Davis (and all his other books too); *The Inquisition in New Spain, 1536–1820: A Documentary History* translated and edited by John F. Chuchiak IV; *Explorers of the Amazon* by Anthony Smith; *River of Darkness: Francisco Orellana's Legendary Voyage of Death and Discovery Down the Amazon* by Buddy Levy; *Don't Sleep, There Are Snakes: Life and Language in the Amazonian Jungle* by Daniel L. Everett; *The Sixth Extinction: An Unnatural History* by Elizabeth Kolbert; *Countdown: Our Last, Best Hope for a Future on Earth?* and *The World Without Us* by Alan Weisman; *The Southern Gates of Arabia: A Journey in the Hadhramaut* by Freya Stark; *In Miserable Slavery: Thomas Thistlewood in Jamaica, 1750–1786* edited by Douglas Hall; *The Secret Diary of William Byrd of Westover*; Marco Polo's *Travels*; John Mandeville's *Travels*; *The London Practice of Physic* by Thomas Willis; *Don Quixote* by Miguel de Cervantes (the Smollett translation); *The Voyages and Adventures of Ferdinand Mendez Pinto* by Fernão Mendes Pinto; *The First New Chronicle and Good Government: On the History of the World and the Incas Up to 1615* by Felipe Guaman Poma de Ayala; and *The True History of the Conquest of New Spain* by Bernal Díaz del Castillo.

I owe a special word of thanks to Peter Carey, whose *True History of the Kelly Gang* started me on the whole thing. Jam is Ned Kelly's direct literary descendant.

Thanks to everyone who read drafts of this book: David Blanton, Zacc Dukowitz, David Weimer, Michael Hofmann, Audrey Thier, and Peter Murphy. Special general thanks to Padgett Powell. Thanks to my agent, Cynthia Cannell; to my exceptional editor, Rachel Mannheimer; and to Sara Mercurio and the rest of the folks at Bloomsbury. Thanks to Paula and Sam Thier, without whom we are helpless, and again to Audrey Thier and Peter Murphy, without whom we are helpless. Thanks also to Stacy and Eric Cochran and the other members of the Park Street Literary Arts Council for the year-long residency during which this book was written.

And to my wife, Sarah Trudgeon, who reshaped this novel many times and whose love and support is a precondition for every enterprise I undertake, large and small, and without whom I am helpless: I have written this book for you. It is a way of almost saying what cannot be said.

## A NOTE ON THE AUTHOR

AARON THIER was born in Baltimore and raised in Williamstown, Massachusetts. He is a columnist for *Lucky Peach*, a regular contributor to the *Nation*, and the author of one previous novel, *The Ghost Apple*, a semifinalist for the James Thurber Prize for American Humor.